The clock ticked

A Klaxon somewhere dee... ...power plant began its mournful clang as Bolan and a security guard ran toward the control room door.

The lock had already been destroyed, although the door remained closed. Bolan stepped back and planted a sharp kick just above the damaged lock. The door swung back with a crash. The room was empty except for the bloody bodies of two men lying against one wall.

Bolan turned to the guard. "Do you know anything about this reactor? Can you work the controls?"

"No," the guard said quietly, shaking his head.

Two more lights joined the carnival of flashing colors across the control panel. Bolan and the guard felt the rumble before they heard it. It grew slowly and sounded as if it would never stop.

In seconds the reactor would blow.

TRADE Books & CD's
BOOK NOOK
01

MACK BOLAN

The Executioner

DON PENDLETON's EXECUTIONER
MACK BOLAN
Meltdown

A GOLD EAGLE BOOK FROM
W❂RLDWIDE

TORONTO • NEW YORK • LONDON • PARIS
AMSTERDAM • STOCKHOLM • HAMBURG
ATHENS • MILAN • TOKYO • SYDNEY

First edition January 1987

ISBN 0-373-61097-1

Special thanks and acknowledgment to
Charlie McDade for his contributions to this work.

Copyright © 1987 by Worldwide Library.
Philippine copyright 1987. Australian copyright 1987.

All rights reserved. Except for use in any review, the
reproduction or utilization of this work in whole or in part
in any form by any electronic, mechanical or other means,
now known or hereafter invented, including xerography,
photocopying and recording, or in any information storage
or retrieval system, is forbidden without the permission
of the publisher, Worldwide Library, 225 Duncan Mill Road,
Don Mills, Ontario, Canada M3B 3K9.

All the characters in this book have no existence outside the
imagination of the author and have no relation whatsoever to
anyone bearing the same name or names. They are not even
distantly inspired by any individual known or unknown to the
author, and all the incidents are pure invention.

The Worldwide Library trademarks, consisting of the words
GOLD EAGLE and THE EXECUTIONER, are registered
in the United States Patent Office and in the Canada Trade
Marks Office. The Gold Eagle design trademark, the Executioner
design trademark, the Mack Bolan design trademark, the globe
design trademark, and the Worldwide design trademark,
consisting of the word WORLDWIDE in which the
letter "O" is represented by a depiction of a globe, are
trademarks of Worldwide Library.

Printed in Canada

Dedicated to the victims of the disaster
at the Chernobyl nuclear power plant
in the Ukraine, April 1986.

THE
MACK BOLAN
LEGEND

Nothing less than a war could have fashioned the destiny of the man called Mack Bolan. Bolan earned the Executioner title in the jungle hellgrounds of Vietnam, for his skills as a crack sniper in pursuit of the enemy.

But this supreme soldier also wore another name—Sergeant Mercy. He was so tagged because of the compassion he showed to wounded comrades-in-arms and Vietnamese civilians.

Mack Bolan's second tour of duty ended prematurely when he was given emergency leave to return home and bury his family. Bolan made his peace at his parents' and sister's gravesite. Then he declared war on the evil force that had snatched his loved ones. The Mafia.

In a fiery one-man assault, he confronted the Mob head-on, carrying a cleansing flame to the urban menace. And when the battle smoke cleared, a solitary figure walked away alive.

He continued his lone-wolf struggle, and soon a hope of victory began to appear. But Mack Bolan had broken society's every rule. That same society started gunning for this elusive warrior—to no avail.

So Bolan was offered amnesty to work within the system against international terrorism. This time, as an official employee of Uncle Sam, Bolan wore yet another handle: Colonel John Phoenix. With government sanction now, and a command center at Stony Man Farm in Virginia's Blue Ridge Mountains, he and his new allies—Able Team and Phoenix Force—waged relentless war on a new adversary: the KGB and all it stood for.

Until the inevitable occurred. Bolan's one true love, the brilliant and beautiful April Rose, died at the hands of the Soviet terror machine.

Embittered and utterly saddened by this feral deed, Bolan broke the shackles of Establishment authority.

Now the big justice fighter is once more free to haunt the treacherous alleys of the shadow world.

1

The huge brown circles made an interesting mosaic when viewed from the high slope. Heavy snow underfoot hampered the lone figure's descent as he headed toward the deadly brown scars. He paused to listen and to look when he reached the bottom of the hill. But there was only the wind swirling flakes of snow about him. Somewhere out there in the bone-chilling cold, he knew, were three men. And Mack Bolan wanted them badly. He wanted them dead or alive.

Dunford, Idaho, was a godforsaken place. It was five hundred square miles of nuclear nightmare: plutonium reactors, waste recycling plants, high- and low-level facilities for waste storage. Dunford had it all. The large dead circles, so perfect from above, were signposts. Under each was a storage tank, some holding a million gallons of boiling radioactive liquid; tanks that were too hot to get close to, and too hot to stand a blanket of snow.

And right now, as the moon slipped behind a lowering cloud bank that threatened to dump still more snow, three men were preparing to blow one of those tanks sky-high. The boiling death that would be released by the explosion would kill every living thing it touched. The plant would be contaminated for thousands of years, permanently shutting down one of the keystones of America's nuclear defense system. Bolan couldn't let that happen. He had to find those men. Now.

But where the hell were they? he wondered. Which tank did they want to hit? In his arctic whites, Bolan was well camouflaged, but Dunford was too big for him to cover on his own. There were nearly two hundred tanks, and his prey wasn't likely to be too particular. Any tank would do, just as long as it was full of hot water. Bolan had a list of the full tanks, but so did the men he was hunting. Even knowing which ones were empty, which were full of salt cake, still left him nearly a hundred to watch. He had to move, and keep moving.

There was less than an hour left. The tank was supposed to be blown at three a.m., and it was already after two o'clock. He moved along the aisles of snow between the tanks, crouching to get a better angle of sight, hoping to pick up the silhouette of at least one of the three men against the dark gray horizon.

He stopped again to listen. What was that? he wondered to himself, trying to shake the spooky sensation of being alone in a white hell. He heard it again, this time a little louder. A crunch—someone approaching through the snow. Then he heard voices. They were off to the left, and some distance away.

Falling flat, he inched around to face the direction of the sound. The voices were still unintelligible, but the men were obviously coming his way. Fast. He reached behind to unsling the white-shrouded rifle, careful not to make a sound. The terrain before him sloped away at a sharp angle. He would have to be quick, and deadly. There was no time to race around the frozen hellscape tracking phantoms. He'd much rather make a few ghosts of his own and be done with it.

The first guy came into view about two hundred yards away. He was turning to look over his shoulder. Bolan steadied himself, readying for three quick shots, and then he saw the second man. Steady now, steady. One more, and he could end it. But the first two stopped. One of them turned and waved impatiently, then dumped a heavy pack in the snow and walked back the way he came. The other man waited, looking around nervously. Bolan readjusted the rifle's sight and watched. He'd teach them something about patience. Not that they'd live long enough for it to be of any use. Soon the guy was back, half pushing and half dragging another man.

"Keep it down, for crissakes, why don't you?" the man who had waited cautioned them.

"What are you bellyachin' about? There's nobody within two miles of us. Come on, let's get it done." He was bending for his pack as Bolan zeroed in on him. The target hoisted the heavy pack and shrugged into the shoulder straps, then reached into his pocket. He pulled out a piece of paper, unfolded it and looked around, as if trying to get his bearings.

"One-oh-seven-B ought to be around here somewhere." He surveyed his surroundings for a moment. Satisfied, he stuffed the paper back into his pocket and pointed to his left. "It's right over there. Let's move it."

Bolan wanted to take him out first. He seemed to be the leader of the group. Without him, the other two would be disoriented, easy pickings for the Executioner. Bolan kept the man in his cross hairs and waited as the group moved forward. Soon, all three were visible in his sight. Bolan squeezed off the first shot. The boom of the big Weatherby Mark V echoed through the still night as the target's head shattered. The bloody spray was dark and shadowy against the freshly fallen snow.

Bolan squeezed off another round before the body of his first target had reached the ground. This time he aimed a bit lower, drilling his man through the chest. A dark stain spread across the saboteur's arctics, and he flew backward, his arms windmilling as his nearly lifeless body fought to keep its balance.

But these guys weren't amateurs. The third man had dived into the snow at the first shot, and now he started to scramble back down the slope. Bolan fired a round into the guy's pack. The dull thud of the slug hitting home goosed the guy into a frenzy. He swung his submachine gun into action and sprayed his fire up and down the snowy hill.

Bolan knew the man had no idea who, or where, his target was. Still, the big guy knew a wild shot could kill just as easily as a well-aimed one. Bolan moved off to the right, angling down and away from the line of fire. There was a low mound of snow about thirty feet away. It wouldn't provide much cover, but it meant Bolan was not out in the open.

Bolan held his fire, not wanting to reveal his position unless he had something to shoot at. The guy seemed to have regained his composure. He had stopped firing, perhaps to reload, or maybe just to listen. Bolan froze where he was.

Suddenly he heard footsteps. Somehow the guy had managed to get far enough down the hill to stand without showing himself. Bolan jumped to his feet and raced after the fleeing gunner. Finishing the job was going to be more trouble than he had anticipated. But that was good. It confirmed Bolan's suspicions that he was dealing with something insidious and deadly.

As the fleeing man's footsteps receded into the night, Bolan plunged on in pursuit. Running was sluggish in the heavy snow, and he had to stop repeatedly to make sure his prey was still on the move. The last thing the Executioner wanted was to run right up the barrel of the guy's gun. Off in the distance, the nightmare machinery of the reactors loomed against the dark gray sky. There were flashing red lights atop the cooling towers, containment buildings and steam-belching stacks. Security lamps backlighted the towers, filling the horizon with bulky shadows.

Scanning the terrain in front of him, Bolan finally spotted a thick white figure struggling toward a wooded strip that ran parallel to the security fence. If the running man managed to reach the fence, Bolan knew he would never catch him. The Executioner fell to one knee and sighted in on the fugitive just as the target tripped and disappeared.

As if sensing the presence of death, and his narrow escape, the man did not rise immediately. Bolan waited, patiently scoping back and forth along the perimeter. He would wait until the target got to his feet before making a move. Bolan knew his own position was tenuous. The damn contrast of white and dark would give him away, just as it had given the fugitive away. But Mack Bolan had time. He could wait.

Suddenly a blinding flash lit up the area where the man had fallen. Scoping in on the dying glow, Bolan saw a hole torn in the heavy wire fence. Loose earth darkened the snow on both sides. The guy had used a grenade to tear an escape route through the wire.

In the distance, Bolan heard the dull whumping of the rotor blades of a chopper. It grew steadily louder. Probably a routine patrol, but the Executioner knew he had to move fast.

"Come on, damn it," Bolan whispered, urging the guy to move. If he didn't get the man before the chopper patrol got there, he might not get him at all. The big guy couldn't afford to be captured on restricted property. He couldn't afford to be captured at all. And he couldn't shoot at the patrol. They were just men doing their jobs. Bolan was simply giving them some help they didn't know they needed, but he didn't have time to explain that to them.

The chopper was coming closer. It was flying low, following the fence. Twin searchlights speared out, dancing along the security perimeter. His guy would likely stay put until the chopper passed, unless the patrol spotted the hole in the fence and came down to check it out. And they were getting closer.

Boring into the scope, Bolan counted. If the guy didn't move by the count of ten, he'd have to risk it.

Eight...

Nine...

Ten...

Bolan fired a shot into the muddy hole at the base of the ruptured fence. He was up and running, zigzagging to keep the guy off-balance. The footing was treacherous, and Bolan had played right into the guy's hands. The first burst from his SMG had sprayed wildly, the second narrowly missed. He knew the guy was expecting him to dive. But the hell with that.

Bolan knew his target would be through the fence and gone before he stopped sliding. The Executioner dropped to one knee and sighted on the hole just as the guy began to struggle up the muddy bank toward the safety beyond the fence.

The guy skidded as he tried to get up the slippery bank. If he fell and landed on the pack, the explosives would likely blow. The guy would be gone, sure, but Bolan would be locked in. Tight. The chopper would call for backup, and the place would crawl with security.

Bolan aimed high, a head shot. It was risky, but he had no choice. He waited until the man reached the fence and then he squeezed the trigger. The guy lost his head as the big Weatherby's boom rolled into the night. The chopper was only five hundred yards away now. Bolan knew they couldn't have heard the shot, but there was no way they'd miss the busted fence. Or the large body plugging the hole.

Bending low, and sprinting, Mack Bolan reached the fence. The chopper was hovering, both searchlights focused on the same spot. They had seen something. Or someone. Bolan didn't know. It bought him some time, and that was all that mattered. The chopper's engine roared, and it started to climb. The searchlights went out just as he stepped through the fence.

He paused long enough to kick some snow over the headless corpse and loose earth. Grabbing some scorched wire torn loose by the blast, he pulled the two ends of the fence together. It wasn't great, but it just might give him extra time.

The chopper was hovering about three hundred yards up the fence. As he ran into the trees outside the plant, he heard the engine roar. The searchlights snapped back on. A burst of automatic weapon fire turned them right off again. Permanently. The engine sputtered, roared and died altogether. Spinning wildly, the chopper plunged behind the trees.

Whoever it was the chopper had flushed obviously didn't want to be caught. Any more than Mack Bolan did.

The darkness ruptured, and tongues of orange flame climbed above the trees. It was too late to help the soldiers in the chopper. But not too late to nail the ones who were responsible.

Bolan jogged through the snow, unzipping his whites as he ran. The Weatherby was nearly empty, and he didn't have time to reload. Pulling his .44 AutoMag free, he ran toward the flames. Some of the trees were already burning, and heavy smoke from the chopper fuel billowed into the sky.

Through the glare that filled the cockpit, he could make out the bodies. Then the swirling smoke closed in, and the chopper was obscured for good.

A hundred yards from the holocaust, Bolan saw a small white 4x4, just off the service road that ran along the outside of the fence. Two men, armed with SMGs, were rushing toward it, and toward Mack Bolan. Toward certain death.

The men had nearly reached the 4X4. They were laughing. Laughing as if the burning wreck of the chopper was nothing more than a holiday bonfire.

Bolan reached the rear of the 4X4 just as his quarry reached the front. He stepped quickly to the right, his AutoMag locked in both hands. As the passenger door opened, Bolan fired once, blasting bits of bone and brain right through the mud-streaked window glass. The driver didn't have time to react. Bolan squeezed gently, almost tenderly, and Big Thunder bucked once. And again.

Then Mack Bolan was gone, as suddenly as he had come. There was still too much work to be done.

2

The office was tastefully appointed. And anonymous. Hal Brognola didn't much care for its lavishness and was obviously ill at ease in the borrowed surroundings. Brognola chewed on his cigar as he paced before the large picture window. Outside, the snow was getting heavier, and Bolan was already two hours late.

Idaho was a state the Fed rarely visited. If he had his way, he wouldn't be coming back. Sure, the mountain view was gorgeous. But he was used to buildings, pavement, the sound of traffic. It was so damn quiet here that he could hear his heart beat.

Brognola knew the man they called the Executioner better than anyone else. They weren't exactly friends, but then Mack Bolan probably didn't have any friends. Hell, the man didn't even have a family except for his younger brother, Johnny. Friends were a luxury for a man in Bolan's line of work. His years in Vietnam and his subsequent intelligence work had created a network of sources, allies, snitches and comrades. But not friends. Brognola knew he was the closest thing to a friend Bolan would ever have.

At times it bothered him that he never socialized with Mack. But Brognola knew that the Executioner could not afford to let down his guard at any time. Too many people wanted his ass. Badly.

Brognola sat down and propped his feet up on the oak desk in front of him. He reached forward and put the cigar down in the massive glass ashtray before returning the chair to an upright position. He started poring over the sheaves of papers in a dozen file folders stacked in one corner of the desk.

Each one bore a small brightly colored label on its raised tab, and each was stamped SECRET in the no-bullshit kind of lettering preferred by guys who were deadly serious about their line of work. Without exception, the colored label bore the name of an American nuclear installation. The folders were on loan from the Nuclear Regulatory Commission, and only one other person knew they were in Brognola's hands. That man had refused to part with the papers at first. He relented only when Brognola had sworn to return the documents within forty-eight hours. Uncopied. And unaltered.

And Brognola didn't blame the guy, once he got a look at the files. Not a bit. More megatonnage was sitting right there in those folders than had been dropped on Hiroshima. And Nagasaki. The intel was that explosive. Critical, actually. And right now Brognola could barely contain his anxiety, waiting for Bolan to report back on a related piece of intelligence the Fed had received that morning.

Each folder laid out, in painful detail, recent nuclear accidents. What was clear, and what the files proved beyond reasonable doubt, was that the "events," as they were tidily called by the NRC, were no accidents. None of them. This morning's information concerned an incident that had not yet happened, and if Bolan got there in time, would never happen.

No way.

Bolan never failed when it really counted. But Brognola couldn't help but wonder where he was.

As if tired of the unspoken question, the Executioner stepped into the office, still wearing his arctic whites. He crossed the room quietly and sat wearily on the edge of a sofa across from the desk. Brognola waited a moment. When Bolan said nothing, the big Fed prompted him.

"Well?"

"Your intel was sound."

"And? Come on, man, don't make me pry it out of you. What happened?"

"Somebody planned to blow one of the high-level waste tanks."

"Well?"

"They didn't make it." Bolan sounded tired. Whether it was from the night's work or the nature of his business, Brognola couldn't tell. And he didn't really want to know. It scared him to contemplate what things would be like without the big guy around. Bolan was practically an insurance policy on the nation's health. The damnable thing was that so few people knew it. But the Fed knew it had to be that way.

Bolan brought his mentor up to date on the night's activities, pausing briefly before describing the fate of the chopper, and of the men who had been in it.

Brognola reached for his cigar and then got up from his chair to stretch. He paced back and forth in front of the window, until finally, unable to endure the silence any longer, he spoke again.

"And tonight is only the beginning. I didn't have time to tell you earlier. What was supposed to go down out at Dunford wasn't the first phony accident. And it isn't supposed to be the last, either."

"Tell me about it," Bolan said. The tiredness in his voice was gone as Brognola confirmed his suspicions. Bolan had seen something out there in the snow he didn't like. If there was a chance it could happen again, he wanted to do something about it.

Damn right.

"What I've got," Brognola said, patting the stack of folders on the desk, "is proof positive. A dozen incidents at a dozen different locations, hundreds of miles apart, all nuclear installations. The statistical odds against any one of them being accidental are enormous. And when you figure the odds on all twelve, well..."

"Hal, we don't have time for a math lesson. I know probability theory. What are the particulars? What's going on? Who's behind it?"

"That's where we've run up against a brick wall, Mack. We know what, but we don't really know who. We can guess. You can, too, I think. But what we need is the goods. We need to make a case, and make damn sure it will stick. We want these bastards handled, and we don't much care how. Or by whom."

Bolan jerked forward, then stopped as Brognola waved a hand.

"No. I know what you're thinking, but no. The President hasn't given me specific authorization to put you on this thing. But he sure as hell knows I will. And," Brognola said, winking broadly, "he didn't tell me not to."

"That's it?" Bolan asked.

"Best I can do, Mack. Sorry."

Sorry. It seemed to Bolan he'd heard it a thousand times since Stony Man. He was good enough to do their dirty work for them. Oh, yeah. Just as long as he didn't tell them about it. He was a back-door man, somebody your servants dealt with. Take what he's selling, just don't let him in the parlor. That was for polite company only.

He'd seen it all before—during the Mafia wars. Nobody wanted to acknowledge him then, either. Oh, sure, some did—a good cop here and there, a grateful citizen now and again. But everybody else said, "Do what you can. Just don't bleed on the rug. Not *my* rug."

And Mack Bolan did it. He did his job. He did it because it was his job. And he did it because it had to be done. Stony Man had been that way, until some Soviet fox had gotten into the henhouse. And Mack Bolan had been the only guy man enough to crawl through the shit to get him out.

Now some new evil was trying to eat away at America, to devour the good. This time they were atomic chickens, laying nuclear eggs. No way Mack Bolan would let this one slide. No way. No matter how he felt. No matter how tired of all the crap he had become. This was his job. It was his job, and he would do it. Because he had to, and above all because he was Mack Bolan. The Executioner.

"Okay, Hal, I want it all. Everything you know. Everything you suspect."

Brognola ran down the incidents one by one, leaving the chaff aside. Every incident was analyzed. Common threads, of which there were several, were highlighted. Possible reasons were discussed, probably scenarios considered. What it all boiled down to was that someone wanted to cramp America's nuclear style. There had been attempts to sway public opinion before, of course. Most of them were honorably motivated. But this was different. This one smelled, badly. It stank of vodka and borscht. It smelled of KGB. You didn't have to look too deeply to find them under most rocks. There *would* be rocks, of course. Rocks labeled Cuba, Libya, Nicaragua. But they were only rocks. It was the thing that crawled out when you kicked one over that Bolan hated most of all. And this rock would probably be lettered in Arabic. But the return address would be Moscow.

Of course.

"Did you look into the antinuke groups?" Bolan asked.

"Yes. There's something there, but I'm not sure. There's Arab money, of course. But that doesn't prove anything. It's legal. And why shouldn't there be, after all. Hell, if I was sitting on all that oil, I think I'd want all the competition on the run. Including flashlight batteries. Nuclear power could put them out of business."

"Sure, Hal. But what I saw tonight was not fair business competition. There were two good men in that chopper. Somebody killed them. And somebody's got to pay for it. Yeah, I nailed the gunners, but I want the people who paid them. What they're up to isn't legal."

"Look, I know how you feel, but we have got to play this one carefully. We have some people inside. Good people. We have to make damn sure they're covered."

"You know better than that, Hal."

Brognola looked at the big guy for a few seconds before he answered. "Yeah, I do."

Whatever else Mack Bolan was, he wasn't a hothead. No way would he compromise somebody on the inside of a deal like this. There was too much at stake, and nobody would know that better than the guy right there on the firing line . . . or on the wrong end of the gun.

"Look, the best thing you can do is read these files. When you're done, I'll try to answer your questions. There's a lot here, but there is a hell of a lot that isn't. And I have to have those papers back by tomorrow night. We don't have a lot of time."

Brognola paced while Bolan flipped through the files one by one. Once in a while he'd ask a question, then push on. His jaw grew tighter with each file. When he was finished, he pushed them into a neat pile and stood up to stretch.

"Not a pretty picture, is it?" Brognola asked.

Bolan didn't answer.

"I want you to meet our best source of information. She can tell you more than I can about some of the groups that might be involved in this business."

"She?"

"Rachel Peres. She's damn good. Been with us a long time. Former Mossad."

"Former? Come on, Hal, that's too damn risky. I can't afford to rely on somebody who might be playing both ends against the middle in this thing."

"No way. She's solid. I can vouch for that. And we really need her. It's taken too long as it is to get somebody on the inside. I can't go back to square one on this. Not now."

Bolan stepped to the window and pulled the curtain aside. Beyond the glass was a second curtain, this one made of snow.

"Mack, you have to trust me on this. I know what you're thinking. But this is too big. And too damn important. You'll need her help."

Brognola was right, of course. And Mack Bolan knew it. And he knew he had to protect himself. He knew Mack Bolan would not be working with Rachel Peres. No. Her partner would be the Executioner.

"Where do I meet her?"

"Right here. She should be in the reception area," Brognola answered as he checked his watch before moving to open the door.

Bolan turned in surprise to stare at the slender dark-haired woman who stood in the office doorway. Her eyes were even darker than her hair. As she walked toward him, Bolan decided there was a no-nonsense look about her, and her grip was firm when she reached out to take his hand in her own.

"I've heard a great deal about you, Mr. Bolan. And to set things straight from the beginning, I assure you, I can take care of myself, and of you, too, if it should come to that."

"I believe it," Bolan said, relaxing somewhat. "Let's get to work. We have a lot to do."

"More than you know, Mr. Bolan."

"Call me Mack."

"Fair enough."

Bolan was impressed by Rachel Peres's grasp of detail as she outlined the information she had gathered. Her efficiency reminded him of someone, someone it was too painful to remember. A woman who had made the supreme sacrifice for him. A woman who had given her life for him. April Rose.

But this woman was something else. As Bolan's thoughts returned to the present he decided that working with her was not going to be that bad.

Not at all.

3

Robert Hanley was nervous. When Hal Brognola had returned his files that evening, he had told him that someone was coming down later with more questions. Brognola hadn't said anything specific, but Hanley knew something big was happening. You could see it in the man's eyes. Hanley had asked, but Brognola had all but ignored the question.

"You don't want to know," Brognola had said.

And Hanley didn't want to know. It was spooky, sitting alone in the big house. His wife and kids were safe at least. They had gone to her sister's in Phoenix. But the darkness of the Virginia countryside was no comfort. If anything, it made Hanley feel more vulnerable.

He wanted to look at the files again. But first he had to make sure the house was secure. He turned on the outdoor floodlights, but a glance at the wide front lawn didn't reassure him. There were too many shadows. The trees that had been his pride and joy could hide anything. Or anyone.

Locking the windows one by one, Hanley felt cold shivers slip down his spine. On the way up the sweeping semicircular staircase, he thought he heard something on the front porch. A thud maybe. Or a footstep. He went back down to peek through the thick glass of the front door. There was nothing there.

Returning to the top of the stairs, he checked the bedroom windows one by one and then the sitting room. As he moved toward his office, he thought of the papers again. So much anxiety over them meant there had to be something in them. Something he hadn't seen the first time. A pattern, some link that bound all the accidents together. Whatever it was, he wanted to find it.

After all, Robert Hanley knew he knew more about nuclear safety than anyone in the country. If there was something in those files to upset Brognola, he'd find it. He'd be ready for Brognola's emissary. He could do it even without knowing what Brognola knew. He didn't need any help. He was the best.

The door to his office was locked as usual. He had taken to keeping it closed, not so much for security, but because of the kids. It was off-limits to them, even for hide-and-seek. When the lock clicked open, he pushed through the door and felt for the light switch with his left hand.

Across the large office the broad window was bright. The outdoor floodlights cut through the thin curtains, which moved gently in the evening breeze. The window was open, and the thick bands of shadow cast by the lighting squirmed like a tangle of snakes. The side window was rarely opened, but he glanced at the heavy draperies for a second. They were still.

When the overhead light clicked on, the shadows on the curtain disappeared. Hanley crossed the room swiftly, pulled the sliding glass closed and locked it. He flipped on his desk lamp and went back to the doorway to shut off the overhead light. He returned and sat down at his desk and pulled the folders toward him.

Opening the first file, Hanley felt another chill. He knew it wasn't the breeze; it was the file itself. He started to examine the thickest of the documents. It was the detailed report of a research team that had explored the causes of a reactor shutdown in the Ohio Valley.

The Nuclear Regulatory Commission, for all the flak it took from outside, was proud of its research. Meticulous and thorough, the NRC examined every nuclear "event," and issued a comprehensive analysis. The public, especially those opposed to nuclear energy, might argue with its conclusions, but never with its science. The fat sheaf of papers before him bore out the depth of the NRC's scrutiny.

Hanley sometimes believed the research teams gathered too much information. It was often difficult to know why things happened, when you had so much detail on *what* happened. The Pitt General reactor event was no different. Midway 2 was a medium-sized pressurized water reactor. It was older than most, and Hanley knew age could have been a factor in the malfunction. That had been the conclusion of the NRC, in fact. Now Hanley wasn't so sure. Neither was Brognola apparently.

"Good reading?"

The question so startled Hanley that it took him a minute to react. The visitor moved out from behind the heavy draperies at the side window before Hanley could say anything. He was tall and slender, but his features were obscured by the shadows cast by the desk lamp. Hanley didn't recognize him. But he knew a gun when he saw one. And the one in the man's left hand looked very deadly.

"Who are you?" Hanley demanded.

"It doesn't matter who I am, Mr. Hanley. It's what you do for a living that counts."

The man moved to the easy chair at the left of Hanley's desk. He sat down, keeping the gun pointed at his reluctant host. Seated, his features were visible at last, but that meant little to Hanley. He had never seen the man before. The intruder took off his slouch hat and dropped it to the floor beside his chair. The man's hair was sparse in front and thinning everywhere else. He ran the fingers of his free hand through it once or twice, arranging the stray hair in a way that was supposed to conceal his baldness.

"I asked if your reading was interesting. Is it?"

"Who are you and why are you here? This is my home. You have no right to be here."

"You're right, of course," the visitor said.

His manner was nearly apologetic. Hanley found this more annoying than the rudeness he had expected.

"Still, there are things I must know, Mr. Hanley. Things that you already know."

"What things?"

Ignoring the question, the man said, "Someone visited your office this afternoon. He returned some papers to you, did he not? Important papers?"

"What business is that of yours?" Hanley was beginning to sweat. The longer the intruder remained polite, the more uneasy Hanley became.

"This time I must disagree with you, Mr. Hanley. It most definitely is my business. Now, if you continue to make things difficult, my assistant and I will have to change our demeanor. I will, at least. My assistant, as you will see if you remain obstinate, has few manners. In fact, he barely has any of the social graces. Otto?"

While the intruder spoke, Hanley watched his face intently. He barely noticed as the closet door behind the man's left shoulder slid open. The intruder's assistant had made his appearance. He moved quickly across the floor to stand behind his superior. The hulking newcomer was massive. Otto's broad shoulders were clearly used to heavier work than supporting his hairless, bulletlike head.

"Otto, Mr. Hanley seems reluctant to tell us what we need to know. Do you think you can persuade him to be more cooperative?"

Otto grunted. His thick lips parted slightly in what Hanley took to be Otto's best attempt at a smile. He stepped around the seated man and swept Hanley's desk clean with one swipe of his thick forearm.

"Otto, you should be more careful. Mr. Hanley's papers are of some value to us."

Hanley leaped to his feet, but Otto was quicker than he looked. He reached across the desk and caught Hanley by one shoulder. With a grunt, Otto lifted the smaller man in the air, then slammed him down heavily in his chair again.

"All right, Otto. Let me ask Mr. Hanley a few questions. I'm sure he understands now how serious I am."

The hulk returned to his place with a second parting of his lips.

"What do you want?" Hanley asked. "Why are you here? What is this all about?"

"I want to know who your visitor was. I also want to know why he wanted the papers he returned to you."

"It was nothing. Just a routine investigation." Hanley sounded desperate, and he knew it. But he also knew these men wanted information they shouldn't have. He'd be damned if he'd give it to them.

"No, Mr. Hanley, it was not routine. Your files are very sensitive. They never leave your office. Never. At least not until two days ago. I find that very interesting. So do my associates."

"Your associates?"

"Mr. Hanley, I am losing my patience with you. You are a bureaucrat, Mr. Hanley. No match for Otto's persuasive skills, I assure you. Give Mr. Hanley a demonstration of your technique, Otto."

This time Otto laughed. He walked swiftly to the front of Hanley's desk and hauled the man to his feet. Without bothering to move around the desk, Otto grabbed Hanley's left arm and gave it a sudden yank, dislocating the shoulder. Hanley screamed, and Otto shoved him back into his chair.

Hanley moaned. His shoulder felt as if it were on fire. He reached up to rub it with his right hand, but the pain was too great. He wiped cold sweat from his forehead. He knew that they were going to kill him if he didn't cooperate with them. It struck home for the first time. They would kill him unless they got what they had come for. And they would most certainly get it. If he stopped resisting, maybe they would let him live. What was the point of suffering if he was going to tell them what they wanted to know?

"Are you prepared to answer my questions now?"

"Yes," Hanley said, his voice cracking under the strain of the situation.

"Good. Otto, get Mr. Hanley some water, please. His throat seems a little dry."

The big goon lumbered out into the hallway. Hanley could hear him searching for the bathroom. A dim light flashed on, and soon Otto was back, carrying the blue glass tumbler from the upstairs bathroom sink. The huge man held the tumbler out, and Hanley reached for it gingerly with his good arm. When he held it securely, Otto caught the hand in his own. And squeezed. Glass cracked, and so did bone. Hanley fainted and collapsed back into his chair. Otto smiled at the bright, wet puddle on the desktop.

"A nice touch, Otto. But can you revive Mr. Hanley?" the intruder inquired.

Otto grunted. He lifted the unconscious man easily. Carrying Hanley as if he weighed no more than a rag doll, Otto went down the hall to the bathroom again. Inside, he dumped his burden into the tub. He turned on the cold water tap, then sat on the edge of the tub. The water revived Hanley, who moaned and tried to sit up. He shook his head groggily. He started as he realized where he was.

Otto reached down and caught Hanley by his left shoulder. Hauling the injured man roughly to his feet, he lifted him free of the tub, holding him at arm's length to avoid the water streaming from Hanley's clothing. Otto dropped the smaller man to the floor, nudging him with one foot.

Hanley got to his feet slowly. He stumbled when Otto shoved him toward the door, hitting his dislocated shoulder on the doorframe as he passed through.

Hanley knew he was going to die, no matter what he told his captors. As they reached the head of the staircase to the ground floor, the NRC man leaped. He landed halfway down the stairs, his feet flying out from under him. He grabbed the handrail with his left hand, but the pain in his shoulder was too intense. He let go with a groan, falling the rest of the way to the hallway below. Otto bounded down the steps behind him as Hanley crawled toward the front door. Before he could get the door open, Otto was on him. The big man stepped on Hanley's back, pressing the fallen man into the carpet.

Hanley twisted to one side far enough to see the figure of the other man descending the stairs. He was almost casual in his descent; there was something delicate, almost feminine in the graceful walk.

"I am disappointed, Mr. Hanley. I had hoped you would be more cooperative. This is very unfortunate."

"Go to hell," Hanley said. His teeth were clenched against the pain, but his captors had no trouble understanding him. Otto pressed harder with his foot.

"This could have been so much easier for you, Mr. Hanley. But now..." He shook his head. "Otto, Mr. Hanley's papers are in a mess upstairs. Perhaps you should gather them up. There is a briefcase beside the desk. Put them in it and bring it down."

Otto nodded, but didn't remove his foot from the small of Hanley's back.

"Now, Otto. We have to hurry."

Reluctantly Otto climbed the stairs. Hanley could hear the rustle of the papers as Otto swept them together. He looked at the intruder, trying to decide whether he *had* seen the man before. It might not make any difference now. Still, for some reason he now looked familiar.

Otto was back, a briefcase in his hand. He stood to one side, docile as a dog at heel.

"Otto, take the papers out to the car and wait for me. I won't be long," the intruder said as he looked directly into the terror-glazed eyes of Robert Hanley.

4

Mack Bolan hated flying into Dulles. The convenience never made up for the noise. But when a man was in a hurry, Bolan knew he couldn't always have it his way. And Mack Bolan was in a hurry. He had some questions for Robert Hanley. Hard questions. The incident at Dunford made it obvious that something was very wrong with American nuclear security. And the files Brognola had shown him were frightening; their implications were even more frightening.

When Brognola had flown back to Washington, Bolan had spent the night in Idaho. There had been a great deal he wanted to know, and Rachel Peres was the only one who could tell him.

Rachel Peres had said nothing to reassure him. For the past several months, she had been working her way into the heart of one of the more radical antinuke groups. Like most fringe movements, it was loosely allied with several others, to the point of having a few members in common.

But there had been more. If Rachel Peres was right, somebody was orchestrating a nightmare, and the incident at Dunford was just the overture. The curtain was about to go up on the deadliest grandstand play Bolan had yet encountered. And when that somebody phoned home, they were picked up in Moscow.

Peres had gotten involved because of the interest shown by Arab terrorist organizations in U.S. protest groups. There was no doubt that some of the support money was coming from the more rabid OPEC countries. And still more from a couple of countries that thought OPEC policy was too tame. Mossad no longer pulled her strings, she said, but she was still a patriot.

Brognola believed her, but Mack Bolan didn't buy it. He'd go along, for reasons of his own, but the Executioner was calling the shots on this one. Starting now.

As the big 747 circled for its approach into Dulles, Bolan considered his options. The first stop had to be at Robert Hanley's. His files were extensive, but some of the material was too technical. Bolan wanted to ask some straight questions, and he needed simple answers. Too much was riding on this one. He couldn't go off half-cocked. And time was tight; the enemy was obviously ready to strike. He couldn't afford a wild-goose chase. One mistake might be all he'd have the chance to make.

Once the plane had landed, Bolan made his way to the car rental counter, where he picked up the keys to a Camaro. He wanted wheels with a little muscle. Something told him he was going to need it. It was already seven-thirty, and he wanted to get to Hanley's before the scientist went to bed. The hour drive would take him to Chantilly, in the northwest corner of Fairfax county, where Hanley lived.

Once behind the wheel, Bolan felt better. At least he was moving. He drove as fast as he dared, keeping to a solid seventy. Twice he had to slow to avoid attracting the attention of a state police patrol car that he'd spotted hiding on the far side of two underpasses.

Dusk soon changed to darkness as he drove farther into the countryside. The open fields were broken by stands of trees, and the Camaro's throaty rumble echoed off the woods as he barreled through. At 8:25 he entered Chantilly. Hanley's place was two miles on the far side of the small town. Bolan gassed up to make sure he'd have a full tank for the drive back, asked the way to Morgan's Turnpike and pulled out in a hurry.

At the entrance to the tree-lined drive leading to Hanley's renovated farmhouse, Bolan paused. Something seemed wrong. His sixth sense told him Hanley wasn't the only one there. The outdoor floodlights burned brightly and everything seemed serene, but Mack Bolan knew such scenes could explode without warning. He left the Camaro on the road and entered the driveway on foot.

As he neared the house, he thought he heard a scream, but he was too far away to be sure. He opened his jacket and slid the solid comfort of his Beretta 93-R into his hand. Avoiding the crisp gravel of the driveway, Bolan swiftly slipped into the trees to his left and approached the house. At the edge of the broad lawn, cover vanished. There was no way to cross the expanse of greenness without being seen. He'd have to waste time now to circle the house. He had to know what, and whom, he would be up against.

The lighting was more subdued along the side and toward the rear of the two-story fieldstone building. A quick look in the garage revealed only one car, Hanley's, if the government parking sticker meant anything. He was sorry now that he hadn't called from the airport, but it was too late for second-guessing. If anyone was in the house with Hanley, he had gotten there on foot or he'd come with the scientist.

The rear patio was dimly lit, and Bolan slid against the house. Pressing himself flat, he edged up to the nearest window and listened. This time there was no mistaking it. There were voices, a thump and then silence. Whoever had called on Robert Hanley was not a friend.

Bolan reached above his head to unscrew one of the two floodlights aimed on the patio. Falling to his knees, he crawled beneath the windowsill to the far side and then doused the second. Pressing his face to the window from the darkness, he could see through to the entrance hall. Bolan could make out the figures of three men, two near the front door and one at the top of the stairs.

They were talking, but the words were too soft to be intelligible. There was no way in through the back that would give him the element of surprise, and he couldn't risk a shot through the glass until he knew who was who. The only other way in was through the front. Swiftly Bolan made his way back along the side of the house, rounding the corner in time to see a huge, bald man carrying a briefcase enter the trees. Probably going to get the car, Bolan thought.

The big man would go first. He was already outside, and taking him out was the least risk to Hanley. Once he was no longer a threat, Bolan could go one-on-one against the remaining man. Unless there were others waiting in the car, who would come running at the first shot. Quickly Bolan crossed the front porch and followed his quarry into the trees. The woods of Virginia were no match for a man who had survived the jungles of Nam.

The woods were dark, and there was heavy underbrush just a few yards into the trees. Bolan could hear the big guy crashing ahead like a bull elephant. After they had traveled about seventy yards, the brush thinned a little, and moonlight filtered through the branches. Bolan could make out the bulky shape of his prey as he passed among the trees. Suddenly the big guy was in open meadow. Bolan was about twenty yards behind and closing the gap. Fast.

Across the open field, Bolan could make out a large Buick. The big guy waved the heavy briefcase high in the air. There *was* backup. That changed things a little. How much would depend on how many goons there were.

The Executioner, with practiced ease, threaded a sound suppressor snugly onto the Beretta and checked the action. There could be no screwups now. Hanley's life might depend on how well Bolan handled this end of things. It wasn't possible to follow the hulk into the open without giving away his presence. Bolan dropped to one knee and waited for the right moment. It came quickly.

As the large man lumbered ahead, the ground began to slope sharply downward. At the start of the lug's descent, Bolan fired a burst. Three dry coughs, no louder than a gentleman clearing his throat, and a small, tight triangle of death smashed into the big man's skull. The rainbow of blood and bone was quickly gone. Without a sound, he fell like a poleaxed steer. If Bolan got lucky, the guy in the Buick would think he'd tripped. When the hulk didn't get up, the other guy would come to see what happened. And the Executioner would be waiting.

Bolan didn't have to wait long. The dome light winked on and off as the second man left the car. Bolan could see his shadow, dark against the side of the car. The man hesitated, uncertain whether to climb the split-rail fence around the meadow.

Finally the guy made his move. He climbed through the fence and walked cautiously toward the bottom of the slope. He looked back toward the car once, as if trying to decide whether to go back and wait or to push on into the dark meadow. Bolan heard him as he called for his friend Otto.

Otto didn't answer him.

He called again, this time as he began to climb the slope. Still no answer, and the guy was getting nervous. He was carrying a machine pistol, sweeping it back and forth in front of him as he advanced. If he didn't get a little closer, it would be a tough shot with the Beretta. Bolan slipped the smaller gun back into its holster and unslung Big Thunder. He'd have to risk a shot from the skullbuster and hope the guy back at the house was too busy to notice.

Otto's pal was now halfway up the slope, and he knew something was wrong. He looked around helplessly, then crouched as he continued up the grassy rise. Suddenly he froze. He must have seen Otto's body.

Big Thunder bucked, and the 240-grain slug tore a hole the size of a quarter in the guy's chest wall. He went down like two hundred pounds of dead meat. Bolan watched the car down at the road. Nothing moved. He pushed through the remaining shrubbery and out into the meadow, crouching just in case. When he reached Otto's body, he turned it over. There wasn't enough of the big creep's face left to identify. The other gunner lay on his back. His face registered a look of surprise.

THE INTRUDER WAS NOT a patient man. Otto was slow. Hanley was uncooperative. It had been rather an annoying evening so far. And then he heard the gunshot.

At its sound, he bent forward, using the barrel of his pistol to brush aside the wet hair plastered to Hanley's forehead. It was almost a caress. The cold metal barely made contact with the skin. Hanley shuddered. He knew what was coming. The gun barrel swayed before him like a cobra waiting to strike. Then it was over. Robert Hanley felt nothing as the bullet blasted through his forehead. It was over so quickly that he didn't hear the shot that killed him.

The killer straightened and looked distastefully down at his victim, nudging aside a few skull fragments with the toe of one Italian Loafer. He wiped the blood on Hanley's shirt, then slipped through the door, leaving it open in his haste.

BOLAN BENT TO RETRIEVE the briefcase, and sprinted back through the trees toward Hanley's house. When he reached the main lawn, he noticed that the front door was wide open. Approaching it carefully, Bolan paused to place the briefcase against the base of a tree. He slid the Beretta out of its holster and sprinted to the broad stone porch.

Creeping softly, the gun extended, Bolan reached the doorway and spun through it. The house was deathly silent. Bolan watched the stairwell in front of him as he stepped deeper inside. Hanley's body lay off to one side. Keeping an eye on the stairs, he knelt to feel for a pulse. There was none. The ugly hole in Hanley's temple told Bolan all he needed to know.

Bolan stepped back to the doorway. He strained to peer into the darkness of the trees. Whoever killed Hanley might still be out there. Waiting. For him. He could be anywhere in the trees, just sitting on a clear shot. Bolan wouldn't give him one.

He bolted to the top of the stairs and stepped into a bedroom. It was full of stuffed animals. A kid's room. And the kid's father lay dead at the bottom of the stairs. Somebody would pay for that. Those two guys dead in the meadow weren't enough compensation. Bolan wanted the guy who had pulled the trigger downstairs.

Bolan could see nothing moving as he peered through the window. If there was anyone out there, he was awfully patient. Good, Bolan thought. Let him wait. Sprinting back down the stairs, Bolan searched for the floodlight switches. He found what had to be them behind the open main door. With a single swipe of his hand, the outside plunged into darkness. Now let that son of a bitch look out.

Bolan rushed to the rear door, slid the bolt back and stepped into the darkness of the patio. Swiftly he crossed the rear lawn and melted into the trees. Moving silently, he circled back toward the front, stopping every few yards to listen. If there was anyone in the trees, he could move only when Bolan moved. To keep the guy off-balance, Bolan staggered his pauses. He had nearly reached the driveway that marked the halfway point in his circuit of the house.

As he stepped into the clearing to cross the driveway, a slug whistled past his ear. Down at the bend in the driveway, where it swept to the left before meeting the road, Bolan saw a car. It was gone in an instant, but it looked like the Buick. The guy must have run for the car, then sneaked back while Bolan had been in the house.

The Executioner knew it was useless, but he snapped a burst through the trees at the end of the drive. The squeal of peeling rubber told him he had missed. He sprinted for his own car, knowing there was no way in hell he could catch the killer. There were too many roads winding through the woods and farms. The guy would be gone before Bolan had even reached the end of the drive.

But he couldn't stay here. It was too late to do anything for Hanley, and there were other things to do. His own car was still where he had left it. He slipped in, keyed the ignition and...silence. Releasing the catch, he got out and opened the hood. Everything was intact. Everything that was there. The distributor cap lay back like a dead octopus. The rotor was gone.

The killer was home free. Angry and dispirited, Mack Bolan walked back up the driveway to the house. He knew he had to call Brognola anyway, so he might as well do it from Hanley's. He wasn't looking forward to the conversation. He was looking forward to something else, though. Retribution. The bastards who had killed Hanley had done it for one of two reasons: either they enjoyed it or Hanley had known one of them. Otherwise, there was no point in killing the man. Not when they'd gotten the papers they'd come for. Not when the guy didn't have a gun and couldn't defend himself. Nope. This one was going to eat at him until he found the men responsible.

For Hanley.

And for the kid who collected the stuffed animals.

5

Paydirt, at long last. Rachel Peres was about to attend a meeting, one she had tried to be invited to for nearly a year. Working her way into the bowels of the antinuke movement had been tedious. So many times, just as she thought she was about to reach the inner circle, she had come up against another wall. The movement was like an onion. The more she peeled away, the smaller it got. But there was always another layer, and another. But now she had made it.

Her feelings were contradictory on the eve of victory. She had met several people she liked, and some she didn't. Like any loose coalition, the movement was constantly shifting. People came and went. Some saw and heard things they didn't like and formed splinter groups. Others simply never returned.

The one thing she was sure of was the constancy of a small group who never seemed to lose faith. And they never seemed to need money, despite the fact they didn't work for a living. If Peres could find out where their backing came from, she knew she'd have the lead she was searching for. And now she had it. The engraved invitation to become part of their inner circle.

Don Patterson, the man she had become the closest to, had set it up for her. The minute he'd opened his mouth, she'd known what was happening. Don was a hanger-on, always at the fringe. But he knew everybody. He was innocuous enough, and he never lacked enthusiasm. That made him useful as a messenger and a gofer. Don was the ultimate tool. Whether he realized it or not, Rachel didn't know. She was sure it wouldn't matter to Patterson anyway. He only wanted to see and be seen, to get coffee for the movers and shakers. He couldn't have cared less if his exploitation were announced in a full-page ad in the *New York Times*.

Rachel, too, had used Patterson. But her reasons were impersonal, even noble. Patterson was the key, and she had to unlock that final door before she could blow the whole business out of the water.

Last night Patterson had called. He had asked her if she wanted to meet Malcolm Parsons. She had jumped at the chance, but had kept her cool. Parsons was the heaviest antinuker around. He seemed to be everywhere at once. Not a week went by when his picture wasn't in the papers. He was always giving speeches, leading demonstrations, going to jail or getting out of it. If she could get next to Parsons, she would be in a position to learn everything. Sure, she had hunches, suspicions, guesses. But Peres knew she couldn't put anybody away with that kind of ammunition. And if she was right, Parsons was dangerous. He was a manipulator.

Parsons had organized several of the most disruptive demonstrations in the past year, including a thirty-four-day sit-in at the gates of the Willham power plant on Long Island. He had been behind a break-in at the NRC regional offices in New York City, during which low-level radioactive waste had been strewn around the offices and dumped into the file drawers. And that was when Peres had gotten suspicious. If Parsons had access to that kind of material, what else could he get his hands on? And how?

The meeting was set for a party, celebrating Parsons's release from jail after leading a flotilla of small boats into the path of a U.S. nuclear carrier. It had been all over the television for three days. One of the antinuke sailors had been killed when he'd fallen overboard and was struck by a Coast

Guard cutter escorting the big flattop. One man was dead, and several others were still in jail. Parsons, though, was out on bail—heavy bail. Rachel Peres wanted to know where the money had come from. So did a lot of other people, including Hal Brognola.

At seven o'clock, Rachel was ready to go. Patterson wouldn't be there for another half hour, but she was anxious to get on with it. If she was right, a year's work might finally pay off—if she was careful. Parsons was dangerous, but just how dangerous she didn't know.

When Patterson finally arrived, he wasted no time bundling her out of her apartment and down the stairs.

"What's the big hurry, Don?"

"Malcolm doesn't like to be kept waiting, Rachel. He's a busy man."

"I know, but it's not like he's the President, for chrissakes."

"Don't be too sure about that."

Outside, the dingy streets of the East Village looked a little better than usual, covered with the city's first light snowfall. Patterson's beat-up Chevy was parked at the curb, the engine running. In the back seat were two people she didn't know.

When Patterson closed the door behind her, one of the men in the rear reached forward and slid a blindfold over her eyes. She ripped it off and turned to confront him.

"What the hell's that all about?" she asked.

"Just a precaution, Rachel," Patterson reassured her. "Not too many people know about the house we're going to. Malcolm doesn't like people he isn't sure of to know where it is. If everything's okay, you won't have to wear it on the way home."

"Okay? What the hell do you mean, okay?"

"I mean, if Malcolm likes what he sees."

"And if he doesn't? Then what?"

"Let's cut the bullshit. We're late already." The man in the back reached forward again with the blindfold as he spoke. He pulled it down over her eyes and tied a small, hard knot in the dark cloth.

"That too tight?" he asked.

"Yes," Rachel answered.

"Good! Let's move it, Patterson."

The car lurched away from the curb, its wheels spinning slightly on the snowy street. After nearly an hour, Rachel had a splitting headache. The cloth was biting into her flesh and cutting off circulation. Her temples throbbed, and the back of her skull felt as if it was ready to explode. She was about to reach up and loosen the blindfold when the hardguy in the back seat said, "Take the next left. Past those trees."

"I know. I've been here before, don't forget," Patterson snapped.

"Yeah, I know, although I don't understand why."

The other stranger, who hadn't said a word during the trip, finally spoke. "Why don't the whole lot of you shut up? You're worse than a bunch of high school kids."

"He doesn't have to talk to me like that," Patterson said.

"Nobody's saying anything until we get inside. All of you, shut the hell up!"

The car bumped into a rutted road, and Rachel could hear snow blowing through trees on either side. It was coming down a lot harder now. The wind had picked up, and the snow scratched at the roof of the car.

"Here we are," Patterson announced.

"Can I take this damn thing off?" Rachel Peres asked. "Or do you want me to spin around three times first?"

The man behind her snapped her head back hard and jerked the blindfold off without bothering to untie it. The rough cloth scraped the skin as it came away.

When they were out of the car, she turned to the man and smacked him across the face. He raised a fist, but the less talkative of the two strangers caught his arm.

"Leave her alone, Bert. It won't accomplish anything."

Bert rubbed his cheek, trying to ease the sting. He glared at Rachel, but said nothing. She could tell by the look in his eyes that he wouldn't forget it.

"Let's go. I need something hot to drink," Patterson said. He sounded as eager as a Boy Scout on a camping trip.

Rachel's eyes were used to the dim light by now. She looked around and was surprised when she couldn't see a building. Three cars and a van were parked in the clearing. Otherwise, there was nothing but trees. Trees and snow and, off to the right, an open field sweeping uphill toward another line of trees.

"Where are we?" she asked.

"Almost there. We have to walk from here because the road's no good," Patterson told her.

Bert led the way through the snow, turning now and then to glare at Rachel over his shoulder. A half-mile trudge through the trees brought them to a large frame house sitting on a hill. It was surrounded by wide lawns, which even under a covering of snow obviously hadn't been tended in a long time. Clumps of weeds sprouted everywhere.

Inside, the house showed the same neglect. They tossed their coats in a heap in one corner, stamped the snow from their shoes and entered a large kitchen. A huge fireplace filled an entire wall. It held a small fire, and there wasn't much heat. The windows were glazed with ice even on the inside.

A large round table dominated the center of the room. Three men, drinking from chipped mugs, were seated around it. They ignored the newcomers. At a counter two women were talking softly. One poured coffee into several mugs identical to those already on the table.

The taller of the two, a slender blonde, winked at Bert. "You guys must be freezing," she said. "Have some coffee."

The blonde took a seat at the table. Her companion added milk and sugar to one of the mugs and carried it over to the table to sit next to one of the men.

"Who's the girl?" she asked.

"Some friend of Donny boy here," Bert said.

"Rachel Peres," Rachel said. "Nice to meet you."

"I'm Connie, and that's Alice," she answered, indicating the blonde. Pointing at each of the men in turn, she continued, "And these guys are Moe, Larry and Curly."

"Put a sock in it, Connie," Bert snapped. "Where's Malcolm?"

"Upstairs, sleeping."

"Well, wake him up. He wanted to meet this broad."

"Broad?" Connie asked, raising an eyebrow. "You been reading detective stories again, Bert?"

"Nah," Alice said. "Bert can't read, Connie. You know that."

The three stooges at the table laughed. Bert stomped out. They could hear him climbing the stairs, cursing as he went. In a few minutes he was back, followed by a tall, gaunt man. Rachel recognized him immediately. She had seen his face on the front page more than once and had attended several meetings that Parsons had spoken at.

Parsons nodded to the others before turning his attention to Rachel. "Ms Peres. How nice to meet you. I've heard so much about you."

"Oh? From whom?" Rachel asked. She didn't want to be too brusque, but she also knew Parsons was tough. Everything she had heard told her that he admired toughness in others.

Parsons smiled. "So, you're as sure of yourself as I've been told."

"Is that bad, Mr. Parsons?"

"On the contrary. And it's Malcolm."

"Okay. Malcolm."

"You and I have a great deal to talk about, Rachel. Why don't we get started? Please join me in my study."

Parsons turned to lead the way out of the kitchen. Down a long hall, he turned to the left. Rachel followed him into a room that was actually a large library. Its shelves were crammed with books at all angles, some upright, some stuck in lengthwise. Many of the shelves were full of papers covered with notes. There was a second fireplace, this one with a huge fire raging in it. Parsons dropped onto a sofa, lying back in a luxuriant stretch.

"Please, make yourself comfortable," he said, indicating a pair of overstuffed easy chairs.

"What do we have to talk about?" Rachel asked.

"I have plans, my dear. Big plans. I can use someone like you."

"Nobody uses me, Malcolm. I won't allow it."

"Let me rephrase that. There is a real need for someone like you in our organization."

"How do you know that? You don't know anything about me."

"That's where you're wrong, Rachel. I know everything about you. I have many friends, as you might have guessed. I've had my eye on you for quite a while now."

"Why?"

"As I said, because I need someone like you. Someone intelligent, someone with courage. I have had you watched for a couple of months. Closely. At the Big Falls sit-in you didn't panic when things got rough. That alone makes you special. Most of the members ran around like lost sheep when the police moved in."

"I never cared for getting hit from behind," Rachel said. She smiled stiffly. Parsons nodded. "I gather you're planning something special."

"Oh, yes, indeed. Something very special, Rachel. Nothing like it has ever been tried before."

"What is it?"

"All in good time, my dear. It's time to explore some of your other qualities."

"Like?"

"You are a very attractive woman, Rachel."

"I see. Is this your idea of initiation?"

"You might say that, yes."

"And if I agree? Then do I get to hear about your special project?"

"You're very curious about that, aren't you?"

"Sure I am. I've never considered a roll in the hay as a political statement. If I'm going to make a difference in this world, I can't spend too much time on my back."

"Oh, you'll make a difference, all right. We all will. If I can pull this off, it will be the end of nuclear power in this country. Perhaps in the world. That's something worth doing, don't you think? Something worth enduring 'a roll in the hay' for? Besides, you might enjoy this more than you think."

Malcolm Parsons looked every inch the scholar. A shock of wild, white hair drooped over his brow. His skin was lined and leathery looking, yet pale. It had the doughy pallor of someone who lived under artificial light. Despite his age, his features were strong, accented by his gauntness. He looked like a poet should look. He was the kind of older man an impressionable sophomore might find attractive—if she were a romantic, and if she didn't look too closely.

He extended his arms. Rachel got up and walked to the sofa. She knew there were some things you just had to do, no matter how distasteful you found them. Enjoy it, hell. The only thing she would enjoy about Malcolm Parsons was watching the sleazy bastard fry.

She pulled her sweater over her head. What would Mack Bolan think if he knew what she was about to do?

6

Leaning toward the front of the cab, Peter Achison snapped at the driver. "Move it, can't you? I've got a plane to catch."

"Keep your shirt on, pal. Everybody's got a plane to catch. That's why there's so much traffic."

Achison was too distracted to appreciate the cabbie's irony. He was already in hot water. He hadn't gotten Hanley's papers, Otto and Jameson were dead, and now he was going to miss his plane. He'd be lucky if he kept his head, let alone his job.

Achison had taken a bus from Washington to Philadelphia, switched to the train in Philly, looked in on Malcolm Parsons, and then laid up at a cheap hotel in the Times Square area for two days. No one knew yet whether he had succeeded or not. Communication was strictly personal. No phones, no telegrams, no letters. And no papers. Unable to sleep soundly, he had passed the time in the hotel with whiskey and television. Now his nerves were stretched to the breaking point.

As they neared Kennedy International, the traffic got even heavier. A light rain, which had melted any remaining snow from the city's first storm of the season, had made the road slick, and the cars were moving gingerly when they moved at all. His flight was still an hour away, but check-in was a lot more complicated than it used to be. Ironically it was the threat of terrorism that slowed the process to a crawl. He would be a casualty of his own beliefs. Lateness was not expected of someone in his line of work. Nor was it appreciated.

"Hey, pal!" the cabbie hollered. "I said what airline? Ain't you in such a big hurry, after all?"

"BEA, and step on it."

They pulled into the terminal approach road, and cars began to peel off the line as passengers found the appropriate airline. The traffic was still sluggish, but moving with more purpose now. As the car pulled up to the BEA terminal, Achison fiddled with the buttons on his coat, removed his wallet and then jumped out of the cab. After closing the door, he handed the driver two twenties. "Keep the change," he said, extending the money to the cabbie.

"Yeah, pal, thanks," he said. He watched Achison enter the terminal, then pulled away, muttering, "I break my butt to get him here on time and he gives me a buck tip."

Once inside, Achison went right to the check-in counter, checked his bag and got his boarding pass. The clock overhead showed ten minutes before boarding time, so he found a cigar stand, bought a pack of English Ovals and a newspaper, then went to the lounge to wait for his flight.

Once on board, he ordered three drinks, added them to the several he had drunk before leaving the hotel and fell asleep. When he woke, they were beginning their approach into Orly. He called the flight attendant for a hot towel to freshen up and ran a nervous hand through his thinning hair. He was to be met at the airport, and he wanted to make a decent impression. His fastidiousness had deserted him under the pressure of the past few days, but it was an asset, and he struggled to restore a sense of control over events.

The terminal at Orly was crowded. The mob scene around the luggage carousel put him on edge, and he had to remind himself that he was in control. When his bag finally showed, he snatched it hurriedly and went to the main lounge. It was eight o'clock. Time to go. Right on the dot, he stood and folded his newspaper three times, tucked it under his left arm and picked up his bag. A man seated across from him also rose and followed Achison into the main lobby. Achison stopped abruptly. The second man bumped him and continued walking. Achison followed.

Out in the cold air, Achison followed the man to a dark green Renault in the parking area and got in the passenger side. His companion started the car and pulled out into the exit lane before speaking.

"How'd it go?"

"Well enough, I expect."

"You expect?"

"Yes, I expect. I'll let Andrey make the final evaluation." Achison's tone was abrupt. He resented the questions. This clown was not someone to whom he owed any sort of explanation.

"Oh, he'll do that. I expect." The man smiled, but Achison ignored him. "He's anxious to look at those papers, you know. He's worried they may be getting onto us."

"I don't think so," Achison said.

"Andrey does."

"Just drive. I'm tired. I don't want to talk."

"Suit yourself."

On the outskirts of Paris, the driver pulled into the driveway of a large estate. A brick wall surrounded the well-manicured lawns. It was topped with broken glass that glittered in the security lights mounted at thirty-yard intervals. The estate was the headquarters of an international trading firm, and the rather extensive security was considered a necessity. Too many industrialists and executives had been kidnapped in recent years for the precautions to seem unusual.

After the Renault had passed through, a uniformed guard pulled a heavy iron gate closed behind it. The Renault continued up the drive and pulled around to the side of the house. Achison got out, taking his bag. Before he could close the door, the driver leaned across to the passenger side and said, "Andrey's in the library. He'll want to see you right away. I expect." Achison slammed the door on the man's harsh laughter.

The huge walnut side door opened as Achison approached. An attractive dark-haired woman greeted him politely and took his bag. After he hung his coat on a rack, she led the way into the dim exterior of the large house. She stopped at a double-doored archway, indicating that Achison should enter. He stepped into the gloomy room, only vaguely aware of the doors closing behind him.

"Sit down, Peter."

A flickering flame broke behind a large desk. Achison could discern the outlines of a large leather chair. As his eyes adjusted, the chair spun. Andrey Glinkov finished lighting his cigar and snapped his lighter shut.

"Did you get the papers, Peter?"

Achison sat down before answering. "No, there was...uh...there was some trouble." Despite his intention to remain calm, he could hear the quaver in his voice.

"What kind of trouble?"

"Someone else was there. He...uh...he killed Otto and took the papers."

"But he didn't kill you? That's very interesting. I should imagine Otto posed more difficulty than you would."

"I don't know. I wasn't there. I mean, I was there, but not when he got Otto. I sent Otto to the car with the papers. Before I left the house, somebody attacked us. He killed Otto and Jameson. He was coming back for me, but I got away. I took a shot at him, but I missed."

"I'm not surprised. It's rather difficult to hit a target you're running away from. I am disappointed, Peter. Very disappointed."

"I know how much you wanted those papers."

"But you did kill Robert Hanley, didn't you?"

Achison relaxed. "Yes, I did. At least that went okay."

"No, Peter, it did *not* go okay. Your orders were only to get the papers. I said nothing about disposing of Mr. Hanley. This unfortunate matter has called too much attention to affairs we would prefer were unnoticed."

"I don't understand what you mean. How?"

"By disposing of Mr. Hanley as you did, you have called attention not only to him, but to his work, Peter. If the papers were the cause of his death, as will most assuredly be assumed, thanks to you, people will naturally look very closely at those papers. Won't they, Peter?"

"Yes. But I thought I had the papers. Then it wouldn't have mattered. There wouldn't have been anything to look at. It would have looked like a burglary. Would have, if that big bastard hadn't interrupted."

"Tell me about this man."

"I don't know much. I didn't get a real good look at him. He's about six two or so I guess. Dark hair. Hell of a shot. He must be a real pro to take Otto out that easily."

"Yes, he is. You have no idea how good."

"You know who it was?"

"Let's just say I have my suspicions. And if I'm right, Peter, your job is going to be much more difficult than any of us thought."

"Who is it then?"

"If the same man you met was behind the unpleasant failure at Dunford, and I believe he was, it sounds very much like the work of a man known as Mack Bolan."

"Who?"

"Never mind, Peter. Just think of him as the Executioner. He may very well be yours."

"Who the hell is he?"

"All in good time, Peter. All in good time. I have a few more questions to ask before I answer any of yours."

Glinkov's calm was a lie, and Peter Achison knew it. There had been much expected and little delivered. At their last meeting, Glinkov had outlined the KGB's current efforts to destabilize American energy programs. The Kremlin knew, as did anyone who thought about it clearly, that American independence from Third World oil was crucial to a continued American presence on the world stage. If she had to kowtow to every backwater nation with any significant amount of crude underground, the United States would be unwilling to step on toes.

What the Kremlin wanted, and what it was Glinkov's job to deliver, was an American public frightened of nuclear energy. Once that was accomplished, the Soviet Union would have a free hand throughout the Middle East and much of Africa. Andrey Glinkov wanted to deliver, and Peter Achison was letting him down.

Unable to keep silent any longer, Achison cleared his throat. "Do you want to ask those questions now, or shall I come back in the morning?"

"Will your answers be any different tomorrow?"

"Well, no. No, they won't—"

"Then kindly wait until I am ready to continue. We may as well get the whole sorry mess over with this evening." Glinkov picked up a folder and spun his chair away from Achison.

The Russian was a cool one; Achison had to give him that. Andrey Glinkov was already notorious throughout the European intelligence community. On both sides of the fence he had a reputation for his ruthlessness and cunning. As near as Achison could tell, he was no more trusted by his Red comrades than he was by Western agencies. The son of an assistant to Lavrenti Beria—the most dreaded secret police chief—he had parlayed his father's bloodthirsty reputation into a career of his own. Beria's influence had long since faded, but the mention of the name still sent shivers down Soviet spines.

Glinkov knew it and was not above trading on it. The prevailing opinion in KGB circles was that one should stay on Glinkov's good side . . . if only one could find it.

Glinkov's current position gave him a free hand to draw on recourses from any directorate, any section, at will. He was determined to make the most of it. And if Achison couldn't help him, he'd have to find someone who could. Glinkov turned back to face his worried agent.

"You know my reputation for impatience, Peter?"

"Yes." Achison swallowed hard. He didn't want to hear what was coming.

"Well, it's all true. One might say I have worked very hard to earn that reputation. However, even a man as impatient as I am can be patient when the situation warrants. This is such a situation. You have done well in the past. I am sure your latest failure is, shall we say, a momentary lapse. I want to give you the chance to redeem yourself."

"Thank you, Andrey. You won't be sorry."

"No, I won't be. But if you fail me again, my friend, you most assuredly will be."

"I understand. What do you want me to do?"

"This man Bolan must be eliminated."

"That might not be so easy. How do I find him?"

"The trick, dear Peter, is to let him find you. And we are already taking steps in that direction. We have a number of operations planned. Nothing major, of course. I want Bolan out of the way before we unveil our masterpiece. But Bolan will be given the opportunity to learn of these minor plots. Sooner or later he will, no doubt, attempt to interfere. When he does, you will be waiting for him. And . . ." Glinkov ground finger and thumb together as if squashing a bug.

"How can you be sure he'll take the bait?"

"Quite simple, really. We have already recruited someone who will tell him. An Israeli woman who is working for the Americans. Our friend Parsons is making sure that she will pass the correct information to Bolan. You will do the rest. Won't you?"

Achison nodded. "Just one thing, though. Aren't you putting Malcolm Parsons at risk?"

"We are all at risk, Peter. We all have our jobs to do. We all have sacrifices to make."

"Does Malcolm know this?"

"Malcolm Parsons is an idiot. He has been useful, and will continue to be, for now. That's all. I'll be in touch with you."

"I see."

Glinkov spun away in his chair again. Achison rose to leave.

"Just one more thing, Peter," Glinkov said without bothering to turn around. "If you should fail to eliminate Mack Bolan, and if he doesn't kill you in your attempt, there will be no place for you to hide. Do I make myself clear?"

Achison knew better than to answer.

7

There was something in the air. Mack Bolan could sense it. Ever since the previous evening, when he had received an urgent message from Rachel Peres, his mind had been racing. The message, of course, had been brief, and coded. But for some reason the young woman had a hold on his imagination.

And now it seemed like she might have something more than that. She just might have managed to get them the break they needed. Bolan was aware of how hard she'd worked to get into the inner circle. The going had been slow. Wary of being set up, Rachel had had to push deeper without seeming to. Every step she'd taken had had to seem like one she had been asked to take.

The minute anyone in the organization felt she was pushing, they would back off. Not only would her access to information be cut, her life might be and probably would be in danger.

Bolan, unlike Brognola, was not convinced that Rachel's ties with Mossad had been cut. But as long as they were after the same thing, he knew it didn't matter. And if there ever came a time when it did matter, he thought he could trust her. Probably.

There were still two hours before their meeting, and Mack Bolan had things to do. No action meant no progress. Since the attack on Robert Hanley, he had felt like a blind man in a fun house. Rachel had fed him enough to convince him that there was something big in the works. He wanted a piece of it. Now.

There was something hypnotic in his preparations. Carefully cleaning the .44 AutoMag had become second nature. The concentration was total. Pure. His life—and the lives of others—would depend on the weapon. It had been that way so many times in the past that it had become a given.

There was an irony in the situation that never escaped him. But he seldom dwelled on it. That something so lethal could also be life-giving was just one more of life's contradictions. The Beretta was less awesome, more like an old friend than a skull-busting ally. The three had been through some tough times together. And that was the key—together.

Tonight, Bolan thought, he might depend on them again. Rachel's news would be important. Of that there could be no doubt. That it could be a setup was more than a possibility, though. Her success had been extraordinary. It had been quick and, apparently, total. What Bolan didn't know was why.

Rachel Peres was a professional. Bolan had accepted that. So were the boys she was playing with. And it was possible for her cover to have been blown in a hundred ways. Some of them she would recognize, some would escape her. So Big Thunder would be riding his hip, just like always. And the Beretta would tag along.

When the guns were cleaned and oiled, he slipped them into their holsters. He had under an hour now, and it would take twenty minutes to make the rendezvous point. It was time to go. As always, Mack Bolan wanted to be early. There were too many loopholes, too many places for people to hide. If a man wanted to stay alive in this line of work, he plugged the loopholes, and flushed out the hiding places *before* it mattered. Otherwise it could be too late.

The meeting had been set for the southwest corner of Central Park. There were too many eyes in New York, too many people could see you when you couldn't see them. The safest place to be was someplace where only a fool, or a criminal, would go. That meant Central Park at night. In the winter.

Outside his hotel, Mack Bolan caught a cab for the ride to Columbus Circle. He watched the traffic, but there was no sign that he was being followed. At the Circle he left the cab, attracting little, if any, attention. The fountain plaza was less crowded than usual. Even society's derelicts sought refuge from the cold.

Rachel was going to wait for him in the park on the bridle path. The shadows under the roadway overpass would be appropriate cover for their meeting. Most New Yorkers avoided such places even at high noon on a summer day. No one with legitimate business would be around. Bolan entered the park followed by jeers and a sales pitch or two, most of which would have been offensive if they had been intelligible. He watched carefully to see whether anyone had paid more than the expected attention. Even a drunk should have noticed a well-dressed man entering the park at night. No one seemed overly interested.

Once inside, it was immediately dark. What few lights there were had long been dead. Vandals accounted for their fair share, and muggers had done away with the rest. The leaves underfoot crunched in the cold, and stray papers blew across the pavement. The wind was brisk, and that was bad. The noise would make it easier for a tail to hide his presence.

At a fork in the walk he paused against a light stanchion to survey the area to his rear. Anything—a flitting shadow, a thud, even a breaking twig—could make the difference. Satisfied that no one was following, he moved deeper into the park.

Bearing to the right, he approached the bridle path. The black dirt was frozen, and the crust looked undisturbed. No one had passed that way recently. Once on the path, he increased his vigilance. The walkway was overhung by trees on both sides, making it a gloomy tunnel. For some reason that escaped both the New York police and Mack Bolan, people insisted on walking that way at night, and muggers kept right on waiting.

After about seventy yards, Bolan's attuned sense of hearing registered something. It was a whisper. That meant one of two things. Either someone was talking to himself or, more likely, two people were hidden in the trees to his left. Bolan turned to look behind him.

The prick of cold steel on his cheek came as no surprise. Holding an urge to retaliate in check, he waited for the second punk to step in front of him.

"Hey, man, you lost?" The sneer was obvious, even in the shadows.

"No. Are you?" Bolan felt the knife a second time.

"You looking for drugs, I bet. You ain't out for the air, is you my man?"

"As a matter of fact I am."

Bolan dropped quickly to the bridle path, spinning on his back as he did. His left foot flashed out and caught one punk in the groin, doubling him over. The second mugger stepped forward, but he was too slow. Bolan caught his extended arm, reaching in behind the blade. He pulled forward, using the momentum to snap the punk's arm at the elbow.

He looked at the two of them, no more than kids, and shook his head in disgust. "You guys shouldn't be out here. Don't you have anything better to do?"

"Man, you broke my goddamn arm. What'd you do that for?"

"If you want to keep the other one, get out of here, and take that garbage with you. Now."

"Let's go, man," the nut-busted mugger groaned. "That son of a bitch'll kill us, man."

Bolan watched them stagger off toward the light and wondered if they'd ever know how lucky they'd been. Another night, and he might have taught them a lesson they'd never forget. This one they'd probably just chalk up to experience and maybe take it out on their next victim. Maybe. There was nothing Mack Bolan could do about that. Not now.

He quickened his pace to make up for lost time. Reaching the overpass five minutes before the appointed hour, he gave it a quick once-over. Rachel wasn't there yet. No reason she should be. And, better yet, the place was deserted. He pressed back into the shadows to wait.

On the dot of nine he flicked his lighter on and off. An answering glow flashed among the trees, and a moment later Rachel joined him.

"You all right?" Bolan asked.

"So far."

"What's up? Your message was urgent."

"I'm not sure. There's a lot going on, and I'm not sure I like it. It's too easy."

"What do you mean?" Bolan knew what she was going to say.

"I can't believe they trust me as much as they seem to. It makes no sense. They're up to something big. I know that. But I don't know what. On the other hand, they've let me in on some penny-ante stuff."

"Such as?"

Rachel quickly sketched the details of three operations that Malcolm Parsons had personally briefed her on. All were scheduled for the next two weeks, and none seemed particularly momentous. Bolan didn't like it.

Not a bit.

"What do you think they're up to?" he asked.

"I don't know. There was a new guy around. I never saw him before. He and Parsons locked themselves up in the library, sometimes for hours at a time."

"Any idea who he is?"

"No. I don't even know his name. They call him Peter, but that's all I know. He's tall, thinning hair. Sounds English, but I'm not certain."

"Try to find out what they're up to. Don't take any unnecessary risks, but do what you can. I think we're being set up."

"But how? Why?"

"How, I don't know. Why I can guess. They're onto me, and they want me. They're trying to smoke me out. The guy at Hanley's, the one who got away. He must have gotten a better look at me than I thought. If they ran that past the boys in the Kremlin, they probably got a make on me. I don't know. It's just a hunch."

"What about me?"

"Watch yourself. They don't trust you. That's obvious. And they'll try to use you to get to me if they make a connection. Are you sure you weren't followed tonight?"

"As sure as I could be. There's always a chance, of course."

The darkness of the overpass suddenly deepened. Bolan glanced toward the mouth of the tunnel and saw two men advancing toward them. Two more entered at the other end. It was a trap, and a good one.

"Get back against the wall and lie down," Bolan hissed, pressing Rachel against the stone. "We've got company."

He unslung the Beretta and dropped to the ground. Their only chance was to clean out one end of the tunnel, fast. And that would just reduce the odds. Bolan hoped they didn't have lights.

As if on cue, one end of the tunnel was bathed in illumination. He snapped a shot at the hand-held torch. He missed the light, but not the man behind it. With a groan, the man dropped the lamp, falling forward to cover it. The Executioner fired again, aiming between the twin points of light escaping from under the man's body. The slug hit home.

Looking over his shoulder, he gauged the distance to the other two men, who seemed to have waited at the mouth of the tunnel. Turning his attention back to the first team, he sighted in on the remaining gunman. So far the newcomers hadn't fired a single shot. But Bolan knew he couldn't count on the situation remaining one-sided. He fired twice, the Beretta whispering death from the shadows. The slugs found their target. They punched the guy twice, once in the forehead and once in the throat. He fell backward, slamming his head against the frozen earth of the bridle path.

The remaining pair still blocked the other end of the overpass. It was almost as if they wanted Bolan and Rachel Peres to escape. But Bolan knew the best defense was a good offense. What's true in football is also true in war, Bolan thought. He couldn't let the two men escape. They could confirm that he had met with Rachel. Suspicion was one thing; proof was another. It would finish her career with Parsons, and it would endanger her life.

The Executioner rolled across the cold earth to the opposite wall. So far the surviving team hadn't produced a light of its own. Maybe they thought they'd need only the one. Okay, Bolan thought, so they'd learn something.

Against the far wall Bolan peered into the darkness. That end of the tunnel, the park end, was much dimmer. The shadows of the two men were motionless, almost indistinguishable from the surrounding gloom. As he watched, he heard the whine of a slug. It narrowly missed him, chipping the stone just above his head.

These guys were pros. No noise, no light. Just spitting death. At him. He'd have to move in, and quickly. Setting the Beretta for a three-shot burst, he aimed into the heart of the darkness. The surprised hiss told him he'd found his mark. The dark shape slid down the wall. It didn't move.

He wormed forward, trying not to rasp his clothes against the wall. The guy couldn't see him. If his opponent heard him, Bolan would be in trouble. The guy was barely visible, and then he was gone. Bolan heard footsteps. The gunner had split.

Unless he was waiting just beyond the mouth of the tunnel.

If Bolan rushed into the light, he'd be a sitting duck. Or a dead one. Well, there was no other way, Bolan thought. He stood up and yanked Big Thunder from its sling. He slipped the Beretta under his coat and ran for the opening.

The guy's footsteps were pounding on the bridle path straight ahead. Bolan raced after him. He was gaining ground rapidly. The guy was out of shape. He didn't even have sense enough to head into the trees.

As the Executioner narrowed the gap, the guy tried to sprint, but he didn't have it in him. Bolan caught up with him at a fork in the bridle path in a thick stand of trees. The guy was a game one. He turned and aimed his weapon as Bolan leaped. Aiming a fist at the guy's jaw, Bolan bore into him with a shoulder. They went down in a heap.

Bolan knew that it would be useful to hang on to this one. He could tell them a lot they needed to know. Getting to his feet, Bolan grabbed at the guy and hauled. The man was breathing like a beached whale. All the fight had gone out of him. This was going to be easier than Bolan had hoped. Suddenly the guy sagged, and the weight was more than Bolan could handle. And then Bolan caught the scent of almonds.

Cyanide. The guy *was* a pro. And for somebody heavy. Bolan bent over the supine body and clicked his lighter. The man's features were twisted by the poison, but there was no mistaking their origin, or that of the ill-fitting suit. They were Eastern cut. Bulgaria probably. That made one thing certain: hit men of this caliber weren't sent out just to keep an eye on some wayward antinuker. They were onto Rachel.

And onto Mack Bolan.

8

"Shit, I hate physical inventory." Dave Jennings slammed a clipboard onto his desk and flipped his pencil high in the air. He missed the catch, sending the pencil skittering off into a corner of the office.

"You don't like anything physical, Dave. Inventory or otherwise." Pete Collins was anything but sympathetic.

"Hell, I'm as physical as the next guy. In the right circumstances. But putting on a rubber suit to stand around and count tubes of hot metal isn't physical. And it isn't fun."

"Maybe not, but we got to do it, so let's get it done." Collins laughed quietly while he slipped on his protective gear. Jennings was having trouble getting into his own suit, but Collins enjoyed the scene too much to offer to help.

Jennings was still fuming. "You know, every three months, we do the same damn thing. And every three months we come up with the same numbers. Since Number 2 went down, we haven't used a single fuel rod."

"Maybe not, but how would we know that if nobody counted 'em?"

"You're starting to sound like one of those NRC guys, Pete. You doing some sort of consulting work on the side?"

"Wish to hell I did, man. You know, consulting is where it's at. You get paid big bucks and all you got to do is tell somebody something he already knows."

Jennings finally smiled. Both men were ready to enter the fuel dump. Collins secretly agreed with his partner. The work was boring. There was rarely any suspense to break up the monotony, and there was certainly no glamour. But rules were rules. And the rules were that you counted the radioactive material in your possession. You counted carefully and you counted often.

Like Jennings, Collins sometimes wished that a discrepancy would show in their figures. It would mean they'd have to go back and do it all over again. But at least the numbers would mean something. In the three and a half years since the TVA Station 2 reactor had been out of service, they had been getting the same result every time they counted.

"You ready, Pete?" Jennings asked.

Collins noaded. Jennings punched the combination into the electronic lock on Fuel Repository Number 1 and waited for the huge door to swing open. Collins stood to the side with a calculator in one hand and a clipboard in the other. When the door was open, the men stepped through and Collins punched in the closing combination.

Neither man knew both combinations. The theory behind this security measure was that it would make theft and sabotage more difficult. There was no real reason for it, since the problem was not access to the fuel rods as much as getting them past the heavy security and radiation detectors at the main gate. The rods were long and pencil thin. You couldn't disassemble them, and you sure as hell couldn't hide them under your clothes. And if you did, you wouldn't get any closer than fifty yards to the gate without setting off an alarm.

Neither he nor Collins was in the same room with the fuel rods. They were on the other side of a thick concrete and steel wall, but the TV equipment they used to monitor the fuel supply was off-limits to most personnel. The fuel was so hot that they were required to wear protective gear. Collins often complained that he had to wear the outfit "Just to watch TV."

As soon as he began his count, Jennings knew something was wrong. He adjusted the contrast on his monitor just to be sure. When he had the focus as sharp as he could get it, he whispered to Collins. "Pete, come here. We've been robbed."

"Sure," Collins said, laughing. "I got to hand it to you, my man. That's a new one. You've tried just about every way a man could to make this more exciting than it is."

"I'm not kidding, Pete. Look for yourself. Punch up A-28."

While Collins directed his camera, Jennings left his own screen to join his partner. "Okay, a little higher and to the left. There. What do you see?"

"Holy shit. Holes. Fucking holes. We *have* been robbed. Must be sixteen, eighteen rods missing."

"Twenty-one. I counted."

"Damn! We got to get hold of McAndrews. He's going to have a stroke, man. A fuckin' stroke."

THE FIRST TIME THE NEEDLE JUMPED, Dave Steinberg thought he was imagining things. He rubbed his eyes, and watched. The needle was normal. He took a quick look at the bank of warning lights. They were all dark. The readings on all the other gauges were ordinary.

The temperature needle jumped again. This time it stayed against the right-hand peg. Something sure as hell was going on. Steinberg punched into the main PA and called his supervisor. While he waited for Mike Orlando, he watched the needle. It was starting to fall back toward the normal range. For a second he thought he'd call Orlando back and tell him to forget it. When the needle jumped a third time, he knew something was wrong.

The main control room door hissed open, and Orlando slipped in. "What's up?" he asked.

"Look at the temperature on sixteen."

"It's a little high. So what?"

"So it buried the needle twice. There's something wrong on that line. No way the temperature should skip around like that. Keep an eye on it."

Steinberg got up, and Orlando slid into the empty chair. He watched the gauge for several minutes without speaking.

"It still seems okay to me. A little skittish maybe, but—"

The bank of warning lights exploded into color. At the same time, the needle went off the high end.

"That's it, Davey. Hit the alarm. And check the cameras. Make sure there's nobody down there. Where's Patty?"

"She was going to check out Tower 3," Steinberg said, punching up the monitor for her location. A small figure in a bulky radiation suit appeared on the screen. "Christ, Mike. She's still down there."

As the men watched, a cloud of steam came into view at the bottom of the screen. It billowed like the fog in a monster movie, rising a foot or two, falling back halfway, then climbing again.

"Get on the radio, Davey. She doesn't see it."

Steinberg tried to raise her. It took him a few seconds. Finally he heard her voice.

"Hi, guys. What's happening?"

"Patty, don't panic. Just look behind you and tell me what you see."

"Quit clowning around, David."

"I'm not clowning, Patty. Do it. Now!"

Steinberg could see the figure on the screen halt. It bent to the side and down. "Holy shit! What's going on? Where the hell did all that steam come from?"

"How bad is it, Patty?"

"I don't know. The whole bottom of the tower is full of it. Is it hot?"

"I'm getting eighty rems per, Patty. You have to get the hell out of there. Now."

"What's happening, David?" Her voice began to break. She had been with them only six months. She'd never seen anything like this. Hell, none of them had. And if she didn't get out of the tower, she'd never see anything like it again.

"I got another needle hopping here, Davey. It's on the same line." Orlando was yelling to make himself heard over the klaxons blaring throughout the power station. "She has to get out of there."

The steam was growing as if it were alive. It followed Patty as she clambered up the ladder. The woman turned again to check her location. As Steinberg watched, the steam mushroomed upward, and Patty was obscured from view for a moment. The steam thinned a bit, and Steinberg could see her struggling to keep her grip. By now she was probably hysterical. He never should have told her how hot the steam was.

The ladder would get tougher and tougher to hold on to. It would get slippery with condensation. Then, in one breathtaking moment, it happened. The woman's left foot slipped off the ladder as she put her weight on it. She hung suspended by both arms. Her feet whirled helplessly in the air as she sought to regain the ladder. Then she was gone from the screen.

"Oh, God," Orlando groaned. "Oh, my God."

"Patty," Steinberg screamed. "Patty." He clicked the mike on and off, trying to raise her again. But he knew there was no way. No one could survive the steam, never mind the fall. And who knew what was at the bottom of that infernal cloud. The klaxons continued to blare. The lights flashed like a Christmas tree. One by one, the needles on the Tower 3 cooling lines began to waver, then to climb.

"Attention, all personnel," Orlando roared into the PA mike. "We have an event in progress. Repeat, event in progress. L.O.C.A. in progress."

Steinberg stared at the empty monitor, now completely engulfed in steam. "It all sounds so routine, Mike. Loss of coolant accident. L.O.C.A., my ass. What the hell are we doing here?"

THE HUGE FLATBED TRAILER RUMBLED up Third Avenue, bouncing over every pothole. The deadweight strapped to its middle rocked precariously. Every bounce threatened to sever the heavy steel bands that clamped the load in place. There was little traffic, other than the trailer and its two escort vehicles. A police cruiser was in the lead and another followed the truck at a respectable distance.

The patrolmen in the rear had been given the standard briefing. They knew the lead-lined steel canister was supposed to be tightly sealed and accident proof. They didn't believe it, but not because they were in the habit of mistrusting their superiors. They didn't believe it for a far simpler reason: if the official version was incorrect, they were dead men. The canister contained plutonium so radioactive that a single speck lodged in a lung would mean certain death.

Among them the four patrolmen had thirty-seven years of experience on the streets of New York. They had seen death in all of its urban forms. Blood was just a color to them now. Brighter than some perhaps, but not unusual. But this time they were scared stiff. The transport of this cargo had been on again, off again for years. Enough people had had enough reasons to delay the passage of radioactive material through inhabited areas so that the case had been tied up in the courts for years. It had finally been approved, but the losers died hard.

Each of the cops knew there were dozens of groups who had their own reasons for wanting an accident in the city.

Some because of the warning it would represent, others for the havoc it would wreak. Some even wanted, hoped, to get their hands on some of the deadly metal. There was enough fissionable material on the tail of the truck to make a half-dozen small tactical nuclear weapons. Everybody knew there were people dying to get their hands on it. The Libyans wanted it, and the Israelis thought they needed it. A dozen countries would love to have it, and twenty terror groups would kill to get it. Yeah, the cops were scared.

At Fifty-third Street, a white van ran a red light, narrowly missing the tractor, and just squeezing between it and the lead car. The backup car peeled out and slid sideways across the avenue. Buck Foster was out of the cruiser and on the divider, pumping a shell into his shotgun before the car stopped rocking. He sighed when the van kept moving. He didn't know whether he was relieved or disappointed. Probably both, he thought, knowing that he couldn't take much more tension. He hopped back into the patrol car, and Dan McGuire gunned it into a roar, caught up with the caravan and punched his horn twice. The driver honked the truck's horn in acknowledgment.

"Buck, I don't know about you, man. But the sooner we turn this baby over to some other jurisdiction, the happier I'll be," McGuire said.

"Hell, yes, Danny. It's enough to make a no-nuker out of you. The crap in that truck scares me shitless."

Neither man really felt like talking, but neither one could help doing it. At Sixty-sixth street, McGuire shot ahead of the truck, and the lead car fell back. The men weren't supposed to rotate their positions, but everybody agreed it would help cut the tension.

At 110th Street it started to rain. And by 125th Street it was impossible to see more than twenty yards ahead. The wipers clacked, and the wheels hissed on the slick pavement. McGuire was getting edgy as he slid to the right-hand lane to wait for the backup car to rotate forward. Three blocks later, he was still waiting.

"Something's wrong, Bucko. Where's Rodriguez? He should have made it up here by now."

Foster craned his neck to see past the rear of the flatbed. There was nothing but wet pavement.

"Holy shit! Rodriguez is missing."

"What the hell are you talking about?" McGuire whispered.

"It's us and the truck, man. That's all. There ain't nobody else behind us."

"Where the hell are they?"

"You're asking me?"

McGuire never answered. The window on the driver's side mushroomed inward. He was dead before the car plowed into the front of a rib joint at 133rd Street.

Foster reached for the two-way and yelled into the static. The mike was as dead as McGuire. The surviving cop kicked open his door and fell to his knees as the truck disappeared into the night.

Down Third Avenue he recognized a cruiser. Its roof lights were blinking sporadically. He got to his feet and struggled toward it. He had to get this on the radio as soon as possible. He didn't understand why the other car hadn't notified McGuire it was bailing out.

When he got to the cruiser, he found out. Rodriguez was slumped over the steering wheel. His head hung at a crazy angle—what was left of it. His partner in the shotgun seat was just as dead. Foster grabbed the radio and clicked it open. Nothing but static.

ON A ROOFTOP at 127th Street, Peter Achison watched, waiting for Mack Bolan. He watched Buck Foster struggle down the avenue searching for a phone. It was cold and rainy, and Mack Bolan hadn't shown. Achison nodded to the two men with him. He whispered into his small walkie-talkie, dispatching three shadows from the roofline across the street. He watched Buck Foster stagger south for another half block, shook his head and stepped out of the rain. Maybe Foster would tell Bolan enough to get him interested.

9

All right, they wanted to play games. Mack Bolan liked games, too. And he played for keeps. The missing plutonium would be round one. Brognola's sources had learned that the stuff had already been sold. But Bolan knew it sure as hell had been stolen to get his attention. And the thieves had it.

The Fed's sources had told him that the hot stuff had been off-loaded and the truck ditched north of the city. The plutonium had been taken to West Virginia and hidden in a cave. It was there waiting, waiting for somebody to come and get it. Sure, it was sold, and the Libyans would still have been happy if they had had to pay twice the price. It was a steal.

But Brognola was concerned that somebody else might be just as interested. That much fissionable material was bound to attract some attention from a number of parties. And there were too many people with questionable connections moving in and out of Malcolm Parsons's group.

Modesty wasn't part of Parsons's character. He'd been bragging about the coup. Bolan was determined to break the thing wide open, and to do it quickly. The last thing he needed was to walk into a free-for-all. Taking on Parsons's clowns would be a picnic. But if the KGB moved in, or one of the terrorist groups thought it was an easy score, Bolan wouldn't have time for sandwiches.

The West Virginia mountains were honeycombed with caverns, most of which weren't on any map. Some were regularly used by moonshiners, some hadn't been visited since the Revolutionary War. The limestone of the Alleghenies had been dissolving for millions of years. In fact, geologists thought it might even be possible to travel from northern Pennsylvania all the way to Georgia without coming up for air.

The intel had even been able to pinpoint the cave. A little footwork had paid quick dividends. It had been easy to find, but Bolan knew it wouldn't be easy to get close to without tipping his hand.

Once he left Morgantown behind, the winter woods surrounded him. Thick stands of trees rolled on and on over mountains. As he drove deeper into the forest, the towns got smaller and more dilapidated. Bolan wondered how Parsons had known such a place existed. Why he had chosen it to hide the plutonium was obvious.

Two miles from Pine Grove, close enough to walk, Bolan pulled his rented Blazer into a logging road overgrown with weeds. Two hundred yards in, the vehicle would be invisible from the road. He edged the Blazer into the brush to avoid blocking the road, although it looked as if it hadn't been used in years.

It was getting dark. The cold was biting, and his breath clouded in front of him as he walked. The Weatherby Mark V was slung over his shoulder, its scope covered to protect it from becoming scratched.

The going was tough. Every breath stung as he drew it. Uphill was the worst; downhill not much better. The terrain was rocky, scattered with weathered boulders. Fallen branches and leaning trunks of long-dead trees littered the grounds. The Executioner felt right at home. It wasn't jungle, true enough, but he was hunting the usual game.

Bolan didn't know for sure what he was up against until he had a chance to watch the cave. If he was lucky, there would only be a small force. Heavily armed, for sure, but small numbers would make it an even match. He'd have to take the cave on his first assault.

On the ridge above, Bolan picked out a break in the trees. It would be a perfect vantage point from which to survey the opposition. The cave mouth was two hundred yards dead ahead across the shallow valley. He lay flat against a dead tree and used his night glasses. No one was visible, but there was a dull glow from deep within the cave.

He scanned the logging road that ran back away from the cave. Vehicles would give him an idea of what he was up against. About three hundred yards down toward the main road, two 4X4 trucks sat in a small clearing. Probably two men each, Bolan thought. Count the driver of the truck and there were at least five, maybe more. They probably wouldn't post a heavy guard—maybe only one man. It was unlikely they expected an attack in the middle of the night. A raiding party would make a racket, and one man would never try it on his own. It made no sense—to anyone but the Executioner.

The immediate problem was time. Bolan knew from the intel reports that the Libyans were coming to pick up the plutonium. They would truck it to Philadelphia where it would be loaded onto a freighter and shipped God knows where. The Libyans were desperate for a bomb. They'd tried to buy one, and to steal one. They didn't have the technology to build their own, but there was more than one country that would be happy to take the plutonium in exchange for a sample of the finished product.

Mack Bolan realized he had only two options: get the stuff back now, or wait and try to take the Libyans with it. The first was easier, no question about it. But which was better? He might never have a second chance to take a little wind out of the Libyan sails.

His decision made, Bolan settled in for a long night. The switch might be made under cover of darkness, but he didn't think so. The logging roads were little more than ruts. Only a fool would try to negotiate them in the dark with such a cargo. And Mack Bolan knew his enemies were no fools. Otherwise his fight would long since have been over. It was precisely because they were so good that Bolan still found himself watching mankind through a rifle sight. It wasn't pleasant . . . just necessary.

By dawn, he was chilled through. Flurries during the night had added to his discomfort, and he had slept only sporadically. At first light, he settled his binoculars on the cave mouth again. One of the goons was stretching himself. A big guy in white coveralls did a few knee bends to loosen his joints, and then a few jumping jacks. While Bolan watched, the gunner took his own glasses and checked the logging road. That meant it would be soon.

Bolan started working his way down toward the bottom of the valley as soon as the sentry had gone back into the cave. He wanted to be close. If he was going to pull this off, it would have to happen swiftly. Time was a luxury Mack Bolan rarely had.

As he reached the foot of the opposing ridge, a muffled rumble echoed through the trees. They were here to make the switch. Bolan hurried up the rocky slope, checking the road behind him twice. He heard a door slam before he saw anyone. There were only two of them. Good, Bolan thought. That cut the odds a little.

Working his way closer, he watched the newcomers climb toward the cave. Bolan put the glasses on them. Dressed in jeans and denim jackets, both men were armed, and they weren't bothering to hide the fact. The weapons were assault rifles, probably Kalashnikovs. About fifty yards away from the cave, one of them stopped while the other continued on up to the cave mouth. He stepped inside and called to the others, then walked back to join his companion.

Maybe luck was with him, Bolan thought. If they all came out in the open, it would be a hell of a lot easier, provided he could get between them and the cave. He scrambled up the slope to a niche in the rocks. He had a better angle now. All it would take was patience.

A minute later three men came out of the cave. The goon in coveralls was followed by two smaller men in combat fatigues and parkas. They walked down to the newcomers. Bolan sighted in on the man closest to the cave. If he took him out, the others would move away from the cave. They'd have cover in the trees, but that didn't bother the Executioner.

The Weatherby was cold in his hands, but it steadied him. It seemed appropriate. Death, too, was cold. Steady. Now! Bolan squeezed and immediately sought a second target. The guy in coveralls flew backward. The impact of the rib-crushing Weatherby slug slammed him into a boulder. The sound of the second shot was lost in the deadly reverberation of the first.

A puff of parka down, and two were gone. But the rest weren't going to be as easy. The first shot had stunned them; the second galvanized them. The three remaining men dived for cover. They had no idea where Bolan was. One by one, they poked their heads out, desperately seeking the source of the hellfire.

If he were lucky, he'd nail a third before they spotted him. Keeping an eye on the cave mouth, Bolan waited. And waited. A shout echoed in the cave, but no one showed. Whoever was inside, and however many there were, they knew to stay put.

One by one, Bolan located the three men in the open. They still seemed bewildered. He could hear them talking among themselves. But they were too confused to mount a counterattack. Backing more securely into the niche, he picked his target. The guy didn't know it, but he had been sticking his head up a little too far for his health.

Bolan squeezed gently. The slug homed in, taking the guy just above and to the left of his nose. Bolan heard the bullet strike. A pale cloud of bone and brain tissue rained silently behind the rock. He was dead before his body hit the ground.

The remaining two had seen Bolan. A sudden chatter of automatic fire chewed eagerly at the rocks around him. He couldn't stay where he was for too long. A ricochet might nail him, even if he kept his head down. They knew where he was; they didn't have to see him now to kill him.

Both weapons were firing at once. The men would have to reload at the same time. If he could get their timing down, he could get out of the rocky vise before it became his coffin. There was a lull in the firing. At the next reload, he would make his move.

Bolan reached into his heavy coat for the .44 AutoMag. Getting out was going to take some firepower, and the Weatherby was too tough to handle on the run. The spray of bullets and fragments of rock was merciless. The whining of the slugs seemed as if it would never end. And then it came—the pause he was waiting for.

Scrambling to his feet, Bolan darted out from behind his cover. Big Thunder's deadly eye scanned back and forth, watching for an opportunity. To the left, there was a small stand of trees. Squeezing off several rounds, Bolan dived into the shelter of the trees, landing on one shoulder and rolling among needles and leafy litter.

Finding a small hollow, Bolan swung around to face his foes. Stationary, he could use the Weatherby. He refilled the magazine and sighted it on the mouth of the cave. It was time for the rest of the boys to join the fun.

Staying down, Bolan slithered through the prickly needles on the forest floor. He wanted to angle around and down and get himself in position to pick off anyone unlucky enough to get careless in the cave mouth. They still didn't know whether he was alone. For the time being, they would assume he had help. They'd be cautious, and slow. But Bolan knew that wouldn't last.

The two gunners down the slope had quit firing. The denim cowboys were getting it together. Swinging his glasses around, Bolan swept the area where he had last seen them. There was no movement. Either they were playing a waiting game or they had moved. Scanning the cave mouth, he picked up a shadow on the far wall. He put the glasses down and trained the Weatherby scope on the shadow, then moved it to the rocky edge of the cave mouth.

After thirty seconds, someone dashed out of the cave. He got about five yards before the Weatherby boomed. The shot caught him in the side of the chest. Thrown sideways, he sprawled face downward on the rocky scree and slid another ten yards before smashing into the base of a tree. His legs kicked convulsively, and then he lay still. Four down. But how many to go? Bolan wondered. Three? Four? Did it matter? Bolan knew he'd have to get them all, or he wouldn't get out alive.

A flash of light caught his attention. Down below, among the rocks, someone was moving. The reflection was barely discernible. The morning light hadn't really burned through the overcast of the night before. But it had been enough. Again the reflection. This time closer. One of the gunners had spotted him. Rather than risk a shot at long range, he was moving in.

Okay.

Showtime.

The guy was good. In covering seventy-five yards he hadn't made a sound. It was too bad they were on opposite sides. Mack Bolan was the consummate warrior. And like the best in any field, he acknowledged skill, even in the enemy. It wouldn't help the guy any, though. Not now. Bolan realized the guy was good, but he was going against the best.

He was close now. Maybe twenty-five yards away, and still he hadn't made his move. There he was, his rifle to his shoulder. Bolan sighted in on him. His finger found the trigger. He began to squeeze, but something stopped him. The guy was aiming, all right, but not at him. Bolan was watching so intently that he flinched at the sound of the shot. Instinctively he turned to find the target, in time to see another gunner fall from behind a tree. What the hell was going on?

The rifleman turned and gave Bolan the thumbs-up. Then he signaled for Bolan to cover him. The guy crawled toward him, expertly using rocks and the trunk of a fallen tree to cover his approach. When he joined Bolan in the trees, he grinned.

"What the hell is going on?" Bolan asked.

"I'll tell you later. We've still got work to do, pal. There's three more in the cave."

"How do you know?"

"'Cause I slept there last night."

"Who are you?"

The guy grinned again, extending a gloved hand.

"Name's Cohen, Eli Cohen."

"That may be your name, but I want to know who you are."

"Sure you do. Let's just say we have a mutual friend. That cave is a natural fortress. We'll have to go in after them."

The stranger rammed a new clip into his Kalashnikov.

"Wait here a second," he said, scrambling back down the slope. He was back in a minute with a second AK-47. "This is a little more appropriate for what we have to do." He handed the Russian weapon to Bolan. "Know how to use it?"

"I've seen my share of these babies," Bolan said.

"I'll bet. Let's go. There's a back door."

Cohen slipped deeper into the trees, Bolan following. When the cave was out of sight, Cohen began to climb the slope. He moved quickly, showing no signs of exertion. Bolan was curious.

"Where are we going?"

"There's a secondary tunnel down into the caves. It's on top of the ridge. They know it's there, but they *don't* know I'm here. I think that gives us a bit of an edge."

At the ridge line, Cohen gestured for silence. He worked his way toward a cleft in the face of a low, rocky wall that ran parallel to the ridge. The two men flattened themselves against the wall, one on each side of the opening. There was a low, moaning wind venting through the rocks, but not another sound.

Bolan nodded, and Cohen stepped into the opening. There was no light in the cleft. The footing was secure, but a little slippery. Bolan took careful steps and felt his way along with one hand on the wet wall. The dull shape of his new ally was a few feet in front of him.

After they had traveled eighty or ninety yards, the opening grew wider and bent to the left. A faint glow was now visible ahead of them. Cohen slowed his pace. Putting a finger to his lips, he motioned Bolan forward. They could stand abreast, their shoulders just brushing the walls on either side.

As Cohen sketched the layout in silence, Bolan watched intently. Dropping to his stomach, Cohen edged forward, taking care not to scrape his weapon against the rock.

Bolan was uncomfortable. The big guy was used to being in command. It made sense, and he needed help, but he was the one who usually gave the orders.

The light was growing brighter. Bolan thought he could make out the roof of a large truck, just below them. That would make the cave floor an eighteen-foot drop. The passage was wider now, opening out like a funnel. Here and there were the marks of a pick. A natural passage had obviously been widened by hand.

A short distance from the opening, Cohen waved Bolan forward. He pointed out the location of each of the three defenders. The one most exposed from the rear would go last. They had to synchronize their shots and take two of the three down. Hard. And fast.

Cohen picked a large man in a heavy overcoat against the left wall. The target had an Ingram MAC-10 in his hand. A small mound of extra magazines lay on a rocky ledge behind him.

Not so smart, after all, Bolan thought. If the guy had to move fast, he'd have to leave his ammo sitting there. Bolan's own target was against the opposing wall. Armed with a Kalashnikov, he was considerably smaller than Cohen's man. His movements were nervous and agile. He might be trouble.

The third man was farther back along the same wall. Squeezed into an opening in the rock, he looked more frightened than alert.

"On three," Cohen whispered. "One...two...three..."

Both weapons opened fire, their hammering squeezing Bolan's eardrums unmercifully. He punched a small figure eight, using more than half his magazine. No fewer than five of his slugs found their mark, stitching his man from the left of his chest to his right abdomen. The little guy bounced as he hit the hard rock of the cavern floor. Blood oozed from several holes in his nylon jacket, mingling with the cold, dark water pooled on the rocky floor.

Cohen aimed higher, hitting his man twice above the neck. The first shot took off the lower jaw. Spurting blood chased bits of broken teeth down the front of the man's overcoat. The second hit plowed through his temple, shattering the skull as if it were an overstuffed piñata. The dead man slid down the wall, his snagged coat hiking up toward his shoulders.

The third man seemed stricken. His palsied shaking was the only movement he was capable of. His eyes darted around the gloomy cavern. He didn't understand what had hit his companions. A short burst from Cohen solved his problem. For good.

"Okay, let's check this truck out," Cohen said, slipping feet first down into the cavern. Bolan followed. As he reached the tailgate of the truck, Cohen pulled aside a burlap curtain that hung across the upper half of the trailer.

"You'd never guess what was in this baby, would you?" Cohen shook his head in wonder.

Bolan nodded grimly. "The main thing is, we got it. I have to let my people know."

Cohen said, "Listen, you never saw me. Understood?"

"Saw who?" Bolan smiled.

Cohen turned and stepped out into the cold, bright mountain air. When Bolan left the cave, Cohen was already gone.

10

Malcolm Parsons liked to live high on the hog. It was an aspect of his personality that had attracted a great deal of media attention. He was lavish in his treatment of people in a position to do him some good, more lavish still in his treatment of himself. It was this, more than anything else, that made Peter Achison hate him.

The ostentation of Parsons's life-style, public or private, was purely self-indulgent. And Peter Achison longed for the opportunity to indulge himself. Looking around at the faded opulence of the country estate where Parsons secreted himself, he felt only contempt for the antinuke leader.

Drumming his fingers on the tabletop, Achison felt his temper rise. Parsons was forever pointing out, at times subtly, at others with arrogance, that he could pull Achison's strings. But the bastard didn't know half of what was going on around him. By design.

He was useful, sure, but annoying, And things hadn't been going well lately. For all Achison knew, Parsons had something to do with that. First, four men, imported heavy hitters, had been lost in the bungled Central Park ambush. Now another screwup. It would be interesting to see how Parsons reacted.

Nominally his superior, Achison was unable to control the more flamboyant Parsons, who believed his prominence entitled him to ignore the guidance and discipline that Achison sought to impose. Parsons believed himself indispensable. Only the knowledge of just how wrong that was kept Achison from exploding when Parsons finally appeared.

"Have you been waiting long, Peter?"

"You know damn well how long I've been here."

"How was she?"

"I don't understand...."

"Do you really think I don't know what you've been doing while I sat here twiddling my thumbs?"

"I'm sure I have no idea what you think I was doing. However, that's not why you're here, is it?"

"No, it isn't."

"Well, then...why have you come?"

"We lost the plutonium."

"You what?"

"You're not listening to me, Malcolm. That's a very bad habit to develop. I said *we* lost the plutonium."

"In heaven's name how?"

"I was hoping you could tell me."

"That's preposterous. How should I know?"

Parsons got to his feet, one of his nervous habits. He paced back and forth along the length of the large walnut table between them. Looking for something to occupy his hands, he grabbed a poker to stir the ashes in the earth, then busied himself with rebuilding the fire. Finally, unable to stall any longer, he returned to his chair.

"Tell me what happened."

"I don't know what happened. The plutonium left West Virginia, but it never got to Philadelphia. None of the men have returned, and there's no one at the rendezvous point."

"No one?"

"That's what I said." Achison, sensing he had Parsons on the defensive, stood up. Crossing to the other side of the table, he stood behind Parsons, placing his hands on the back of the seated man's chair. "There was nothing, and no one, there."

"I knew something like this would happen. I just knew it. I told you no one was to be hurt. Those policemen, you shouldn't have done that."

"I already told you. We had no choice. Besides, that's spilled milk. What matters is the plutonium."

"How did you find out?"

"When the shipment didn't show up in Philadelphia, our clients contacted me. Understandably, they were upset. They thought, perhaps still do, that someone was trying to pull a fast one on them. Of course, I reassured them on that score. I only wish I were as certain as I claimed to be."

"What is that supposed to mean?"

"It means that until I know what did happen I have to assume anything could have, might have."

"Are you suggesting that I had anything to do with this?"

"You knew where the plutonium was, didn't you?"

"Of course. I was the one who organized the transportation. You know that."

"How about your people? How trustworthy are they?"

"I can vouch for them all."

"What about our little snitch?"

"What about her? She didn't know where the stuff was."

"Are you sure?"

"Certain."

Achison hoped that Parsons was getting the distinct impression that he was being grilled. He knew the antinuke leader didn't like it. He wasn't used to being in the hot seat. Achison rather enjoyed watching the erosion of the man's confidence. He kept the pressure on, partly to make certain that Parsons was telling the truth, but mostly because he enjoyed watching Parsons squirm.

Neither man noticed the door open.

"How pathetic you are!"

Achison turned, his mouth hanging in midsentence.

"Who the hell are you?" Parsons demanded.

The new arrival walked to the table and sat down. "Why don't you introduce us, Mr. Achison?"

Achison shuffled his feet. "Malcolm Parsons, Andrey Glinkov."

Parsons looked at Glinkov. "Who the hell are you? I don't know you. What are you doing here?"

"You idiot," Glinkov spat. "Who do you think pays for all of this?" He swept his hand around the kitchen, a gesture meant to encompass far more than their immediate surroundings. "You work for me, Mr. Parsons. So does Mr. Achison."

Parsons turned to Achison. "What the hell is he talking about? Who is he? What's going on here?"

"Like the man says, Malcolm. We work for him."

"The hell I do. I'm my own boss. Always have been. You better leave while you still have the opportunity."

Parsons stood up angrily. He walked to the end of the table and called into the room beyond. "Bert, get in here! Now!"

Silence. Either Bert hadn't heard or he was part of this outrage.

"Sit down," Glinkov said. His voice was soft, almost gentle. But there was no mistaking its steely edge. "I am more than a little annoyed at what has happened."

"What are you talking about? Annoyed at what? What business do you have being annoyed at anything?"

"I pay the bills, Mr. Parsons. And right now I don't believe I'm getting my money's worth. Where is the plutonium?"

"How did you ... would you please tell me what's going on here?"

"That's precisely what I want you to tell me, Mr. Parsons. What happened to the plutonium?"

"I, uh ... I don't know. I didn't even know it was missing, until a few minutes ago. Isn't that right, Peter?" He turned to Achison for support, but the latter merely shook his head.

"I don't know, Andrey. I was just trying to find that out myself when you walked in."

Glinkov leaned back in the chair. He sighed with equal parts of exasperation and disappointment. "Oh, Malcolm, what are we to do with you?"

"What do you mean?"

"Obviously you have bungled your assignment, at least insofar as Ms Peres is concerned. You were supposed to make good use of her, Mr. Parsons. But it seems she has made more use of you."

"She didn't even know about the plutonium."

"Can you prove that?"

"I swear she didn't know. I let her leak some information, like Peter wanted, but she didn't know where the stuff was hidden. There's no way she could have told anyone. She didn't know."

"Then what happened, Mr. Parsons? Who did know? Who told Mack Bolan?"

"Who's Bolan? I don't know anybody by that name." Parsons looked helplessly from Achison to Glinkov and back.

"Peter will brief you on him later. Right now I'm more interested in seeing to it that he doesn't interfere in any more of our activities."

"But..."

"Shut up, Mr. Parsons. Shut up and listen. This is what I want you to do."

Quickly Glinkov sketched his plan. Rachel Peres was to be taken to a "people's prison." There was to be no announcement. In due course, Glinkov knew, the underground would buzz with the story. Sooner or later, it would reach Bolan. But no effort was to be made to ensure that it did, lest Bolan realize he was being set up.

Glinkov knew that, being uninvited, Bolan was certain to show. Their silence was designed to attract his interest. It would, of course, be a trap. Achison was to be in charge.

"I hope I have made myself perfectly clear. Any questions, Peter? Mr. Parsons?"

Each man shook his head. Whether they understood was less certain than that they wanted Andrey Glinkov to disappear for the rest of the evening. Parsons felt a surge of gratitude that Achison had been present. Something in Glinkov gave him the chills. There was such certitude in the man's voice. Obviously he wasn't used to having subordinates fail him. Parsons chose not to think about what might happen should this latest effort end abortively.

Achison, on the other hand, was glad to see Parsons ground under Glinkov's thumb. The bastard had it coming. As many times as he'd tried, he had been unable to ruffle Parsons's feathers. Glinkov, master of the art, had had no trouble at all. And sharing the burden of Glinkov's icy stare made the room seem warmer by half. His contempt for Parsons hadn't been diminished, but he had discovered a reluctant kinship. It must have been like that for enemies chained to the same bench in a Roman galley. The lash bit everyone with equal indifference. A shared hatred made allies of the oddest kind.

Glinkov sat silently. He despised both of them. Neither was more than a tool for the KGB man. And tools were made to be used, then thrown away, replaced by newer, better tools. He stood abruptly. "Peter, you'll be hearing from me. Goodbye, Mr. Parsons." The Russian left as suddenly as he had come.

Parsons turned angrily to Achison. "What the hell did he mean when he said I work for him? I don't work for anybody."

"Tell him that, why don't you? The next time you have the chance. And the nerve." Achison laughed. "I think we should tend to Ms Perés. Where is she?"

"Upstairs, sleeping."

"Get her down here. Now. Bert?"

Bert came into the kitchen.

"Where the hell were you ten minutes ago?" Parsons demanded.

"In the living room, why?"

"Didn't you hear me calling you?"

"Yeah, I heard you." Bert smiled.

"I see. So that's how it is?"

Bert nodded.

"Mr. Glinkov has deep pockets, doesn't he?" Parsons asked of no one in particular.

No one answered. No one had to.

"What did you want, Malcolm?" Bert asked. There was a certain impatience in his voice.

"I want you to take Ms Peres for a ride. Take her clothes. She'll be staying awhile."

"She's not here, Malcolm."

"What do you mean she's not here?"

"She left a few minutes ago. With Mr. Glinkov, Malcolm."

Achison laughed, and Parsons turned to him. He stepped toward the larger man, his fists clenched.

"I wouldn't if I were you, Malcolm," Achison said.

Bert laughed out loud.

"This just ain't your night, Malcolm," he said. He laughed again and walked back out of the kitchen. The others could hear him chuckling as he mounted the stairs.

Parsons was about to say something when the door opened with a bang. A small athletic-looking man stumbled through the open door and collapsed at the foot of the table. His face was badly bruised, his clothes torn and dirty.

"My God, what happened to you?" Parsons shouted, kneeling by the fallen man.

"Ambush," the fallen man mumbled. "Somebody jumped us. They got the stuff."

"Who? Who was it?" Parsons demanded.

"You already know that," Achison whispered. "Bolan."

"Who the devil is this Bolan? Everybody talks about him as if he were the Angel of Death or something. You all sound like a bunch of superstitious savages."

"Take my word for it, Parsons, you don't want to know. And if you ever do meet him, I dare say you'll write a few prayers of your own. If you have the time."

"Forget that now. Help me get him upstairs."

Parsons turned the now unconscious man over and took him by the shoulders. Achison grabbed his feet, and together they strained to lift him. He was slight, but the deadweight was a challenge. They passed through the door and navigated the broad hall. At the foot of the stairs, Parsons laid him down.

"Wait here," he said. "I'll go get Bert. We'll never make it by ourselves."

Parsons mounted the stairs two at a time, returning with Bert a moment later. The big man effortlessly hoisted the prostrate form and reclimbed the stairs.

"Poor guy looks like he's had a rough time. Who is he?" Achison asked.

"A new addition to our little family. He was one of the West Virginia team. His name's Eli Cohen."

11

Pacing back and forth, Hal Brognola waited anxiously for Mack Bolan. He was not looking forward to telling Bolan the latest news. Rachel Peres had disappeared. She had missed her last two check-ins. She had not been back to her apartment. No one had seen her.

Brognola knew Bolan had become fond of the young woman despite the short time he had known her. Bolan talked about her in a way he hadn't talked about a woman in a long time. It was all couched in terms of professional appreciation, of course. But there was something else. Something in his voice, something approaching affection.

And now she was in trouble. Brognola knew that she was too good not to get word to him, somehow, if she was going to miss a meet. That could only mean she hadn't been able to. Either she was a prisoner or... The big Fed didn't want to think about the other possibility.

Rachel Peres's disappearance also meant that a year's work was in danger of going down the tubes. And if Rachel's instincts were right, they were getting close to something, something a lot bigger than they had expected. Parsons was going to make a move. That much was certain. It was going to be big, and it was going to endanger a lot of people. There were too many possibilities, too many places to cover. Brognola knew he needed Rachel's help. Where the hell was she?

Where the hell was Bolan?

The big guy entered the office on cue. Mack Bolan took a seat and watched Brognola expectantly.

"What the hell are you staring at, Mack?"

"At someone who obviously doesn't want to say what's on his mind, but knows he has to."

Brognola tried to smile. "You don't make it any easier. You know that?"

"The day it's easy, is the day you don't need me anymore."

"I guess you're right."

"So tell me."

"We've lost Rachel."

Bolan held his breath before asking, "What do you mean, lost her?"

"I don't know. She missed her last two check-ins. Nobody's seen her. Not for three days."

Bolan stood, sat down, then stood again. He crossed the room to pull open the heavy drapery. His back to Brognola, he watched the empty street for several minutes. The white-knuckled hand on the drapery told Brognola all he needed to know.

"Tell me what you *do* know, then." The voice was husky. Brognola hadn't heard him sound like that in a long time. The voice wasn't Mack Bolan's. It belonged to the Executioner.

The big Fed sighed. There was so little to say that it made him feel inadequate, stupid. There was no excuse, and he offered none. He sketched the details in a dull monotone, his eyes riveted to Bolan's broad back. When he finished, he sat on the sofa and waited.

"It must have been West Virginia. They must have figured it out. How else could they have gotten onto her?"

"I don't know. But what could we have done? We couldn't let that stuff out of the country."

Bolan turned to face him. "I know." Turning back to stare down at the empty street, he continued, "Why didn't you tell me about Eli Cohen?"

"Who?"

"Eli Cohen. Who is he?"

"You tell me. I've never heard of him."

"Hal, you don't play with me. I know the games you guys play. I've been there, remember?"

"I swear I don't know what you're talking about. Help me out. Tell me something I can use."

"He was there, at the cave. Said he was part of the team on the inside. When it got a little rough, he threw in with me. Led me into the cave through a back route. When it was over, he was gone, but he left his Kalashnikov. Why didn't you tell me you had a man on the inside?"

"Because we don't *have* a man on the inside. It's that simple. I have no idea who he is. Or who he works for."

"Then how did he know who I was?"

Brognola shrugged helplessly. "I don't know, Mack. You have to believe me."

"Yeah, I do. Look, I'm wasting time. Where is Parsons? He's the guy to start with."

"That's just what they want you to do. You understand that, don't you?"

Bolan ignored the question. "Has there been any word at all, from anybody? Anything that suggests they're trying to set me up?"

"No..."

"Then I'll take my chances. Just tell me what I want to know. And don't tell me I'll blow her cover. It's already blown. And I'm sure as hell no secret, either."

"All right."

While Brognola talked, Bolan listened with half an ear. His mind was already sorting through options, discarding the complicated and the improbable. Direct action was the best. Take it to them. Hard. Hit them where they breathed.

Before Brognola finished, the Executioner already knew what he was going to do. Tonight.

Bolan left Brognola's office, and by the time he reached the George Washington Bridge, he knew what he had to do. He owed it to her. And he was going to pay up. In spades.

The Palisades Parkway was beautiful at night. The moon was almost full, the trees bare, ghostly in the silver light. As he drove farther away from the city, the Hudson's shimmery glow replaced the fading lights of the town.

By Exit Fourteen, it was solid country, nothing but trees and open fields. A startled deer froze at the sound of the rented Camaro's engine and then hightailed it to the safety of the forest. The trees were covered with a thin, icy glaze, and they sparkled when the headlights hit them. Huge boulders, left behind by glaciers, glittered under the ice, their cold fires reflections of the hellfire that blazed in Bolan's eyes.

It was cold and clear, the kind of night when death went walking. And it would, if the Executioner found the scum responsible.

Parsons's hideaway was in the country near Middletown. Country living must appeal to him, Bolan thought, and the people of the area had seen it all: Moonies from Harvard, hippies from San Francisco, even groups that practiced witchcraft. Parsons and his friends wouldn't even rate a raised eyebrow. Comings and goings were regular events.

The farmland was rich. Apple orchards and horse and dairy farms were numerous. And late-nineteenth-century estates were cheap. Too far from the city for an easy commute, they were now maintained as country homes by the wealthy or turned to more profitable use by small businesses. Or converted to retreats by dozens of cults, movements and activist groups.

As he neared Goshen, Bolan could almost smell the nitrate he knew would soon fill his nostrils. It was a smell that would violate the clear, cold air, which was free of car exhaust and factory smoke. The country road was rough. Wary of patches of ice formed by snowmelt runoff, Bolan slowed the car.

At the turnoff to Parsons's place, he left the Camaro in a small clearing that had been plowed flat and rutted by heavy use. The road, little more than twin ruts among the snowy weeds, wound through the trees. He would use it until he got closer to the estate. It would save time. The moon had begun to slide in and out of cloud cover, which darkened the woods a bit. Not enough to cover his approach completely, but enough to make it easier.

Up ahead, twin columns of smoke rose above the trees and dispersed in the stiff wind. Bolan had one hundred yards to go. Time to leave the path and use the woods for cover. The brittle crust of snow crunched under his feet. Twigs and branches, hidden under the snow, snapped with every step. In the silence of the forest, the snapping sounded like a pistol shot.

Two small outbuildings offered some cover. Bolan angled behind them, then made a painstakingly slow circuit of the house. He wanted some idea of what would greet him once he got inside. And the Executioner knew that he would get inside come hell or high water. The place was large, mostly fieldstone, and brightly lit. A broad porch occupied much of the front of the two-story building. A deck had recently been added to the back and there were three doors.

Occasionally a shadow would pass by the curtains that shrouded all but one of the windows. There had only been two cars down at the main road, but it was impossible to tell how many people were inside. Bolan knew it was possible that the cars were communal property. There could be a dozen hardmen inside, or nothing but women and children. Only time would tell. And time was running out.

Mack Bolan had to make his move. Easing around the side of a small fieldstone stable, he inched forward, using shadow and the momentary dimming of the moon to cover his approach. Small evergreens dotted the side lawn and offered some protection as he neared the house. The hard snow crunched as he moved.

The last thirty feet would be the toughest; there was no cover. Heading toward a curtained window, Bolan sprinted to the wall directly beneath it. At the base of the wall was a bed of tangled shrubs and vines covered with snow, making a mound two feet deep and three feet high.

Bolan was forced to stay back from the wall and to keep low. Working through the heavy drifts, he moved toward the back of the house. The stairway to the deck would get him close, but he'd have to take his chances on which room to enter. The stairs were covered with ice that crunched with every step. Slowly, slowly. One at a time, Bolan climbed to the broad deck. Even in the cold, the smell of the new lumber stung his nostrils.

Once on the deck, he drew Big Thunder from its sling. He inched to the nearest window and paused to listen. Inside, there was silence. This was going to be easier than he had hoped. The storm window was up, and the screen was plastic. A quick slice of his knife, and it fluttered to the deck. The inside sash was locked, but the blade slid up and over. The lock clicked open, and he was home free.

Slipping the knife back into its sheath, he pushed on the sash with his left hand. It resisted for a moment, then the ice that held it gave under the pressure. With a dull thud of its sash weights, the window slid open. Pulling aside the curtain, he listened. Bolan could hear voices from deep within the house but the room was vacant. He pushed the curtain all the way back and slipped inside.

A dim light filled the room, and a brighter light spilled through a crack under the door. It was a bedroom, with two large double beds. It was neat, but showed signs of regular use. Books and papers filled two rows of shelves on one wall, and clothes hung in the open closet. Opening the door a crack, he could hear the voices more clearly. Soft piano music obscured the words.

The hallway outside was bright, too bright for him to take a chance on being spotted, but he had to get a better idea of what he was up against. There was a light switch on the wall directly opposite the doorway. With any luck, it controlled the hallway lamps. Pulling the door wide open, Bolan listened. The hall was deserted. Quickly he reached for the switch and flipped it, plunging the hall into darkness. Someone would notice it sooner or later, but at least he would be harder to spot.

Swiftly he stepped to the end of the hallway, pausing for a moment to listen at each door. Silence. Everyone must be downstairs.

Making his way to the stairs, he checked the door at the head of the stairwell. That room, too, was silent. He listened again, hoping to get an idea of the numbers he was up against. The voices continued at a constant level, and the piano droned away. He could tell that there were two men and two women. But Bolan couldn't tell if one of them was Rachel.

He strained to hear, but the piano masked the voices. Softly he began his descent. There was a faint sound behind him, and he turned. The door at the head of the stairs had opened.

"Go on down, Mr. Bolan. We've been expecting you." Peter Achison gestured with a Skorpion machine pistol. To his right, holding an Ingram MAC-10 in his hands, was Bert.

"Place the gun on the carpet gently. Slowly."

Bolan bent to place the AutoMag on the stairs in front of him. Bert laughed, but Mack Bolan never heard it. Someone had climbed the stairs behind him. A rifle butt slammed into the side of his head. The Executioner collapsed and rolled down the stairs.

12

The cold water shocked Mack Bolan back to consciousness. He shook his head to clear it and looked around the room. He was tied to a bench on a wall opposite the doorway. The rope was heavy and well knotted, but there was a little slack.

Two men stood watching him. The same two men who had surprised him at the top of the stairs. The larger of the two was built like a linebacker. He stood about six three and must have weighed two-fifty. In one hand he held a quart of beer, in the other a machine pistol.

The second man was older, less athletic in appearance. His hair was thinning, and he looked at least fifteen pounds underweight.

"Mr. Bolan," the balding man said. "We meet at last."

"You haven't met me yet, pal," Bolan said, spitting his words out between clenched teeth.

"Rather brave words for a man in your position, Mr. Bolan."

"Just exactly what is my position?"

The skinny guy pursed his lips, as if in thought, and made a steeple of his long fingers. "Let's just say you are about to become the *late* Mack Bolan. Would you say that about sums it up, Bert?"

The larger of the two men smiled. "Yeah, I'd say that. Why don't we get it over with?"

"We have to wait for Andrey, Bert. You know that. Mr. Glinkov would be upset with us if we took the law into our own hands."

"I say we're wasting time, Peter. If this guy is such bad news, we're taking a chance keeping him around. Let's waste him and be done with it. Glinkov won't care."

At the mention of Glinkov, Bolan's eyes widened. So there was a KGB connection. The name didn't mean anything, though. Either he was new, or he was special. Maybe both. Either way, it wouldn't matter unless Bolan could get loose before the Russian arrived.

"You won't have long to wait, Bert. I already spoke to Andrey. He'll be here in a couple of hours. Just try to restrain yourself."

"I still don't like it."

"Bert, we're paid very well to do what we're told. Do I make myself clear?"

Bert nodded reluctantly.

"You keep an eye on Mr. Bolan while I go up to the house." The skinny guy turned to leave, then stopped. "Oh, Mr. Bolan. I think it might interest you to know that Ms Peres isn't here." He chuckled and left.

It was going to be a pleasure to waste that creep, Bolan thought. Yeah, a real pleasure—if he ever got out of there. Bert had taken a seat on a long bench on the opposite wall. All four walls were made of stone. Bolan knew he was either in the basement of the house or in one of the outbuildings. Getting free without making any noise wasn't going to be easy.

Rachel had mentioned somebody named Peter. The skinny guy must have been the man she had met—the one who had huddled with Parsons. There was something familiar about him, too. His general build. The way he moved. The face meant nothing, though. And Bert. Bolan knew his kind by type. The no-nonsense hardman. Long on brawn, a little light on brains. It might be possible to throw him off his guard long enough to get free. But he couldn't do it with Bert sitting there staring at him.

The guy was guzzling beer, letting some of it run down over his chin. He'd already had a few. With a little luck, Bolan thought, he might nod off. Or have to relieve himself. Anything to give Bolan a little time. The guy's eyes were heavy, and his head lolled to the side occasionally. He was going to fall asleep, as long as Bolan didn't do anything to arouse suspicion. And as long as the scarecrow didn't come back.

Bolan discreetly surveyed the room, taking inventory. Mostly garden tools and a few bottles and cans of insecticide and plant food. Somebody, Parsons no doubt, was more concerned about the health of his plants than that of his neighbors. It was hard to understand how someone could lavish attention on flowers and yet be willing to unleash nuclear poison.

Assholes like Parsons were so egotistical that they failed to realize they were likely to die in their own traps. They thought they were too smart, that they were above it all. More often than Mack Bolan cared to admit, it *was* the schemers who got off scot-free. It never mattered to them how many soldiers died in a war, as long as the generals were safe.

Bolan had to get his hands free. He bunched his muscles and wriggled his arms slightly, then relaxed. The ropes felt a little freer. Bert roused himself and took another swig of beer, ignoring Bolan completely.

Bolan clenched his fists, unclenched them and clenched again. The ropes on his wrists were the loosest. If Bert would drift into a fog, Bolan could free his hands. He worked silently. Patience was paramount. As long as Bert noticed nothing, it might be possible.

Bert's head fell to his chest, and he started to snore. Bolan tugged vigorously at the rope, chafing his knuckles. A little more leeway was all he'd need.

While he worked, Bolan eyed the contents of the room again. Getting free was only half the battle. As soon as he got up, he'd have to know what he was going to do. Bert might not be sleeping that soundly. Glancing again to a table at one end of the shed, Bolan examined the bottles. He could just make out the letters P-R-U-S-S on a two-quart jar. It had better be what he hoped.

Another tug, and the rope slid down off his right hand. The cord on his upper arms still prevented him from moving but with his free hand he quickly loosened the rope on the other. Bert was snoring peacefully. Bolan wriggled now, stretching against the cord to bring the slack into play around his upper body.

A final shrug, and the ropes fell to his waist. He slid one arm out of their coils, then followed it with the other one. Bending slowly, he worked anxiously at the knots binding his feet. If the other man returned it would all be for nothing. He sure as hell wouldn't get a second chance. The knot was stubborn, resisting his nails and scraping at his fingertips.

Finally, the knot budged. He pulled at the loosened coil. It came away in his hands, just as Bert shook himself. It was now or never. Bolan leaped the length of the shed, searching in the shadow thrown by his own body for the two-quart jar. He found it and turned in time to see Bert raising his machine pistol. With all his strength, Bolan hurled the jar. It caught Bert on his collarbone with enough force to shatter the glass.

The gun fell to the floor of the shed as two full quarts of prussic acid spilled over Bert. It splashed in his face and eyes, beginning its corrosive attack. Bert clawed at his eyes as he emitted a deafening howl. His hands blistered as the acid ate away at his skin. The Executioner moved to the corner, grabbing a pitchfork and charging toward his blinded opponent. Like a medieval jouster, Mack Bolan brought his makeshift lance to his shoulder and then drove it home.

Bert gagged and began to gurgle. Bolan put all his weight on the pitchfork, driving its tines into a wooden window frame behind Bert and pinning him to the wall. Blood bubbled and drooled out of his mouth as Bert gasped for air like a landed trout. A tine of the pitchfork had pierced his throat on either side of the larynx. His eyes bulged as blistered fingers struggled to pull the pitchfork free.

Bolan swept the machine pistol from the floor. Holding it tightly against Bert's chest, he fired a short burst. The rain of death punched through the rib cage into the heart, and Bert struggled no more. His limp body sagged, pulling the pitchfork out of the dry wood of the window frame as he pitched forward, his fall arrested by the farm implement's handle. He paused momentarily, as if in slow motion, then slipped sideways to the floor.

Bolan moved toward the door and opened it slightly. There was no sign that anyone had heard the struggle, or the short burst from the Skorpion. Bert had been more useful as a sound suppressor than as a human being. The moon was gone, and it had begun to snow again. Swirls of snow blew through the open door of the shed, collecting on the floor.

His head ached, but he had to know if the scarecrow had been telling the truth. Crossing the snow-crusted lawn in a hurry, he climbed the stairs to the deck for the second time that night. But Bolan knew this time they wouldn't be expecting him. Slipping in through the same window, he spotted Big Thunder and his Beretta on a night table. He holstered both guns and stepped through the door out into the hallway.

The earlier voices were silent now, and the house seemed deserted. If they were waiting for the Russian, someone should certainly be around. All Mack Bolan wanted was one man, and some information. He had to find Rachel. Now that they thought they had him, Parsons and his men might decide they didn't need her as bait any longer. If she were still alive.

Descending the stairs two at a time, he burst into a lower hallway. Still no sign. He stalked his own shadow down the hall toward an arched doorway. The room was dimly lit, and empty. Where the hell were they?

At the other end of the hall was a closed door. He approached the door carefully, pausing to listen. From inside, he heard the sound of heavy breathing. Deep and irregular, it sounded as if the person were heavily sedated. Turning the knob, he pushed through the door.

There was a small reading lamp over the only cot that was occupied. A man lay on his side, facing away from the door. An open book lay, pages down, on the sheet beside him. The room smelled of medicine and alcohol. It was a hospital smell—an odor Bolan would just as soon never smell again.

He bent over the sleeping man. Ready to smother any sound the patient might make, Bolan hefted a pillow in one hand, his Beretta in the other. As he reached out, the man stirred. Groaning, he rolled onto his other side. Bolan drew in his breath sharply. Eli Cohen had had a rough time of it. His face was badly bruised. Several wounds marked the smooth, dark complexion. Both eyes were black and blue, as if the man's nose had been broken.

What in hell was he doing here?

While he debated whether to risk waking the battered man, he heard the sound of feet scraping on the front porch. There were two sharp, almost angry voices. He recognized the scarecrow, but the other voice was unfamiliar. Probably Glinkov.

There was no way he wanted to risk a shootout under the current circumstances. Rachel wasn't here, that was clear. Cohen was, but he didn't know what that meant. Until he did, he would file that knowledge. It was significant, Bolan knew, but of what? Even if Cohen were on the right side, he couldn't risk compromising him. He had to get out.

Racing back through the room, he closed the door softly behind him and mounted the stairs. Waiting at the head of the staircase, he tried to overhear the conversation as the new arrivals entered the house. There was too much racket: chairs scraping, and the stamping of snow off several pairs of feet. A woman's voice asked who wanted coffee.

As much as he wanted to get a look at Glinkov, it would have to wait. He'd be back. The warrior knew discretion and good judgment counted for much in an unending war. Glinkov would have to keep. First, he had to find Rachel. Closing the door behind him, Bolan slipped back through the window and out onto the deck. The wind had begun to howl, and the snow stung as it whipped across the deck. Already there was an inch of new snow on the ground.

The Executioner was thankful for the turn in the weather. No doubt they'd be looking for him soon, but the privileges of rank meant they'd have their coffee before worrying about whether Bert was comfortable in the outbuilding. And Bert would never feel the cold again.

13

Enough was enough. Mack Bolan was fed up. He'd been pushed to the wall, and it was time to push back. He had to believe that Rachel was still living, and therefore he had to keep searching for her.

He would start at a couple of the safehouses. Tossing them one by one, he would tug on Glinkov's chain a little. Send him a message. If anything happened to Rachel Peres, no place in the world would be safe for the KGB man. Not even Moscow was off-limits to Mack Bolan. He'd been there before, and he'd go again.

The first stop was in the East Village, not far from Rachel's apartment. A flophouse for the disaffected, members of most radical movements had used it at one time or another. As the times had gotten tougher, the place had gotten more militant. Bolan had seen a dozen centers like it over the years.

It was the kind of place where everyone slept with a gun under his pillow. A man could have a roof over his head if he knew the right catchphrase or spouted the current antiestablishment rhetoric. But he had better sleep with one eye open. Few of the groups tolerated one another, no matter how similar their "political" positions. Violence was what they knew best, and practiced most often. Bolan sometimes wondered whether it might not be easiest to arm them all to the teeth, then stand back and let them fight among themselves. And he'd take on the winner for breakfast.

The People's Hostel was about to receive a visitor, an armed transient, like so many others. But they had never seen the likes of the Executioner. Parking around the block, Bolan made sure he had a clean approach to his rented Camaro. He'd be leaving in a hurry. A back alley ran through the block and passed the hostel on one side. Dressed in his nightsuit, Bolan blended with the shadows as he jumped for the lowest rung of the fire ladder. He hauled himself up, the old iron squeaking under his weight.

The five-story building was dilapidated. The window frames hadn't been painted in a long time, and they'd worn bare. Putty fell in chunks from around the glass. Moving swiftly, Bolan climbed to the roof, pausing once at each level to check a window. Most were dark. It was difficult to tell how many people were inside. The more the merrier crossed his mind, but it was too reckless an attitude for the work he had to do.

It was possible that Rachel was inside. But even if she wasn't, it was a place to start. The underground grapevine would blossom as soon as he left. Tales of radical heroism would distort what happened, but Glinkov would read between the lines. And the Russian was undoubtedly looking for him already.

The tar-and-gravel roof was covered with litter. Scraps of snow still lay in the nooks and crannies, but it was possible that the rasp of his shoes might still be heard below. On tiptoe, Bolan moved toward the fire door. Most roofs in the neighborhood were used for drug deals, and the doors were usually open. This one was no different. Its hinges didn't even squeal as he tugged on the handle. Inside, the light was dim. Overhead, a single bulb, more suitable to a refrigerator, revealed the stairs and enough graffiti to cover a subway car.

Working his way down, Bolan stopped at the landing on the top floor. His listened for a moment, but heard nothing. Only one room had a door, and it was open. Checking each room in turn, he found them all empty.

The next floor was wide open. The walls had been taken down, and the place was used for storage. Cartons were piled everywhere. A quick look told Bolan the place was an armory. Guns and ammunition were stacked in one corner. It seemed careless, until he reached the next landing. A steel door barred the way. Before even turning the knob, he knew it would be locked. It was.

He knew there would be grenades and plastique in the storeroom. The latter would come in handy now. Back on the fourth floor, he found the plastique and cut a block of C-4 big enough to take out the door. In a half-empty carton there were detonators, wire and radio transmitters. Rigging the door to blow on the first attempt, he quickly planted the plastique, set up a detonator and reclimbed the steps.

In one open crate he found a half-dozen Ingram MAC-10 submachine guns. Selecting one, he checked it out. It was a bit rusty, so he pulled another from the crate. This one was satisfactory. He fitted the SMG with its bulky sound suppressor. Now for ammunition. On steel shelving against one wall, Bolan found several cases of ammunition. He grabbed several clips and stuffed them into his coat pockets. He was as ready as he'd ever be. Standing away from the stairway, he pressed the button.

Before the smoke had cleared, he was at the bottom of the steps and through the splintered doorway. The Ingram ready, he checked both ends of the hall. Below, he could hear footsteps. The surprise wouldn't last long. He kicked in the first door he came to, but the room was empty. As was the next. In the third, a man was sitting upright in bed, the covers drawn up to his chin. He was groggy, uncertain of where he was.

"What the hell's going on, man?" he asked.

"I'm looking for somebody," Bolan growled.

"If it ain't me, I can't help you, man."

"It's not you, pal," Bolan snapped. He slugged the man in the forehead with the Ingram. The man would sleep through.

Out in the hall, shouts echoed up the stairs. As Bolan kicked in the fourth and last door, two men ran into the hall from the stairwell. Both were armed.

Bolan stepped through the doorway just ahead of a burst of gunfire. Several slugs tore into the wooden doorframe, sending splinters in every direction.

"Cover me," one of them shouted. Bolan could hear footsteps pounding toward him. The guy bounced through the doorway. Like an idiot, he had put himself between his quarry and his companion. Bolan squeezed off a burst from the Ingram. The .45 caliber slugs ripped into the commando, knocking him back into the hall again. Stitched by the hellfire from collar to belt, his spine had been severed in three places. A rain of slugs poured through the doorway. Bolan slid along the wall, making certain he was out of the line of fire.

When the gunner paused to change magazines, Bolan burst through, squeezing off a short burst to keep the guy's head down. He raced toward the stairs and dived headfirst past the opening. Spraying fire down the steps as he sailed by, Bolan caught his adversary by surprise. He waited long enough to be certain that the guy was out of action, and then slipped back to the stairwell. The second gunner lay sprawled on the stairs. His eyes were rolled back, as if trying to look through the ugly, round red hole in the middle of his forehead.

Grabbing the guy's gun, Bolan jammed a new clip into place, then reloaded his own weapon and slung it over his shoulder. Stepping over the dead man, he worked his way down to the second floor. This one, too, had been gutted; the rooms had been dismembered to make way for a dormitory. Three rows of bunks, all empty, filled the space.

Bolan heard a shout as he crossed toward the stairs to the first floor.

Another gunner bounded up the steps and burst into the sleeping quarters. Bolan sprayed lead in his direction and dived for the floor. One of the .45 caliber Ingram rounds shattered the newcomer's right hand. His gun clattered to the floor. Before he could retrieve it with his left, Bolan was on him. Grabbing the man by the collar, he hauled him to his feet.

"Don't shoot me, please," he screamed. Reaching for Bolan's hands, he tried to free himself from Bolan's grip, more in desperation than rage. "Please, don't shoot me."

"I'm looking for somebody," Bolan snarled. "I can see she's not here. But somebody knows where she is. I want that somebody to get a message. Do you understand?"

The young man nodded. "What message?"

"You tell him I'm coming. You tell him I'm going to find him. Tell him that if anything happens to Rachel Peres, he'll wish he'd never been born. Understand?"

"Who... who am I supposed to tell? Who's the message for?"

The young man's eyes were rolling. His voice was barely intelligible through the blubbering.

"You just tell everybody you know. He'll get the message. Understand? Because if he *doesn't* get it, I'll be back."

Bolan tossed the injured man to the floor and returned to ground level, unopposed. If anyone else had been there, he was long gone.

Rousting punks was something Bolan had been doing forever. Or so it seemed. Ever since the Mafia wars, it had been necessary. But the punks had never learned, and this new breed was no different. Just harder to understand. The mob had wanted money, and it did whatever it could to get it. But terrorists were either true believers, or cynics.

The true believers never saw the contradictions. They preached the sanctity of personal freedom and made a living by violating it, or denying it to those who opposed them.

Worst of all were the cynics. They would say or do anything to advance their aims. And when you sloughed off all the rhetoric, ripped the curtain of bullshit aside, it was all about power. Power over people who had precious little of their own. Not over their lives, their futures, not even over the time of their own deaths. The terrorist slime that was spreading over the planet, like mold on a piece of exposed cheese, had to be stopped. But first somebody had to get their attention.

Hell, it wasn't Bolan's choice for a hobby, but somebody had to do it. And with Rachel's life hanging in the balance, he had all the reason he needed. The armory in the East Village would never be the same. But it had seemed like an empty exercise. For all Bolan knew, those guys at the crash pad were blameless. But when somebody comes after you with an SMG, Bolan knew you had better assume he was up to no good.

There was another stop he wanted to make, and this visit would be quick. The whole point was to make it clear that the houses weren't as safe as their residents thought. They had no secrets. Not from the Executioner. The thing they never seemed to understand about a rat hole was that there was only one way in. And sometimes no way out.

Bolan drove across town to the docks. South of Fourteenth Street, New York's West Side was a nightmare after dark. The area consisted of winding streets and row after row of abandoned warehouses. It was so gloomy and oppressive that even the hookers preferred to ply their trade farther north under the lights. It was a place where anything was possible. And where anything could hide.

Hal Brognola knew a great deal about Parsons's little game. And it was becoming increasingly evident that Parsons was little more than the mouth that roared.

Someone else was calling the shots. Bolan's lead on Glinkov looked promising. They didn't have everything yet, but they would shortly. And what they already had told them they were playing with people who operated in the big leagues. It meant Parsons couldn't be in control. He was small time.

Parsons had never been involved in the kind of thing they were turning up. Public disturbance was his ball game, not murder. True, there were links to Parsons, but some of them were merely circumstantial. And some of them looked manufactured. It was as if someone wanted Parsons on the hook. Or already had him there.

Weapons were being stockpiled all over the place. But that wasn't a secret. Bolan knew the best way to get a line on the bastards was to smoke them out. If they ran, they would lead him somewhere. If they stayed put, it could take days, even weeks, to find them. Bolan didn't have days. Neither did Rachel.

The target was a munitions dump just off the river. The West Side Highway was lined with dozens of places just like it. Tiers of broken windows in rotten frames. Rusted doors on rustier hinges. Broken asphalt parking lots. And behind it all, the murk of the midnight Hudson. The river had no glamour in this part of town. In the distance, the dim lights of New Jersey flashed halfheartedly, now and then highlighting a piece of garbage bobbing in the oily water. When Bolan was done, there'd be even more trash in the river.

The place looked like all the others—a monument to urban decay. Single storied, its few remaining windows had been unwashed for years. Leaving his vehicle on a side street, the warrior swiftly made his way through the deserted streets. At the last corner, he slipped into an alley as a police cruiser slid down the off ramp from the highway above. It turned a corner and made its way down one of the winding side streets.

When the cruiser was gone, Bolan sprinted across Twelfth Avenue. At the back there was a loading bay that opened onto a door of corrugated sheet metal. The water lapped at rotten pilings behind and below it. Bolan took a small jimmy from his pocket and wedged it under the ring mount of the door's padlock. The old screws groaned, then squealed as the ring came loose. The chain dangled uselessly, slowly banging against the door. The hollow echo from inside the warehouse sounded like a death knell.

Mack Bolan slid the door open and entered the building. The scurry of rats stayed just ahead of the beam of his torch as he walked among the assorted crates and cartons. Opening a few, he confirmed Brognola's latest intel. There were enough weapons here to equip a small army. Most of them were packed in cartons that belied their contents. Tractor parts had been replaced with automatic rifles, submachine guns and handguns. They were of every make and model, a collection of black market arms worth thousands of dollars. A large crate labeled Generator actually contained smaller boxes of ammunition.

Near the rear door, Bolan's flashlight picked out a small panel truck. His search of the vehicle uncovered two five-gallon gasoline containers, one full, one half empty. Quickly Bolan poured the volatile fuel over the stacks of crates. With the jimmy, he punctured the truck's gas tank, adding its contents to the pyre. Selecting a LAWS rocket from one of the crates, he slipped back through the door, leaving it open to let the wind inside.

Back across the highway, Bolan took careful aim. With a whoosh like the opening of hell's gates, the rocket streaked across the deserted highway, piercing one of the few intact panes of glass. The elevation was perfect. The LAWS rocket blew with a sound like thunder, igniting the gasoline. In seconds the place was a roaring inferno.

Bolan ran up the block toward his car, reaching it just as the first munitions detonated. In minutes the place would be leveled. Bolan regretted that he didn't have time to stay and watch. But as his Camaro roared to life, he smiled grimly. It wasn't only money, he thought, that could burn a hole in your pocket. And when the pocket belonged to the KGB, you could stand and watch or you could fan the flames.

Either way you upped the ante in the game with the highest stakes in town.

14

"That was quite a fireworks display you put on last night. What the hell was in that warehouse, anyway?" Hal Brognola asked the man seated before him.

"You name it," Mack Bolan answered. "If it could kill somebody, it was there."

"I'm catching some heat about it, you know."

"Why? There's no reason to connect you with what happened. You know that as well as I do."

"You're forgetting something, Mack. I told you the President was taking a personal interest in this matter. You've also been around long enough to know that people like Malcolm Parsons get away with as much as they do because they have connections."

"Look, Hal, you brought me in on this, and I've been working closely with you. It's sensitive, I know that. I also think we're onto something. I'd bet you Parsons didn't even know that stuff was there. Time's running out, and I've got to find Rachel."

"I know you feel responsible for the position she's in, but you can't. She knew what she was letting herself in for, and besides, she's okay," Brognola countered.

"For how long, and how do you know she's okay?"

"Because she's not the only one we have on the inside. Look, our information has been right on the money, hasn't it?"

"So far, yeah, it has."

"So trust me on this. She's the ace up their sleeve. If they feel safe, she's safe. But the minute they get the idea that having Rachel isn't going to help them any, they'll kill her. Nobody pays for insurance that's lapsed, Mack."

Bolan knew Brognola was right. Hell, he could ride around the country for a year, blowing warehouses and wasting punks. He'd wanted to send a message. All right, he'd sent it. And they'd gotten it. He was sure of that. The question was, what to do next?

If he lost sight of his primary goal, he wouldn't help Rachel at all. If he lost his cool and got himself killed, it wouldn't matter what his intentions had been. The best way to help her was to put Parsons, and whoever controlled him, out of commission. That had to be first.

"What do you want me to do?"

"First, I want you to tell me everything you learned last night. All of it. What kind of weapons, their place of origin, the works."

Bolan sketched out the broad outlines for the big Fed, stopping occasionally for a question or two. The debriefing took nearly half an hour. When he had finished, Brognola nodded again.

"It all fits. We got a make on your Mr. Glinkov, and there's no question this is KGB. But it's a lot heavier than we thought. Glinkov is one of the big boys. He's got a free hand in operations. His budget is pretty sizable, and he's got a pipeline to the top. We think Peter Achison may be the KGB point man on this."

"What's Glinkov after? Why do I get the feeling that I'm sitting on a nuke, just waiting for someone to set it off?"

"Because that's just where you are. We got a little intel on Glinkov's next move. If we play it right, we can kill two birds with one stone—get Rachel out and shut the KGB bastard down. Glinkov is going for the long ball. You hurt him last night, and I think you gave him a push."

"How deep is your other man?"

"Very."

"When do I get to meet him?"

"You already have."

"Not Eli Cohen?" Bolan stared at the big Fed. Brognola stood up, reaching for his cigar.

"You got it."

"Why didn't you tell me before?"

"It didn't matter before."

"Does it matter now?"

"It sure does. Eli's the one who knows where Rachel is. And he's the one who knows what's on tap. We need him on the inside. I can't take a chance. But trust me, he's a good man, one of the best."

"Mossad?"

Brognola nodded.

"What's their interest in this? And don't tell me it's the same as ours. They spy on us just like we spy on them."

"Nature of the beast. Look, I'll tell you what Eli's been able to get to us so far. That's the best I can do. You already got a leg up. You know what he looks like, and he knows what you look like. When the shooting starts, and believe me it will, at least you'll know not to blow each other away."

"That's cold comfort, Hal."

Brognola spoke quietly for nearly an hour. He had chewed the better part of four cigars before he'd finished. He yanked the fourth out of his mouth, shook his head and tossed it into a wastebasket.

What he said had scared Bolan. It was obvious now that Glinkov, and not Parsons, was pulling the strings. Parsons might dance better than most, but he was still a puppet. Glinkov's puppet. And there was no longer a mystery as to why Mossad was in on the hunt. The stability of the Middle East hung in the balance. It had been that way for so long that no one, not even Bolan, could imagine it getting any worse. Until now.

Glinkov's plan was brilliant. And economical. Its outlines were simple. Terrorists would seize Thunder Mountain, a large nuclear reactor in the Hudson River Valley about fifty miles north of New York City. An ultimatum would be issued, demanding that the United States deactivate all of its nuclear power plants.

Public outcry would be deafening. Those who were already opposed to nuclear power would join the chorus. Even those who weren't would be stunned by the boldness and the ease of the seizure. If the power plants couldn't be defended, then every one of them was a potential powder keg. No one wanted a source of energy, no matter how useful, that had to be defended by military troops.

The kicker was even worse. Unknown to Parsons, another of Glinkov's stooges was going to engineer an "accident" during the seizure that would irreversibly damage the reactor. The result would be a nuclear nightmare that would make the disaster at the Chernobyl nuclear power plant in Russia seem like a high school picnic. Millions of gallons of radioactive waste would pour into the Hudson River, killing everything in its path downstream.

Clouds of radioactive steam would billow into the sky and contaminate hundreds of square miles for decades. The immediate vicinity would be uninhabitable for centuries.

The reactor meltdown that would result when the coolant was siphoned off had consequences that would far exceed the Soviet nuclear accident. The reactor's fuel would get hotter and hotter until it passed the melting point, a temperature high enough to melt through the steel and concrete that usually contained the radiation in a safe area. It had a name, China Syndrome, taken from the ultimate destination of the ball of hellfire an uncooled reactor would become. It would take scientists years to determine the extent of damage caused by the incident at Chernobyl. But scientists might not have the same luxury of time if the KGB plot in the U.S. succeeded.

That was Glinkov's plan. The Israelis, obviously, had to defend themselves against the rising Soviet influence in the Middle East. That explained Eli Cohen's presence. It might even, Bolan thought, explain Rachel's. Former Mossad indeed. No wonder she was good. This mission was top priority. World wars had started with less provocation. And Mack Bolan was in the middle. He even had the advantage of knowing what was going to happen. What he didn't know was when.

Brognola waited patiently while Bolan considered what he'd just been told. When Bolan looked up, the big Fed said, "So that's the story." He chomped on a new cigar, glanced angrily at it, then threw it into the large glass ashtray on the desk.

"Do I get any help on this?" Bolan already knew the answer, but he had to ask.

"This is as far off the record as it can get, Mack. Anything happens to you, as far as the rest of the world is concerned, you were in on it. You were one of them. You don't exist, pal."

Bolan nodded. It had been that way for a long time. Why should he expect it to be any different this time? He stood up and turned to go.

"Mack." Brognola was looking out the window, his back to Bolan. "Good luck."

Bolan nodded to the big Fed's broad shoulders. Luck was such an inadequate word to describe what he was going to need to pull this one off.

Outside it was getting cold again. The sky was dark, the stars hard points of light, twinkling nervously. They seemed so small that it was difficult to imagine their hellish fire threatening anything so placid and serene as the Hudson River Valley. And yet a tiny spark, kin to the huge and distant stars, was already lit just fifty miles away. Ready, willing and, worst of all, able to bore its way through to the bottom of the world. Mack Bolan didn't even try to imagine how many innocent people it would take with it.

15

Not having an exact timetable posed problems. Knowing that Glinkov and his followers were planning something big meant they had to be watched. But watching someone closely, looking for something, anything, to fit in with what you knew, was hard on the nerves.

Mack Bolan didn't like doing nothing. This time, though, he had no choice. His choice would have been to go in hard, tear the place apart and turn his back on the smoking wreckage. It might make him feel better, but it wouldn't help Rachel. And it wouldn't get him Glinkov.

The Russian hadn't been seen, and no one even knew what he looked like. Brognola's people had a few intelligence photos, but they were six years old. And grainy. Glinkov was supposed to be shown in two of them, but no two men looked alike, and there was so little to go on that even computer enhancement hadn't helped. What galled Bolan the most was the possibility that Glinkov might walk in right under his nose and walk right out again. There was so much activity around the place that it was difficult to keep track of the comings and goings.

After thirty hours of close surveillance, he felt like a traffic cop on a day off. He was watching because he couldn't afford not to. It was his instinct. It was natural. And it was frustrating as hell. Bolan had to sit tight because doing anything else might blow the whole operation sky-high.

Parsons was very visible, orchestrating things in the overblown style and with the exaggerated gestures that marked his public addresses. Also prominent was the balding man who had been Bert's companion. Bolan knew that he must be Peter Achison. The guy seemed inoffensive enough, but the few moments he had spent in the outbuilding with the man had convinced Bolan that there was more to Achison than met the eye. His eyes were the giveaway. Even in the dim light, Bolan had seen the flat, deadly glitter. They were killer's eyes. And Bolan was convinced he had seen the man before.

The trees around Parsons's hideaway offered some cover but little shelter from the biting wind. It had been a few days since the last snow, and the sky seemed uncertain about its next move. An occasional burst of sunlight warmed Bolan slightly. At night it was below freezing. By the evening of the second day, Bolan was losing his patience. The big guy wanted, needed, action. Sitting around just gave him time to think. Too much time. The longer he waited, the more helpless he felt. But he knew that waiting was the only thing to do.

After dark he planned to move in closer, check the place out again and see if he could pick up any conversation. If they were getting ready to make their move, they had to be talking about it. If he knew when, he could make his own plans.

As the sun started to slip behind the trees, the sky began to cloud over. It had picked up a deep red color at the horizon, then, as suddenly as if someone had thrown a switch, it was dark. Overhead the clouds pressed toward him. What little light there was came from the house, but by eleven even the houselights were gone. The place looked almost deserted. A single lamp burned in the kitchen, throwing a dull rectangle onto the snowy lawn. Bolan knew that it was time for a closer look.

Inching through the trees, the snow crunching under his feet, Bolan kept his eyes on the house. So far there had been no sign of movement. Everyone must have gone to bed. Tonight obviously wasn't the night. As he reached the out-buildings, the kitchen grew brighter when someone turned on the overhead light. Using the rough stone wall of the outbuilding to his advantage, Bolan boosted himself onto the roof so that he could see into the kitchen.

Parsons moved nervously back and forth across Bolan's line of sight. Pacing with his hands behind his back, he was talking with someone Bolan couldn't see. Shifting his position on the roof, the warrior could just make out the back of the other person's head and one shoulder. Parsons seemed to be arguing, but his voice didn't carry across the broad lawn. Bolan had to get closer.

Sliding off the roof, he landed in a frozen drift behind the outbuilding. Keeping well away from the kitchen window, he moved in. At the house wall, he edged his way to a po-sition directly beneath the partially opened window. A tele-phone rang. Parsons picked up the receiver after one ring. Bolan was able to hear every word of the conversation.

"It's for you, Peter."

The second man began to talk. "Yes, Andrey.... Of course.... No, no.... Of course we will.... Right away." The receiver was replaced with a click. The scrape of a chair ob-scured the man's next sentence.

Parsons responded with some irritation. "Why? I don't see why we have to go out in the middle of the night. I don't mind telling you I'm getting fed up with these childish games."

"You can tell that to Andrey the next time you see him, Malcolm."

"Perhaps I will."

"We'd better get moving."

The voices moved off. They were going to be coming out, but Bolan wasn't sure which door they would use. He couldn't take the chance of being discovered. Sprinting through the snow to the safety of the outbuildings, he pressed himself flat against the wall and waited. A few moments later lights flooded the lawn.

The front door opened, and both men walked out into the cold. Parsons was still arguing, but Bolan was too far away to hear what was being said. He had to follow them. The caller's name had been Andrey. It could only be one man. This might be his best chance to get a look at Glinkov.

The two men headed down the path leading to the parking area. There was only one thing for Bolan to do. He couldn't follow them; his car was too far up the road. The only answer was to get back to his car by the most direct route and then wait for them to pull out. Even tailing them would be risky. At this time of night there would be little traffic on the country roads. He'd have to give them plenty of room.

Struggling through the heavy snow, Bolan felt a natural high, his adrenaline pumping. Finally he could do something besides twiddling his thumbs. If he got a look at Glinkov, the waiting would have been worth it.

As he reached the road, Bolan heard the slam of a car door, followed quickly by another. He got in his own car, closing the door quietly. He was a hundred fifty yards away, but sound carried in the crisp night air. Rolling down his window, he waited for Parsons to crank up his engine. When he heard the whine of the starter, Bolan turned his own engine over. It caught immediately.

Headlights stabbed out into the road ahead. Bolan threw his car into gear. He had to hope they weren't going to head his way. The shadows thrown by the headlights wavered as Parsons's vehicle moved forward and away from him. Bolan breathed a sigh of relief. Once they got onto a more heavily traveled road, he could fall back a bit and not worry about attracting attention. For the time being, though, it was going to be tricky.

The Chevy Blazer driven by the two men would be fairly easy to spot even in traffic. Its height would be an advantage for Bolan. The Blazer moved slowly, trailing exhaust in the cold air. When it had passed from view around the first curve in the road, Bolan put his own lights on and pulled out of the snow onto the road. As he followed behind, he could track the vehicle by the play of its lights among the trees.

The nearest major highway was several miles away, so he could hang back. As the Blazer reached the first intersection, Bolan was several hundred yards behind. He spotted the sweep of the headlights as the vehicle made a left turn, heading north on Route 84. Bolan followed, narrowing the gap a bit. He still hadn't seen another car, and at two o'clock in the morning he knew that it might be a while before he did.

The Blazer didn't seem to be in any hurry. It settled into the right lane and moved at a steady fifty miles per hour. After fifteen minutes, Bolan spotted the blinking turn signal and made ready to follow it off the highway onto a secondary road. It continued northward, slowing a bit to allow for road conditions.

Bolan wondered where Parsons was going. Nothing in his intel suggested there was anything nearby that Parsons and his followers were even remotely connected with. It was too late for sightseeing, and this trip had clearly been connected to the telephone conversation. Parsons had been given orders of some kind; reluctantly he was carrying them out. Bolan wondered what they were and if they were from Glinkov.

The Executioner knew that Thunder Mountain was in the opposite direction, so it couldn't be a reconnaissance trip. There were only two men anyway, not enough to mount an offensive against a well-guarded installation like the nuclear power station. Conjecture was leading him nowhere, so Bolan resolved to wait it out. As long as Parsons and his companion continued driving in the opposite direction, it was unlikely that anything would happen at the power station.

After fifteen minutes, the Blazer signaled to make another turn, this time into a narrow, winding road heading due west. The Blazer and Bolan's Camaro were the only vehicles on the road. Hanging well back, Bolan began to wonder whether Parsons was going anywhere at all. Maybe the men had just gone for a ride to settle their nerves. Maybe Parsons was getting cold feet. The antinuke leader had never been involved in anything as deadly as this plot before.

Suddenly the Blazer made a sharp turn without signaling. It sped off down a rutted side road, traveled thirty yards and then stopped. Bolan couldn't chance following, so he continued past the entrance. He slowed a bit, but couldn't see anything. It appeared as if the Blazer had simply stopped, although the clouds of exhaust told him it was still running. Bolan hadn't seen any illumination other than the headlights, so no one had gotten in or out.

A half mile past the turnoff, Bolan knew he had no choice. He had to chance being spotted. Banking into a small clearing, he made a quick turn and extinguished his lights, then coasted back toward the narrow road, keeping his approach as silent as possible.

He brought the car to a stop and rolled down the window to listen. The Blazer was out of sight, but he could still see the glare of its headlights. He debated about moving in on foot. Bolan knew that it might be worth a closer look. He hadn't seen any buildings down the side road, and there were no other cars in sight. If Parsons and Achison had come here to meet someone, Bolan was at a loss to explain how the other party would have gotten to so remote a location.

While he pondered what to do, the Blazer's engine revved, and the 4X4 began to back out of the cul-de-sac, its engine groaning against the heavy snow. The red glare of its taillights stained the snowy bank on either side, and then the rear of the Blazer burst into view.

The vehicle bounced unsteadily as it backed onto the road. In a sudden hurry, it sped back in the direction it had come. As soon as it was out of sight, Bolan clicked on his lights and roared after it. This time, Parsons drove like a man with a mission. The Blazer was bouncing recklessly, and Bolan had to goose his engine to keep it in sight.

At the intersection the Blazer continued to retrace its route, heading toward Route 84. Bolan was mystified. Nothing had happened. Parsons and his companion had met no one. They had visited a snowbank in the middle of nowhere and now appeared to be heading home. In a hurry.

Moving up on the Blazer carefully, Bolan decided it was time to take a chance. He slowly narrowed the gap between the Blazer and himself. He intended to pass the Blazer and drive back to the Parsons place. It was clear that nothing was going to happen tonight.

As he pulled up on the Blazer, Bolan realized with a start that there was only one occupant. The passenger seat was empty. He had never actually been close enough to know whether anyone had ever been in it. Could Parsons have been alone all night? If so, where was the other man? Had he merely walked Parsons to the car and then gone back to the house?

Bolan drove closer, and as he did, he knew he'd been had.

The Blazer pulled onto Route 84, and Bolan had his chance. The four-lane highway would allow him to pass without calling attention to himself. Not that it mattered, he thought. He had been lured out there on purpose. Bolan's car eased alongside the 4X4, and Bolan glanced at the driver.

It wasn't Malcolm Parsons.

It was the skinny guy, Achison. As Bolan pulled alongside, the man ignored him. Bolan pulled slightly ahead, then eased into the right lane. He glanced into the rearview mirror just in time to see the Blazer veer to the right, bumping over the shoulder. With a roar that Bolan could hear over his own engine, it continued on into the open field and up the side of a hill. Bolan hit his brakes, skidded to a halt and bounced out of his car.

The Blazer was gone.

16

Malcolm Parsons sat in the car, watching Peter Achison drive away in the Blazer. Just as Achison had predicted, a second car, a Camaro, drifted past the end of the driveway. Clearly it had been waiting, planning to follow them. He didn't like Achison, but he had to give the man credit. He certainly knew his job.

Parsons had grown increasingly cynical in recent years. Ideas that had attracted him out of a sincere desire to make a difference in the world, to change it for the better, had lost their meaning. They had become the means rather than the ends. Notoriety had been good to him. He felt warm in the glow of the spotlight; it was an easy way to make a living, and it gave him ready access to young women.

He couldn't say with a degree of certainty when he'd stopped caring, when he'd stopped trying to make things change. He knew that he had become exactly the sort of hypocrite he had once deplored. He had been seduced by the trappings of success.

But lately he felt that things were slipping out of his control. Achison scared him. Without making any overt threats, Achison made it clear that Parsons had better do as he "suggested" if he wanted to continue his activities. In more reflective moments, Parsons wondered just what might happen if he were to balk. But Parsons knew that such a move would put his life on the line.

It had been bad enough, realizing that Achison controlled him. But learning that someone else controlled Achison had come as a shock. The master of duplicity had himself been tricked, not once but twice. He hated the fact that the Arab money he had been spending so freely was not Arab money at all. Glinkov was Russian, which meant he was probably KGB.

Parsons quickly dismissed the thought. The Camaro was long gone. It was time to keep his appointment with Andrey Glinkov. He didn't like the man; his eyes were pools of emptiness. The antinuke leader had encountered that look only once before. It was during a hiking trip in Arizona when he'd stared into the eyes of a rattlesnake that had just bitten him.

Starting his car, Parsons pulled out into the road and headed in the opposite direction. His appointment was for three o'clock, and he had been advised not to be late. He wouldn't dare. If he played his cards right, he might regain control of his organization.

As much as Achison and Glinkov frightened him, he was unwilling to give up the easy life. He had been comfortable for too long to go back to square one. He had fought the good fight, and no one had given a damn where his next meal had come from. Sleeping on the floor of cold-water flats was not for him. No more. He had paid his dues. And if the price of comfort was his soul, what the hell. He'd pay.

GLINKOV'S EYES WATCHED the door of the secluded farmhouse as it opened. The Russian was clearly annoyed.

"You're late, Mr. Parsons. I don't appreciate that. I won't tolerate it," he said before Parsons was barely through the doorway.

"Who the hell are you to talk to me like that?"

"That doesn't matter, Mr. Parsons. What matters is that I can, and do, expect you to be on time. I'm a busy man."

"Yeah, sure. We're all busy. I have things to do, too. Why am I here?"

Glinkov didn't answer. He watched Parsons closely, waiting for the telltale signs. If he knew Parsons as well as he thought he did, the man would begin to squirm. Until then, he would hold his silence.

"I thought you had something you wanted to talk to me about," Parsons said, shifting his feet nervously. "Let's get down to business. I want to go home to get some sleep."

Glinkov leaned back in his chair, still keeping silent. It shouldn't be long. He knew why Parsons was being so antagonistic. Camouflage. Parsons was obviously feeling the strain.

"Look, are you going to talk, or aren't you?" Parsons made a show of walking deliberately back to the door he had just closed. With his hand on the knob, he turned to Glinkov, arching an eyebrow as if giving the Russian one last opportunity to speak.

And Glinkov smiled.

Parsons stood with his hand on the knob. He turned the knob, pulling the inner door toward him. Still watching Glinkov, he reached for the outer door.

Glinkov was still smiling. His eyes had that same flat, empty glitter. Parsons threw in the towel. He knew that he had lost. The Russian owned him.

"All right, look, I'm sorry. I guess I'm a little edgy."

"Sit down, Mr. Parsons."

Parsons did as he was told. He returned to the sofa across from the Russian's easy chair. When he was seated, Glinkov stopped smiling. Finally the Russian spoke.

"Our little diversion was successful, wasn't it?"

"Yes. You were right. There was someone watching the house. Who was it?"

"It doesn't matter, yet. For the moment, as long as we know *where* he is, it doesn't matter *who* he is. It is always the enemy you can't see who poses the greatest threat, Mr. Parsons.''

"Always?"

"Yes, always."

"Why did you want me to come here?"

"To inform you of a few things."

"Such as?"

"And to request a favor of you."

"A favor?"

"We shall get to that later. First, the information." Glinkov glanced at his watch. "As of this very minute, our little adventure at Thunder Mountain is under way."

"What? But how? I mean, I didn't give that order."

"Mr. Parsons, it's time you realized that you are no longer in a position to give orders. It is no longer your prerogative. From now on you will follow them."

"But the plans were for—"

Glinkov cut in. "The plans have been changed. Mr. Achison is in charge of the operation."

"You bastard. You had this all worked out. You didn't want Peter to lose anyone. You wanted me out of the way."

"Not at all. When we are finished here, we will go directly to Thunder Mountain. But Mr. Achison, you will have to admit, is more . . . military minded, let us say. And this is, after all, a military operation, is it not?"

"But we're not ready. We still need some information on the layout of the plant."

"I have that already. I've passed it on to Mr. Achison. I'm sure he'll make good use of it. Your Mr. Reynolds was an invaluable source of information. I congratulate you on finding him."

Parsons was momentarily speechless. Things were totally beyond his control. "I seem to be expendable," he said.

"Not at all. We need you very much, Mr. Parsons. That should be apparent. You will give us the media exposure we want. Your presence will ensure that people pay attention to what we say rather than to what we do.''

"What do you mean? What's the difference?"

"All in good time. We have to hurry. We have things to do. We are to meet Peter in two hours. Inside Thunder Mountain."

"But—"

"First, come with me." Glinkov walked toward the back of the house. Parsons meekly followed. There was nothing else he could do. Entering the kitchen, Glinkov opened a wooden door that hid behind a flight of stairs. Glinkov motioned for Parsons to follow him downstairs.

The basement was illuminated by a single overhead bulb. In one corner, two figures lay huddled against the wall. Alan Reynolds moaned as the two men approached. The other figure, a woman, was lying facedown.

"What happened? What's going on here?" Parsons demanded.

"Mr. Reynolds has served his purpose, Malcolm. It wouldn't do for anyone to learn just how helpful he's been, would it?"

"But what—"

"That favor I mentioned? It's time to deliver. I want you to dispose of Mr. Reynolds. Now."

Glinkov reached into his pocket and withdrew a small automatic pistol. The blue steel of the .22 caliber Walther TPH glittered in his palm. "I trust you know how to use this?"

"I won't do it. I'm not a murderer. I can't shoot a man in cold blood like this. What the hell do you think I am?"

"That's a question you might more appropriately ask yourself, Mr. Parsons. What the hell *do* you think you are? It will only require one shot." Glinkov extended the gun.

"No, I won't. I can't," he argued even as he snatched the gun from Glinkov's hand. He was beginning to sweat. "Don't ask me to do it. There's no point, no reason."

"Of course there is. He's seen me. He can identify me. We can't have that, can we?"

Parsons slowly raised the gun, pointing it at Reynolds and then at Glinkov. "I could shoot you, you know. I could do that."

Glinkov said nothing. He stared unwaveringly at Parsons. He had seen the man squirm earlier. He would do it again now. He was broken. Parsons's last vestiges of self-respect had been stripped away. He would do what he was told.

Slowly, the gun was shifted away from Glinkov toward the whimpering man. Reynolds wouldn't feel anything; he was too far gone. Parsons knew that if he didn't shoot him, Glinkov would. And then the Russian would shoot the antinuke leader.

Parsons closed his eyes and squeezed the trigger. The report bounced off the basement walls. Parsons opened his eyes and looked at Reynolds. The bullet had hit him in the left temple. Blood pooled on the canvas beneath the dead man's head. The wound was raw and ugly. A thin trickle of blood oozed from Reynolds's open mouth.

Parsons turned away. Throwing the gun across the cellar, he bent over at the waist and threw up. A series of dry, racking heaves twisted his gut into knots.

"Well done, Mr. Parsons. You have more backbone than I thought. Perhaps we shall enjoy working together, eh? Who would have thought it?"

"You cold, murdering bastard," Parsons whispered. "There was no need for that."

"No? Then why did you do it? It was you, after all, who pulled the trigger."

"You made me do it."

"Did I?" Glinkov retrieved the pistol and handed it back to Parsons. "Keep it. You'll need it before the night is over."

"What do we do with the woman?" Parsons didn't want to know the answer, but he had to ask.

"We'll take her with us. We will have use for her at Thunder Mountain. Give me a hand."

Glinkov rolled the unconscious woman into a second canvas, then pulled her forward. "Take the other end. We'll take her out to the car."

Parsons bent to grab hold of the other end of the roll. The woman was heavier than he had expected. She had seemed so frail lying next to Reynolds.

The two men struggled up the narrow stairwell. Back in the kitchen, they lowered their unconscious package to the floor. Glinkov reached back to turn off the cellar light.

"What about Reynolds?" Parsons asked.

"We needn't concern ourselves with him any longer. There is nothing to connect us with this place. It will be weeks before anyone finds him, if then. And by that time we will long since have accomplished our purpose. Let's go."

They hoisted the canvas roll again, Parsons grunting under the unaccustomed exertion. They dumped the woman in the trunk, but as Parsons moved to close the lid Glinkov stopped him.

"I think we better make sure she can breathe. Our cargo is rather valuable."

"Why?"

"I'll explain while we drive." Glinkov tugged at the canvas, pulling it down and away from the woman's face.

"Christ. It's Rachel!" Parsons rasped.

Glinkov laughed. "You must miss her on these cold winter nights."

17

Thunder Mountain was the largest reactor complex in the American northeast. Three nuclear reactors, each capable of generating two thousand megawatts, were nestled in the woods high above the Hudson River. Right from the beginning, the plant had drawn opposition, both from local residents and environmentalists. Construction of the project had been marked by riots and sit-ins. The first day the plant had gone on line, three hundred people had been arrested during a riot. Police records proved that few of those arrested lived in New York State. Thunder Mountain was a national concern.

Security measures at the plant were strict. The entire complex was fenced in. Armed guards patrolled the perimeter twenty-four hours a day. But things had been relatively quiet until Three Mile Island had had its accident. Hordes of media people had descended on the plant, and the news reports had been full of footage showing the earlier unrest.

Unlike many of the nuclear installations around the country, Thunder Mountain was located relatively close to a major urban center. Its public relations problems were tricky, and its attention to safety more scrupulous than most. It had been cited by the NRC for its exemplary conduct in dealing with potential accidents on three separate occasions.

That was about to change.

In the heavily wooded area behind the plant, Peter Achison went over his plans one final time. Timing, he kept reminding his small assault team, was everything. The first attempt might be the only attempt. If they failed to breach security and gain entrance to the grounds, the ball game would be over before it began.

The twenty-five members of the team had been divided into squads of three to five, each with a specific task. The greatest burden would fall on the initial attack team. All were heavily armed. Each man carried a Kalashnikov assault rifle. Several of them also carried grenades stolen from a U.S. Army depot two years before.

"Any questions?" Achison asked as he looked from one member of the team to another. He had been drilling them for weeks and didn't expect any questions. He wasn't disappointed. "Everybody should be in position in twenty minutes. The first team should be inside ten minutes later. We'll open the rear gate and let the rest of you in."

Achison felt a rush of excitement. He hadn't felt like this since Vietnam. An Australian by birth, and trained in the Australian military, he had been assigned to U.S. forces for three different tours. Each time he had kept his eyes open and his mouth shut. But much of what he'd learned had been wasted. Until now.

"Remember. No shooting unless absolutely necessary. In order for this operation to succeed, we need hostages. Let's move it."

The assault team broke up and each squad moved quickly to take up its assigned position. Achison would lead the initial attack. The others, including a backup team assigned to crack the rear access gate if the frontal assault failed, were led by Eli Cohen. The remaining members of the team would wait until access had been achieved.

Achison led his men through the woods, circling toward the front gate. They kept well back from the fence, which was regularly patrolled by two-man guard teams in Jeeps.

The perimeter of the plant was large, and the four teams made continuous circuits, passing a given point at half-hour intervals.

The main gate was well lighted and guarded by six men at all times. Security had gotten somewhat lax after the Three Mile Island incident had died down, but Achison knew his task wasn't an easy one. Surprise was crucial.

As they moved through the woods, Achison kept an eye on the fence. He wanted to get a fix on the sweep cycle kept by the patrols. A fifteen-foot strip of cleared land ran along the inside of the fence to allow passage for the Jeeps. On the inside of that strip were more woods, and beyond that, the buildings of the reactor complex.

As they neared their goal, one of the buildings vented steam in a huge cloud. The noise was nearly deafening.

"Shit, no wonder people don't like these things," one of the men whispered. "I wouldn't want to hear that in the middle of the night, either."

"That's why we're here, asshole," somebody laughed. "We're gonna shut it down."

Achison kept silent. Only two other members of the team knew the actual purpose of the raid. It was one of Glinkov's cardinal rules that information be parceled out jealously on a need-to-know basis. Even Parsons had no idea how big the operation was. But that didn't make any difference, Achison thought, because Parsons would soon be out of the picture. He had served his purpose.

"All right, let's slow it down. We're getting close." Achison held up his hand. "I'm going to move in for a look. Wait here."

He slipped into the trees, making a wide arc to his left. Ahead, he could see the glow of the lighting at the main gate. The next ten minutes were critical. They were so close. He didn't want a mistake now.

Worming his way through the trees, he cursed as snow, dislodged by his passage, cascaded down his open collar.

Fifty yards from the access road, he could see the guard station. The main gate appeared to be closed but unlocked.

All six men on duty were present. It was best to know where everyone was. Achison had seen perfectly ordinary missions fall apart because someone had gone off and returned at an inopportune moment. That would not happen tonight.

Achison returned to the rest of his team and filled them in. His intention was to vault the fence and come on the gate from the inside. It would be easier to control the guards and reduce the possibility of a confrontation.

"Look, the next patrol is due in four minutes. When they pass, we'll wait another five. That will give us plenty of time before the next unit comes in. Remember the TV cameras. Louis, I want you to take one out. But just one. Anything more than that will attract attention. Get it now, but keep your eye out for the Jeep."

Louis moved away and headed toward the fence. An electronics specialist, the surveillance camera posed no problem for him. He was back in three minutes, grinning.

"Man, this is gonna be a piece of cake." He rubbed his hands together in satisfaction. "I'm almost disappointed, man. I thought we were gonna have some excitement."

"You want some excitement, just screw up. I'll show you more than you can handle," Achison warned.

"No sweat, man." Louis laughed.

So far everything was going like clockwork. Achison checked his watch. Eli should be in place now, he thought. He hoped his second-in-command didn't have to hit the back door.

A rumble in the trees alerted the men. The next patrol Jeep was making its pass. "Quiet everybody," Achison whispered. "As soon as they're gone, get ready. We hit the fence in five minutes."

The men sat quietly on the snowy ground as the Jeep rumbled past. It was so close, they could hear snatches of conversation from its occupants. Thirty seconds later, it was gone. It was time to go to work. Achison stood and gestured to the others.

"Let's go."

They checked their weapons and moved toward the fence. The chain link was topped with coils of concertina wire. Getting over would be tricky.

"Louis," Achison whispered, "is that wire hot?"

"Nope. And I already cut it over by the camera. Just left it in place so the patrol wouldn't notice anything."

"Nice work." Achison thought the guy was too cocky by half, but he did good work.

"Like I said, man. No sweat."

Louis tossed a grapple over the fence, letting it catch on the inside of the chain link, then hoisted himself up to pull the concertina wire aside. He continued on up and over, landing with a thud on the inside of the compound. The others followed, their Kalashnikovs slung over their shoulders. Twice, a rifle rattled against the fence.

When the five-man team was inside, Achison gave the sign. Swiftly they moved toward the guardhouse at the main gate. All six men on duty were inside. Approaching from the windowless backside, the assault team lined up against the rear of the guardhouse and split in two.

Two men moved to the side away from the gate where they could cover the guards through a window. The remaining two moved to the opposite side, ready to force the door. Achison stayed in the middle where both teams could see him. When the cover team was in place, he signaled the others.

The guards were caught napping. Four men were seated at a table, playing cards. One was making coffee. The sixth man was lying on a cot, watching the card game.

The guardhouse door burst open with a slam, breaking two panes of glass.

"Nobody move. I mean nobody, understand? Hands up. Now! And don't even think about that alarm button, pal." Louis was in his glory. He wasn't even sure there *was* an alarm button, but that's what they said in all the movies. How could it hurt?

Without warning, one of the men at the table pulled his .38 revolver. He got to his feet carefully, backing toward the nearest wall. Partially concealed behind another member of his team, Louis raised his Kalashnikov. The guard reached back with his hand to find the wall.

It was a standoff, until Louis fired a burst. The rifle hammered, its noise deafening in the small room. Louis had aimed high. The burst slammed the guard into the paneled wall behind him. The man grabbed his throat as if to prevent the bullets from striking it. He was too late. Blood spurted from behind his fingers, staining his shirt and spattering the wall behind him.

No one moved, as if they were all waiting for the echo to die. Then Louis said, "I hope one of you guys has a spare shirt. We were counting on those uniforms." He laughed once, a brittle bark from deep within his throat. "Come on, guys, get their guns. We're on a tight schedule here."

Quickly the other guards were disarmed. Forced to strip off their uniforms, they were then herded into the bathroom of the guardhouse where they were bound and gagged. The antinuke raiders quickly put on the discarded uniforms. Achison grabbed a large ring of keys and tossed it to Louis.

"You and David get out to the rear gate. Eli's waiting. Take the Jeep outside. Make it fast."

"Right, chief." Louis snapped off a sardonic salute.

He was beginning to get on Achison's nerves. Either he didn't realize just how serious this was or he didn't care. Either way, he could be a liability. Well, there were ways to handle that, too, Achison thought. He watched the clown hustle out to the Jeep, relieved not to have to listen to him for a while. And he had work to do. They would have to clean the bloody mess to preserve the appearance of order.

The next obstacle would be the Jeep patrols. There were four of them, and each had to be captured and replaced. The best place to handle the switch would be at the back gate. Eli would handle it. Anything, an employee going home sick, an unexpected delivery, hell, even a routine late-shift arrival, could upset their plans.

Achison checked his watch again. Glinkov would be here any minute. And Parsons. Wait until the bastard found out what was in store for him.

Louis roared off to let Cohen and his men in. At the rear entrance he hopped from the Jeep, fumbled with the keys and finally unlocked the gate. Cohen waited in the trees until the gate swung open.

The next patrol was due any minute. "Louis, you and David stay with the Jeep. Put the hood up, like you're having trouble. We'll be in the trees. When the patrol gets here, get the drop on them. We'll back you up. We'll take all the guards out the same way. As soon as that's done, bring the rest of the men to the guardhouse."

"Right."

It worked to perfection. The surprised guards were stripped, bound and gagged, then dragged into the trees. Two of Cohen's men replaced them in the Jeep and moved off. Cohen thought it ironic that, having taken control of the power station, they had also taken on the responsibility to protect it.

"Louis," Cohen said, "I'm leaving you in charge. I have to talk to Peter. Handle the rest of the teams the same way. When you've nailed them all, meet me at the guardhouse. Got it?"

"Sure thing."

Cohen sprinted off toward the guardhouse, keeping toward the trees to avoid the next patrol. He reached the gate just as a car pulled through. It was Glinkov and Parsons, but where the hell was Rachel?

Glinkov got out of the car as Achison locked the gate. It would not open again. "Peter, I see everything is under control. Mr. Parsons ought to watch you carefully. He might learn a few things."

Achison laughed. Parsons might learn something, all right. But it wouldn't do him any good. "How did things go on your end, Andrey?"

"Very well. Malcolm took care of Mr. Reynolds for us. Very neatly, I might add."

Cohen rounded the corner of the guardhouse. Glinkov spotted him first. "Eli, any trouble?"

"No. Everything is going according to plan."

"Good. I have Mr. Parsons, as you can see. The next phase should go rather well, I should think."

"It should. As soon as the perimeter is secured, we better start rounding up the staff. There should be about thirty people on duty tonight. They're spread out, so we'll have to be careful. One reactor's down and one's still under construction. Unit 1 is the only one operating tonight. We'll take the main control room first. From there we can monitor communications and make sure we keep a lid on this until we've consolidated our control."

"Very good. I'll leave that to you then. But I have something else I want you to handle first."

"What's that?"

"A little package in the trunk. It might come in handy later, I should think." Glinkov handed him the keys. "Open the trunk, Eli."

Cohen, curious, did as he was told. "What the hell is *she* doing here?" Fortunately Rachel was asleep, or unconscious. At first Cohen feared she might be dead, but her chest was moving slightly.

"I think our Mr. Bolan might like to see her, don't you agree? He has seemed, shall we say, upset by her disappearance. I should like to dispose of him here where we can control things more readily.'' Turning to Parsons, he continued, ''I think some sort of reference to her presence should be worked into your first communiqué, Malcolm.''

''What do we do with her in the meantime?'' Cohen asked.

''Keep her under tight security, segregated from the other hostages. I want to know where she is, and I don't want anyone, I repeat, anyone to go near her. Understood?''

''Yes, sir,'' Eli said. ''Let's leave her in the car until we secure one of the buildings, then I'll move her inside.''

''Very well. Let's move on. It's getting cold, and I'd like to be enjoying the warmth of a raging fire.''

18

As the Blazer vanished over the hill, Mack Bolan realized he'd been had. But why? He knew that the answer would not be found back at the Parsons place. Parsons wasn't the type to lead an armed assault on Thunder Mountain. But Achison had been in the Blazer. That could only mean one thing: Glinkov.

Bolan floored it, pulling back onto the highway, fishtailing for a hundred yards until the tires gained traction. They were clever, all right. They'd bought themselves plenty of time, but Bolan was determined that it wouldn't be enough.

Thunder Mountain was forty miles away, nearly an hour's drive over winding, ice-slick roads. And Bolan had no idea what he would be up against once he got there. But there was no time to consider possibilities. There was only time for a direct attack.

As he maneuvered the Camaro through the slippery turns, always riding on the thinnest edge of control, Mack Bolan knew that he was the only man who stood between order and chaos, and the only man who stood between Rachel Peres and certain death, unless Eli Cohen was still on the inside.

With less than twenty miles to go, Bolan had decided only one thing. He had to approach the place carefully. There was no margin for error. If he blew it once, the ball game would be over.

Bolan pulled off the road to check a map of the Thunder Mountain installation, but it showed him little he didn't already know. He'd have to trust his instincts, and hope for a little luck, something that had seemed in short supply the past few days. He rammed the car back into gear. The menacing roar of the Camaro echoed through the trees, filling the car, and Bolan's head, with the rumble of combat. Every battle he had ever fought paled before the coming confrontation. Never had the threat to innocent civilians been so enormous.

With five miles still to go, Bolan decreased speed. Glinkov was no fool; he might have more resources than Bolan realized. He had to prepare for the worst, and that was going to cost him time, time he didn't have. But there was no other way to go.

A warning sign on the right told him that the plant was just a mile away now. Bolan began looking for sentries that Glinkov might have posted on the approach road. He hoped the Russian was cocky enough to ignore that precaution. Such arrogance would be Bolan's ally, as it had been so often in the past. Seldom did the outcome of a battle hinge on one major mistake. It was an accumulation of errors that made the difference.

Thunder Mountain's glow lit up the trees now. They were starkly etched against the gray background. Bolan pulled into a small clearing, driving the Camaro past a bend in the narrow road and slamming it hard into a snowdrift to get it as far out of sight as possible.

Approaching on foot, Bolan decided to check the main gate first. It was the easiest point of entry. If Glinkov had taken the plant already, it would be most obvious at the main gate. The cover thinned as he neared the entrance, and the deep drifts among the trees hampered his approach. Finding a vantage point fifty yards from the fence, Bolan noticed nothing unusual. There were uniformed men in the main guardhouse. The gate was closed, and a patrol Jeep stood behind the small building.

While he watched, one of the sweep patrols rolled past, and a guard waved to the gatehouse. The driver beeped his horn, but kept on moving. Bolan had no choice. He'd have to get over the fence and close enough to the gatehouse to hear what was going on. If Glinkov hadn't yet taken the plant he would be stopped. If he already had... Well, Bolan didn't want to make odds on the outcome.

Pulling back into the trees, the Executioner followed the fence as he moved away from the gate. Bolan checked for the next Jeep patrol. Moving tightly against the heavy wire, he noticed footprints. The snow had been trampled by several pairs of feet. Above his head, the concertina wire dangled uselessly where it had been severed.

Footprints on the inside of the fence moved in the direction of the guardhouse. He was too late. The plant had been taken. But the attackers hadn't bothered to repair the fence. That might mean they weren't expecting anyone, at least not so soon. They were cocky, all right, maybe just cocky enough to give Mack Bolan the edge he needed.

Vaulting the fence, Bolan landed lightly on the inside and moved swiftly toward the guardhouse. Approaching from the rear, he flattened himself against the building. Pressing an ear against the wall, he could make out the hum of conversation, but the words were obscured. Moving toward a window, he kept an eye peeled for the patrol Jeeps. The engine noise would give him some warning, but his position was exposed.

Directly beneath the window, Bolan could hear the conversation more clearly. Two men inside were playing cards. There was no way to tell whether they were legitimate guards unaware that their defenses had been breached or Glinkov's men relaxing just a little too soon. There was another window, and Bolan slipped along the rough wall to a spot directly beneath it. The window was lighted, but no sound came from within the small room.

Stretching to his full height alongside the window, Bolan strained to hear, but the room was silent. He'd have to chance a look. Inside, several men, bound and gagged, lay on the floor. There was no blood visible, and they appeared unharmed. But there was no way to get them out without going through the front. It was too risky. Bolan would have to try another tack.

Watching for the next patrol, Bolan sprinted along the fence, leaving the guardhouse behind. Just ahead was a stand of trees that approached the fence, creating a small gap through which the Jeep would have to pass.

Bolan headed for the trees, pulling at his Beretta while he ran. Once in the trees, he could watch, unseen, and nail the first Jeep that came along. Cutting down on the patrols would limit the possibility of discovery before he could get some help. He had to find Eli Cohen.

The Jeep rumbled into view from the direction of the guardhouse. Its two occupants seemed more concerned with their conversation than they were with surveillance. Bolan knew there were supposed to be four patrols. If Glinkov had kept to that practice, that meant eight men. There were several men in the guardhouse and probably several more elsewhere in the plant. It meant Glinkov had a substantial force at his command. Bolan didn't like the odds, but he knew he had no choice.

The Jeep was rapidly approaching. The men continued their conversation. The Executioner set his Beretta for a three-shot burst and crouched among the trees to take aim at the driver. The Beretta whispered, and all three slugs punched through bone and brain. A spray of death's shadow flew from the driver's skull, raining on the passenger who flew forward as the Jeep careened into the trees.

Bolan moved swiftly, reaching the Jeep just as the second guard scrambled to his feet. A second burst from the

Beretta slammed into the man's chest and found his heart. He fell like a tree, slamming his head into the frozen ground. His feet kicked spasmodically for a second and then he lay still.

Bolan wasted no time in celebration. Quickly he hoisted the dead man and tossed him into the rear of the Jeep. The driver was slumped forward over the wheel. The Executioner shoved him aside, slipping in to restart the stalled engine. He had to get the Jeep out of sight before the next patrol came along. The engine coughed reluctantly, then caught. Slamming the Jeep's transmission into reverse, Bolan gunned the engine and backed away from the trees. The radiator had been punctured by the impact with the trees, and a cloud of steam billowed around the struggling vehicle.

Sputtering and choking, the Jeep labored into the woods, back away from the fence. When Bolan was sure it was out of sight, he killed the engine. As he leaped from the Jeep he grabbed the passenger's Kalashnikov. He checked both corpses for ammo and additional weapons. Three clips for the AK-47 and a pair of fragmentation grenades evened the odds. A little.

The key was whether these guys would be missed. What he had so far seen suggested they wouldn't be. Two down, but Bolan knew he had a long way to go. Before he could make up his mind what to do next, he heard the roar of another Jeep. It was heading his way fast.

It was too early for the next patrol. No one could have heard the suppressed fire of the Beretta. What the hell was going on? Moving silently toward the fence, Bolan spotted the Jeep hugging the fence and running flat out in his direction. Like its predecessor, it would have to pass through the narrow gap between the trees and fence. The Executioner resumed his former position, bracing for round two.

The Jeep slowed suddenly, then veered into the trees. The driver was looking over his shoulder, as if expecting pursuit, or working against the clock. While Bolan watched, the Jeep roared into the trees, pushing far into the snow. The driver leaped from his seat as he killed the engine. He reached into the back seat, withdrawing an Ingram MAC-10. The man bent down, out of Bolan's sight for a moment, and when he straightened up, he threaded a sound suppressor onto the Ingram's snub nose.

Crouching low, the man moved back toward the fence, heading in Bolan's direction. Backing off, Bolan watched silently. The newcomer took the position Bolan had just relinquished. He dropped to one knee, examining the snow, then turned slowly, his eyes searching the trees. He had noticed signs of Bolan's presence. Before he could finish scanning the area, the sound of another Jeep filtered through the trees.

It was some distance away and running at a crawl—probably the next patrol. The man turned his attention to the approaching vehicle, looking back to check the trees one more time. He edged forward, placing a small cluster of evergreens at his back, and slipped out of Bolan's sight. He was about thirty feet away, too close for Bolan to risk moving. It appeared as if he was going to ambush the next Jeep, but why?

Before Bolan could answer that question, the headlights of the approaching Jeep stabbed through the darkness, scattering shadows across the snow where Bolan crouched. He couldn't see the newcomer, who hadn't made a sound since taking up his position. The Jeep was close now and had slowed to a near crawl. Bolan could hear the guards discussing something. The Jeep stopped. The passenger dismounted and walked toward the front of the vehicle.

"Look here, Stan. Tracks. Somethin' went off into them trees."

"It's probably nothing. Somebody had to take a leak, I'll bet. Come on."

"You sure?"

"Hell, there ain't nobody here but us chickens, pal." The driver laughed. "Let's go."

The passenger turned to get back in the Jeep. The cough of the Ingram caught him by surprise. The rain of .45 caliber hellfire stitched the driver across the chest, slamming him backward into the seat. Bolan saw the second guard dive for cover. Too late. The Ingram sought him out, catching him in midair. His body slammed sideways as the rapid fire shattered his ribs. He spun, hitting the ground in a roll and coming to rest against the fence.

The hidden man suddenly appeared, crossing behind the Jeep to reach the fallen man at the fence. He grunted, then dragged the body toward the Jeep to dump it in the rear seat. Crossing behind the Jeep a second time, he pushed the driver into the passenger seat.

Reaching into the rear again, he tugged a large piece of canvas from the back seat and dragged it across the snow toward the fence. He rushed back to the Jeep and swung it around, aiming its headlights toward the fence. Using the canvas, he quickly obscured any signs of a confrontation, kicking loose snow from the base of the fence onto the bloodstain that stood out in the bright lights from the Jeep.

Out in the open, the newcomer had his back to the trees. Bolan raised his Beretta and moved forward. The running engine would cover his approach. He reached his initial firing position just as the man finished. Bolan drew a bead on the man's back. And waited.

When he turned back to the Jeep, the man's features sprang into bold relief for the first time since his arrival. The Executioner inhaled sharply. The man was Eli Cohen.

Mack Bolan watched while Cohen got into the Jeep and swung it around. He headed into the trees just as Bolan had done with the patrol he had taken out earlier. But this time there was a difference. Cohen had his own Jeep. As the vehicle disappeared into the trees, Bolan walked toward the area where Cohen had concealed his own Jeep earlier.

Bolan heard the engine die, and the lights went out. In a few moments, he heard Cohen floundering through the snow. Placing the Jeep between himself and the approaching man, Bolan dropped to one knee. As Cohen broke into the clear, Bolan bent to conceal himself behind the rear of the Jeep.

Eli Cohen was nearly out of breath from his exertions. He trudged heavily toward the Jeep. With twenty-five feet remaining, he stopped and scanned the trees. In a loud whisper, he called, "Bolan? Bolan, are you here?"

"Who wants to know?" Bolan answered.

"Thank God!" Cohen sighed, turning toward the sound of Bolan's voice. "We better get a move on. We don't have much time."

Bolan stood up, still holding the Beretta. "Where's Rachel?" he demanded.

Cohen hopped into the Jeep and cranked it up. "Get in," he said over the roar of the engine. "I'll tell you everything I know. But we have to hurry."

Bolan knew he had no choice but to trust the man. He wasn't sure he should, but unless he missed his guess he couldn't win if he didn't. Bolan climbed into the Jeep, keeping the Beretta in his lap. Cohen saw the pistol and smiled.

"Nice gun," he said.

19

The main control room of Thunder Mountain's Unit 1 reactor was crowded. The chaos was getting to Malcolm Parsons. He wasn't used to such a commotion unless he was at its center. He felt like a bystander, and knew that, in fact, that was all he was. Glinkov's men had just returned with the last group of hostages. The Russian was huddled with one of the raiders, stopping occasionally to issue orders. Parsons had had enough. He charged over to Glinkov with his arms waving.

"Do you mind telling me what the hell is going on here?" Parsons demanded.

"Hold your water, pal," the man with Glinkov snarled.

The Russian placed a hand on his companion's arm. "Give me a moment with Malcolm, would you, Steven?"

Grudgingly the man withdrew a few steps, turning his back to watch the disposition of the hostages.

"Malcolm," Glinkov said, trying to soothe the older man's irritation. "I'm very busy. Why don't you wait in that office over there. I'll be with you as soon as I can."

"What's happening here? Who are all these people?"

"In a minute, Mr. Parsons. Kindly wait in the office."

Parsons wasn't happy, but he did as he was told. Glinkov watched him go, a thoughtful expression dulling the forced smile. When Parsons had closed the office door, Glinkov returned to his lieutenant. "Do you have them all now?"

"Yeah. We checked the time cards. Everybody's here. Thirty-two of 'em."

"Not as many as I would have thought," Glinkov said.

"Well, only one reactor's operating, and these damn things practically run themselves. So much automation, computers and all that shit. All that power, and hardly anybody watching it."

"A good thing, too. Our task would have been much more difficult otherwise. It's time for the next phase, Steven. Get all the hostages into one location. Use that backup control room. It will be easy to secure."

"Right."

"All except Ms Peres. I want her separated from the rest. Keep her someplace downstairs that's more difficult to get to. And I want her watched by two men at all times. If Bolan shows up, which I fervently hope, I want some warning. He'll be after the woman first. Put two men on her—expendable men. And let me know where you're keeping her."

"Okay. Anything else?"

"No. Have you seen Eli?"

"He left a half hour ago. Said he wanted to check on the security patrols. You want him?"

"No hurry. Tell him to see me when he returns. I have to see our Mr. Parsons. He's upset, it seems."

Steven orchestrated the confinement of the hostages. The terrified workers were milling about, anxiously watching their captors. Prodded with weapons, they moved quickly into a concrete room with a heavy steel door. When they had all been herded into the bunkerlike holding pen, Steven stood in the doorway.

Grabbing two men, he pointed to Rachel Peres. Glinkov watched as Rachel left with the three men. When they had gone, Glinkov walked toward the office where Parsons could be seen pacing nervously.

Glinkov entered, and Parsons charged forward. "When are we going to get the media in on this?" he demanded. "This can get us some major coverage. It proves how poorly defended these nuclear plants are. I mean, hell, we just charged right in. If a bunch of amateurs like us can do it, just think what trained guerrillas could do. Washington will be made to look the fool over this."

"Slow down, Malcolm. Everything in due course. You must be very careful about what you say, don't you think? It won't do to meet the press unprepared. I think you ought to prepare a few carefully chosen remarks for the morning press conference. I'll make arrangements for that in a while."

"But you don't have to. I have all the contacts we need. There are several journalists sympathetic to our cause. They'll be here as soon as I call them."

"That won't be necessary."

"But—"

"Never mind, Malcolm. Just do what you do best. Get your statement ready. Let me handle the rest of it. I'll call you when it's time."

Glinkov didn't wait for a reply. He closed the door, leaving Parsons staring at a blank sheet of stainless steel. Out in the main control room, the crowd had diminished. A few armed men sat in small groups, smoking and talking quietly. Two guards stood at the door to the backup control room.

Glinkov had no intention of using Parsons any further. There would be no communiqué. He had different plans for Thunder Mountain. And for everyone here. But he wanted Parsons out of his hair for a while. When more important matters were out of the way, Mr. Parsons could be dealt with.

The Russian looked up at the massive banks of dials and gauges on the control boards that were arranged in an oblique U, all visible from the two swivel-based control chairs. A distant hum was the only evidence of the massive power that could be unleashed from the room. A console swept away from the chairs in an arc on either side. The most important work of the power station could be directed, or misdirected, by walking no more than twenty feet to either side of the swivel chairs.

Glinkov sat in one of the two chairs, scanning the wall of gauges and dials, instinctively reaching out for the controls. He didn't even realize that Steven had returned to the room.

"Kind of like *Star Trek*, isn't it?" Steven laughed.

"*Star Trek*?"

"Yeah, you know, the TV show. Starship Enterprise, and all that. This place gives me the creeps."

"I think we better begin the next step, Steven."

"Okay, you're the boss."

"Yes," Glinkov whispered, "I am."

"What do you want me to do?"

"We'll need two men who understand this, what it does." He gestured broadly, sweeping his hands across the range of equipment arrayed before them.

"Why two?"

"We can hardly afford to make a mistake now, can we? And a second man will be able to confirm, or contradict, whatever the first man tells us."

"Be right back."

Steven crossed the wide white floor to the steel door. He paused a moment to open it, then stepped inside. The hostages, who were seated on the floor, stopped their whispering.

"All right, folks, listen up," he snapped.

"We need some help out there, and I'm going to have to ask you to cooperate. That way, nobody gets hurt."

One of the captives rose to his feet. "Do you mind telling us what's going on here? Who are you people?"

"You don't need to know anything about it, pal," Steven said. "Like I said, we don't want anybody to get hurt. Now, are you going to cooperate or not? It doesn't make any difference to me."

"Then we won't cooperate. Not until you tell us what's going on here." A murmur of assent and encouragement greeted the statement.

Steven stared at the challenger a moment. Quietly he unslung the Kalashnikov draped over his shoulder. Holding it casually, almost carelessly, he waved the assault rifle back and forth in front of the captives. No one spoke. No one moved.

The gunfire sounded like an explosion in the concrete room. The Kalashnikov bucked in Steven's hand. Four slugs slammed into the standing hostage, blowing his face in every direction with their impact. Blood sprayed the captives seated behind the dead man's body, and bright crimson flowers bloomed on their white clothing. Shreds of brain tissue clung to the bare concrete wall. There was silence.

"Well, there you go," Steven smiled. "Somebody got hurt after all."

He surveyed the seated audience. "I'll be back in five minutes. When I come back, I want two men who know how to operate this plant ready to come with me. Think about it. Five minutes."

He turned smartly and left the room, closing the door with a dull clang. Leaning against the door, he lit a cigarette. The killer marked time, glancing at his watch as smoke from his cigarette curled silently toward the overhead ventilation fans. When his deadline arrived, he ground the butt underfoot and reopened the door.

"You ready?" he asked.

Two men were standing beside the door; the others were still seated. They stepped forward.

"That's more like it. Come on." He gestured with the Kalashnikov, and the two men preceded him through the door. When it closed again, he said, "I hated to do that, you know. But it's like the old joke about a mule. First you have to get his attention."

He led the men toward the office where Glinkov was waiting. Waving them in, he closed the office door and leaned against it. He nodded to Glinkov, who smiled.

"Gentlemen," the Russian began, "I'm not an engineer, but I have some acquaintance with nuclear energy. I want you clearly to understand that, because we don't have much time. I have much to do and little patience. I want you to cooperate and to answer my questions clearly and quickly. Are you prepared to do that?"

Both men nodded reluctantly. Neither looked at the other.

"Very well then, shall we begin?" He rose and led them back into the control room. Sitting in one of the console chairs, he patted the other. "One of you sit here."

When the hostage was seated, Glinkov continued. "What I want to do is quite simple really. You can direct me or you can instruct me. Either will suffice."

"What is it you want to do?" the seated man inquired.

"First, I want to override the automatic controls. I want this reactor on manual operation. Then, I want to drain the reactor coolant and make sure the flow of additional coolant is shut down. Finally, I want to withdraw the control rods from the reactor. That's all."

"But you can't do that. It, I mean the reactor will—"

"I know very well what will happen to the reactor. And that is precisely why I am here. Now, shall we get on with it?"

The man was shocked.

"So, how do we override?"

The sight of Steven's Kalashnikov was all the man needed to encourage him to talk.

"Push the red button there, next to the computer keyboard."

"That's all?"

The man hesitated.

"I said, is that all?"

"Yes, that's all, but—"

Glinkov interrupted him. "Thank you. Now, which controls open the drainage valves?"

"The blue handles here. Push them up to open, pull them back to close." He looked nervously at his colleague.

"Very well. And which gauges monitor the coolant level and temperature?"

"Up there on the board. That bank in the yellow rectangle marked Number 1 tells you everything you need to know about the reactor's pressure vessel. The other gauges under Number 1 are all secondary functions."

"Thank you. So, if I do this," Glinkov asked, drawing the pair of blue handles toward him, "we will begin to drain off the coolant? Is that correct?"

The engineer nodded. Clearing his throat, he said, "Yes, that's correct." His voice was hoarse.

"I'm sorry you feel compelled to lie to me, Mr.—" he glanced at the engineer's identification badge "—Anderson. Now, I told you I wanted cooperation. And you are refusing to cooperate."

Glinkov stood. "Steven, Mr. Anderson is of no further use to us. Take him back to the others, would you please."

Steven prodded the man in the back with his rifle. Anderson got to his feet. Steven poked him again with the rifle, more deliberately this time, and the man stumbled back toward the backup control room. Glinkov read the second engineer's badge and gestured to the empty seat.

"Sit down, Mr. Robbins. Would you like a cigarette?"

Robbins nodded, and Glinkov withdrew a pack of Marlboros from his jacket. Taking a cigarette for himself, he extended the pack to Robbins. When each of them had a cigarette, Glinkov replaced the pack and took out his lighter. Lighting his own first, he leaned forward to light Robbins's and said, "We can resume as soon as Steven returns." He smiled, exhaling a narrow plume of smoke.

Robbins steeled himself against what he knew was coming. Still, at the burst of gunfire, he could feel a trickle of urine run down his leg. A moment later and Steven returned.

"All set?" he asked.

Glinkov nodded. "I think Mr. Robbins understands his responsibilities in this situation. The controls are color coordinated, are they not, Mr. Robbins?"

"Yes."

"A pity your friend Mr. Anderson thought I would overlook something so obvious. I can understand his reluctance to cooperate. But he shouldn't have taken me for a fool. You won't do that, will you, Mr. Robbins?"

When Robbins shook his head, Glinkov smiled. "I should certainly hope not. I wouldn't want to have to do this all by myself. So, when I pull the yellow handles back, I begin to drain the coolant from Reactor 1. Correct? Good. Next, I want to shut off the flow of emergency coolant. No point in draining it away just to put more in now, is there?"

Glinkov watched the temperature gauge as he followed the engineer's instructions. Soon, he knew, the needle would begin to climb. They were on their way.

20

"I don't have much time," Cohen said as the Jeep bounced along the trail that wound through the sparse trees. "We have to get the other two patrols and get me back to the plant."

"I'm not sure I understand what's going on here," Bolan said.

"I'll explain later." Cohen smiled. "Right now all I care about is getting my sister out of there."

"Your sister? You don't mean...?"

"Yeah. I do."

So that explained it. Sort of. Rachel and Cohen were sister and brother.

The Jeep was angling toward the fence. Bolan was watching for another spot where the trees closed to within a few yards of it. The going was rough. Cohen was driving without lights. He was trying to keep the engine noise down as well. To their left, they could see the eerie outline of the plant through the trees.

"That looks like a good spot up ahead." Bolan pointed to a group of conifers about a hundred yards in front of them. The gap was wider than the last one, but they'd have to chance it.

"No good." Cohen shook his head. "There's a surveillance camera close by. We took one out getting in here. If another one goes down, somebody might notice."

"Suppose I just cripple the sweep mechanism. They're not as likely to realize it isn't moving."

"I guess we can chance it," Cohen said. "We'll have to hurry, though. The next patrol will be here any minute. There's another Ingram in the back. That AK-47 makes too much noise. You might as well chuck it."

Bolan reached into the back seat for the SMG. Its sound suppressor was already in place. There were some ammo clips as well. He grabbed two and stuffed them into the pockets of his coat.

Cohen killed the engine, and the two men sprinted toward the fence. Cohen dropped to his belly and wormed his way forward. Bolan did the same.

"There. See it?" Cohen pointed to a small projection on the top of the fence. It was nearly fifty yards past the spot they had chosen for their attack. "Think you can get it?"

"Watch me," Bolan said grimly. "I'm not ready for a TV career."

Bolan waited to catch the dull flash of the camera lens, which meant it was pointing directly at him. When it came, he counted to ten and then sprinted for the fence.

Positioning himself at the base of the wire under the sweep area of the small camera, he studied the mechanical mount. A small servomotor was housed in the base. The sweep rate was slow. The servo emitted the barest of hums.

The camera was high above him. Getting to it without being seen was going to be tough. The lens was slowly panning back and forth. A small coaxial cable ran out of the camera's body and down the post into the ground. But there was another, smaller wire. It didn't run into the camera at all. It fed directly into the servo mount. The motor was on a separate line. He could cut the line without taking out the camera. It would freeze, but it would still work.

Bolan reached into his coat and withdrew a combat knife from its sheath. The six-inch tempered steel blade was more than enough to sever the power line. Now all he had to do was time it right. As he watched the camera move, he heard the sound of the patrol Jeep.

"Hurry up. Here they come," Eli Cohen urged in the world's loudest stage whisper.

The camera reached its limit and began to pan back away from the oncoming patrol. Wait. Wait. And . . . now. Bolan sliced through the small cable and held his breath. The camera jerked once, then was still. They were home free.

And not a minute too soon. The headlights of the oncoming Jeep danced along the fence. Bolan sprinted back to Cohen and checked his SMG.

"Remember, we have to hit them before they get to that camera," Cohen cautioned. "Ready?"

Cohen made Bolan uncomfortable. The guy was a natural leader. A take-charge kind of man. Two of them working together would lead to friction eventually. But there wasn't time for that now. They had too much to do. And too little time to do it in.

The Jeep cleared the last bend. Coming straight on, its riders looking nervously into the trees.

"You take the driver," Bolan said.

"Gotcha."

Closer, closer. The Jeep was now fifteen yards away, well within the Ingram's effective range.

"Now," Bolan whispered.

If Cohen replied, Bolan didn't hear him. He squeezed the Ingram's trigger and swept a tight figure eight with the SMG's muzzle. It was too dark to see much, but Bolan had no doubt that the guard in the passenger seat never knew what hit him.

Cohen's target was the easier of the two. The driver had turned toward his passenger as if to confide in him. The burst from Cohen's Ingram caught him leaning. A narrow column of death stitched the man's side from neck to hip. The impact of the slugs drove him sideways. The steering wheel followed, and the Jeep careened into the fence.

The man's foot was still on the accelerator. The engine strained against the fence. Cohen was up and running, reaching the Jeep just as the fence post was beginning to bend. Cohen grabbed the driver by both shoulders, yanking him from the Jeep. The engine sputtered, then died.

"Three down and one to go," Bolan said as he joined the Israeli agent.

"Let's get this mess into the trees." Cohen hopped into the driver's seat. He restarted the engine and backed the Jeep hurriedly away from the fence. Bolan grabbed the driver's corpse and threw it roughly into the back of the Jeep, then climbed in beside the dead man.

The Jeep bounced through the snowy undergrowth. Straining through the occasional drifts, the engine seemed loud enough to wake the dead. Bolan glanced at the man beside him and knew it wasn't that loud. Curious, he searched the dead man's pockets. There was nothing but a wallet.

He opened the wallet and flipped through the papers. There was a driver's license, a couple of credit cards, business cards, a matchbook cover with a scribbled phone number, a couple of receipts. In the photo section were several snapshots. Some showed the dead man, a woman who was probably his wife and two kids.

There was always something to make you wonder, Bolan thought. Wonder why a man would do the sort of things this guy did. And, worse, why you did what you did. Why couldn't these assholes make the connection between people they cared about and people others cared about?

The Jeep stopped and Cohen jumped down. Bolan sat, staring idly at the photographs.

"Something wrong, Mack?"

Bolan sighed. He closed the photo section and flipped the wallet closed. He tucked it into the dead man's pocket and climbed from the Jeep.

"No, nothing's wrong. Let's go."

Cohen looked at his watch. "I've been out here nearly an hour. I'll have to get back soon before Glinkov misses me."

Bolan nodded. "Listen, Eli. That son of a bitch is mine, understand? I want him."

"That all depends, Mack."

"On what?"

"Rachel. If she's okay, he's yours, but..."

Bolan clapped a hand on the smaller man's shoulder. He squeezed gently. He didn't have to speak. Cohen turned silently, his shoulders shaking ever so slightly. He shook his head, as if to clear it, and rubbed his jaw. "We got work to do," he said.

The two men walked back to their own Jeep. Each felt alone, and, as they walked side by side, the feeling was intensified by the knowledge of the other's loneliness. Cohen started the engine and backed the Jeep out into a small clearing where he could turn it around. He drove to the fence. Bolan hopped down and covered the evidence of their latest encounter.

Back in the Jeep, he scrutinized Cohen's face, looking for some trace of Rachel. He saw none. None but the ghost of her present situation, which haunted her brother. Bolan knew the Israeli felt as helpless as he did. The odds confronting them were enormous.

And the pain of that helplessness was as old as mankind. Bolan knew that. He knew that the Spartans at Thermopylae had felt it, and the Jews at Masada, too. It must have robbed Roland of sleep at Roncesvalles and lain down beside the farmers' sons at Valley Forge. Hell, for all he knew, the same sense of powerlessness had haunted the Vietcong in the tunnels at Cu Chi. Sure, he knew all that. And it didn't help one damn bit.

"One more and we're golden, Mack." Cohen tried to joke, but his voice betrayed his feelings. Both men knew that the next Jeep didn't mean the ball game. It was just the end of the first quarter. And Glinkov was no rookie.

Cohen revved his engine, and the Jeep lurched forward. Once again, he threaded his way through the trees. "I think I know the best place for our next play." Bolan looked at Cohen, waiting for more. "It's risky, but it will save us some time."

"Are you going to tell me more?" Bolan asked. "Or do I have to guess?"

"What's the matter, Mack, don't you like guessing games?"

"Not tonight I don't."

"All right, you just watch. If you don't know by the time we get there, I'll fill you in. Fair enough?"

"Nothing's fair about any of this, Eli. You know that as well as I do."

Cohen didn't answer. He didn't have to.

21

Malcolm Parsons was in way over his head. It was a truth he had been trying to ignore for too long. One by one, his illusions had crumbled. His control was less than he had thought. His money didn't come from the source he had imagined. He was less a mover and shaker than he wanted to believe. Instead of using people, he had been used. He had fought against the truth, fought long and hard. Now, pacing back and forth in the heart of a concrete fortress, he could no longer deny it.

Being forced to take the life of Allan Reynolds meant little in comparison to this realization. For as long as he could remember, he'd thought he was more important than he really was. Now reality had risen up and slapped him in the face. Now reality answered to the name Glinkov.

It was, he knew, too late to save Alan Reynolds. It was too late to rescue whatever shreds of dignity he had left. It was even too late to preserve his reputation as a man who got things done. And he was afraid it might be too late to save his own life.

Whatever Glinkov was planning, it was clear there was no longer a need for Malcolm Parsons. He had been used by the Russian, skillfully and ruthlessly. Parsons was enough of a tactician to admire the Russian's work. He had used Parsons just as Parsons had used so many others. There was only the slimmest of chances that Parsons could yet pull this one out.

Glinkov stood in the doorway, watching Parsons pace.

"Malcolm, you seem upset," Glinkov said, finally betraying his presence.

"You bastard. You scheming, bloody bastard," Parsons roared. He charged the smaller man angrily. Glinkov smiled, waiting until Parsons was within reach, then smacked the taller man across the face as one would smack an unruly child.

Parsons fell back. He was stunned, less by the blow than by the manner of its delivery. He rubbed his cheek, muttering under his breath. Glinkov continued to stand in the doorway as if nothing had happened. It wouldn't be long before this insufferable egomaniac could be dispensed with once and for all, he thought.

"Get control of yourself, Malcolm. You're behaving like a child. That won't get either of us anywhere now, will it?"

"I ought to kill you, Andrey. I really ought to."

"And why is that?"

"Because you used me. You used me, and you used people who believed in me."

"And I suppose you never used anyone, Mr. Parsons. Is that what you're trying to tell me?"

"Maybe I did, but it was for some purpose. I wanted to make a difference in the world."

"Don't think for one minute that I have no purpose, Malcolm. And don't believe that I won't make a difference. I daresay, before the night is over, I will have made more of a difference than you could ever dream of."

"Not if I can help it, you won't."

"But my dear Malcolm, don't you see? That is precisely why you're so upset. You *can't* help it, and you know it. I understand it must come as something of a shock to you, but you are far too simple a man. Events have been set in motion that are far bigger than anything you could ever imagine. Now why don't you just learn to accept that painful fact? Come along. There is someone I want you to see."

"No. I don't want to see anyone."

"Come along like a good little boy."

"You son of a bitch—"

"Follow me."

Glinkov turned abruptly and left the room. His pace, more than his words, told Parsons how sure of himself he was. The Russian knew that he would follow and that he would put up no further argument. Still rubbing his burning cheek, he rushed after Glinkov.

"Where are we going?"

"You'll see."

Glinkov led the way to an elevator. He pressed the call button and stood with his hands folded behind his back. He paid Parsons no attention. For all the Russian cared, he might have been alone.

When the elevator arrived, it opened with a soft hiss. Glinkov stepped to the rear of the car. Turning to face forward, he indicated the panel of buttons and said, "Press Level 4, if you will, Malcolm."

Parsons did as he was told. Perhaps he had found his true calling. It seemed as if he were fit for nothing more lofty than operating an elevator.

The door closed quietly, and a low hum filled the large car. It moved quickly down, marking each level it passed with an electronic beep. Level 4 was the lowest level, buried deeply beneath the ground's surface. When the door opened, Glinkov stepped into the dimly lit bowels of Thunder Mountain. Parsons followed meekly behind him.

Both men instinctively looked up at the ceiling. It was as if they could somehow feel the massive weight of the mountain, and its deadly burden, pressing down on them. The hallway stretched off into near darkness in both directions. Glinkov turned to the right and moved swiftly ahead.

The size of the tunnel heightened the gloom. Twenty feet overhead, the fluorescent lamps seemed as far away as stars. The wall on the right was marked by an occasional door.

The left wall was a blank expanse of gray concrete. Glinkov moved briskly, his heels tapping on the concrete floor. Parsons, wearing crepe-soled shoes, made no sound. It was almost as if he wasn't there.

When they had traveled nearly two hundred yards, Parsons could make out the figures of two men in the gloom ahead. They stood casually, one on either side of a large steel door. Thirty feet beyond them, the hall ended in a blank wall. A smaller passage met it at right angles.

Neither man was familiar to Parsons. He wondered why it galled him so much that Glinkov had so neatly finessed him. The Russian had been able to pull this off without even bothering to get someone to betray him. How long had he been there in the wings, waiting? Long enough to recruit his own team obviously. And Peter Achison, where did he fit in? Had he been Glinkov's man all along, or had he too been fooled?

Glinkov gestured to one of the guards, and the man fished in his fatigue pockets for a key. The man bent forward in the dim light to fit the key in the lock, then opened the door. Glinkov waved Parsons in before him.

Stepping in behind Parsons, Glinkov turned on the overhead light. "You know Miss Peres, I believe, Malcolm?"

"You know damn well I do."

"Of course, and do you also know that she works for the Mossad?"

"That's preposterous!"

"I think not."

Rachel was sitting on the floor in the far corner of the small room. Her head was slumped forward on her chest, and she seemed not to be aware of them.

"What's wrong with her? What have you done to her?" Parsons demanded.

"You surprise me, Malcolm," Glinkov sneered. "You sound almost as if it mattered to you."

"Well, no, I . . . but you must be wrong. She's no secret agent, no spy, I—"

"And what makes you so sure? How well do you know her? Where did you meet her? Why was she interested in your little band of fools in the first place? Hmm?"

"I don't know, I—"

"No, Malcolm, you don't. But I do. And I can tell you that she is a Mossad agent. But don't feel too bad. She has fooled better men than you, Malcolm. Even the lofty Central Intelligence Agency has been duped by our little flower here. You should learn not to be so careless about women you take to bed."

"What are you going to do with her?"

"Nothing, for the moment. There is someone looking for her. As long as he has a chance to save her, he will keep on looking. As long as she is still alive, his attention will be divided. He is no ordinary man, Malcolm, as I'm sure you will discover if he ever catches up with you."

"What are you talking about? Why should he even be looking for me? Who is he?"

"His name is Mack Bolan. I'm sure it means nothing to you. Yet. He has been called by other names in the past—Sergeant Mercy, Colonel John Phoenix. His file is among our thickest. And right now he is looking for you because he knows you were the last person to see Miss Peres. As far as Mr. Bolan is concerned, you are responsible for her disappearance. That, of course, is just what I wanted. It is about time we closed our file. While he is concentrating on you, I can take him by surprise."

Parsons said nothing. He crossed the room to kneel in front of Rachel. He reached forward and took her chin in his hand. Tilting her head back, he gasped involuntarily. Her face was badly bruised. One eye was swollen closed.

"My God, what have you done to her?"

Parsons got to his feet and turned to confront the Russian. Glinkov remained impassive, the merest hint of a smile hovering at the corners of his mouth.

"It was essential to gain certain information. Circumstances did not permit the use of more... humane methods. But I have my responsibilities to discharge. In a few hours it won't matter anyway."

"What do you mean it won't matter?"

"Surely you don't think I can permit her to live? As soon as Mr. Bolan is out of the way, she will be of no further use to me."

Before Parsons could answer, Rachel groaned. The older man turned back to her. He knelt again, and Rachel opened her eyes, although she couldn't focus. Parsons wheeled on the Russian.

"You really are a bastard."

"Don't be so squeamish, Malcolm. You're in this all the way, you know. She can send you away for a long time. You wouldn't enjoy spending the rest of your life in prison, would you?"

"Why don't you ask him what he really has in mind, Malcolm?" Rachel's voice was weak, but it startled both men.

"What do you mean?" Parsons demanded.

"Ask him what he plans to do here. Ask him what's going to happen. Go on, ask him."

"Well," Parsons said, "what *is* going to happen? Why are you here?"

"Very well. I don't see any harm in telling you now. And it was rather well conceived, even if I say so myself. Ms Peres, thanks to you, has managed to learn a great deal about my intentions. She can fill you in." Glinkov smiled softly. "Go ahead, my dear, tell him."

Parsons turned to Rachel. "What is he planning to do?"

"He's going to sabotage the reactor and pollute the whole area. He'll blow it to kingdom come if he can, or cause a meltdown if he can't. Isn't that right, Mr. Glinkov?"

"Yes."

"Are you out of your mind, Glinkov? Hundreds of thousands of people live around this plant. You're putting them in mortal danger. This was supposed to be a public relations demonstration. We want to teach the people, not kill them."

"That's where you and I disagree, Malcolm. Besides, what could be more educational than a major nuclear accident? If you'll excuse me, I have some things to attend to. Why don't you two get reacquainted?"

Glinkov smiled at each of them before turning to walk through the doorway. Parsons turned to Rachel. "He's serious, isn't he? He really intends to destroy this plant!"

Rachel nodded. "And while you're digesting that, why don't you ask yourself what that means for us?"

"What do you mean?"

"You don't think he can afford to let us live, do you? He's a KGB agent. He's here illegally. There's no way in hell the Soviets want to be connected to this thing. I'm not even sure he's acting on orders."

"But why? I don't understand what's going on here."

"It's quite simple, really. If the U.S. stops using nuclear power, it will have to use more fossil fuels. That makes it more dependent on foreign oil. Which means Arab oil. All the money you thought was coming from Libya was KGB money. They can use the Arabs against the United States and keep their hands clean at the same time. If the U.S. is not self-sufficient, it will become impotent. It looks like he's going to pull it off, too."

Parsons stared glumly at Rachel Peres. "And you, was it true what he said about you? Are you Mossad?"

"Not anymore. I work for the CIA on a contract basis now. He didn't seem to know that, which is about the only thing he doesn't seem to know."

"Why did you do it? Why did you come to me? Surely you don't think I was party to something so monstrous as this?"

"No, not you. But you were ripe for the picking, Malcolm. You set yourself up. Glinkov didn't have to try very hard. You were all set. You were so damn smug, so damn sure of yourself. I'd be willing to bet it's been a long time since you had any doubts about yourself. Am I right?"

Parsons nodded. "You would have been if you had asked me yesterday. But that doesn't matter. We have to stop him. He can't be allowed to get away with this. I'll talk to him."

"It's long past talking, Malcolm. Believe me."

"Maybe not. I can try at least."

"And if it doesn't work?"

"Then I'll have to kill him."

Parsons rose. He closed the heavy steel door behind him as he left the room.

22

The guardhouse wasn't much larger than a garage. But it might as well have been a fortress. Mack Bolan and Eli Cohen stood in the trees, watching. It seemed all they could do at the moment. Bolan began to pace, stomping down the snow with nervous movements. Inside, they had counted four men, each armed with an AK-47. In addition there were the hostages, all bound securely. There would be no help from them.

"You know, it might be time to take a little risk here, Eli."

"No shit. How the hell else can we get in there? But I'm fresh out of ideas. And if I don't get back to the control room pretty soon, Glinkov is going to wonder where I am. He's already suspicious of me."

"Then we have to move now, don't we?" Bolan said. It wasn't really a question, so Cohen didn't respond.

Bolan stopped pacing and stared at the small cinder block structure. As Cohen watched him, it seemed almost as if the midnight warrior were trying to see through the stone.

After two minutes of silence, Cohen laughed. "All right, let me hear what you have in mind. I know I won't like it, but what the hell."

"Look, we're sitting here, wondering what to do, because we know which side you're on, right?"

Cohen nodded. "So?"

"We're forgetting one thing. They *don't* know. As far as they're concerned, you're Glinkov's right-hand man. The boss of security on this operation, right?"

"Go on, I think I see what you're leading up to."

"All you have to do is walk right up to the damn door and knock. They'll let you in. Once you're on the inside everything changes. The odds are in our favor, right?"

"Almost..."

"No almost, Eli, they are. So here's what we'll do. You go on in. Send two of them outside, get them into the trees somehow. Tell them you saw something, or whatever. I'll handle the rest. In the meantime, you can get the drop on the other two. I'll join you as soon as I can. We don't have much of a choice."

Cohen shrugged. "Here goes nothing." He walked out into the open area between the trees and the guardhouse. In a moment he disappeared around the side of the small building.

Bolan heard a heavy rap on the door. Through the window, he saw one of the guards move to open it. There was some conversation, but the men were too distant for Bolan to hear what was said. Cohen was gesturing with his hands. The voices grew louder, as if someone were arguing with Cohen.

Finally one of the men crossed Bolan's line of sight. He disappeared into a corner of the guardhouse, and a coat flew past the window. A moment later the man reappeared, struggling into a heavy parka.

The door slammed, and heavy steps sounded on the hard-packed snow. A few seconds later two men rounded the corner, heading in Bolan's direction. They were walking slowly, like kids on the way to school. Bolan didn't know what Cohen had told them, but they obviously weren't happy about his orders.

They were grumbling sullenly as they moved into the trees. The Executioner faded back into the shadows. He couldn't afford to jump too soon. A mistake now would blow the whole thing right out of the water. Whatever he did, it had to be silent. And deadly.

The men were angry enough to be careless. That was good. But the snow was an enemy here. It hampered Bolan's movements and made silence difficult to maintain. The two men passed within fifteen feet of him. But they were too close to the guardhouse. He'd have to let them get deeper into the trees.

As they continued their reluctant tramp, Bolan could hear their muffled exchanges. The taller of the two was complaining. "I never liked Cohen, anyway, I tell you. There's something about him that isn't kosher. No pun intended."

"You're just pissed because he's got Glinkov's ear, that's all."

"Ear hell! If I didn't know better, I'd think he had Glinkov by the balls. Who the hell is he, anyhow? I never saw him before this thing got started. Did you?"

"Shit, that doesn't mean anything. I never saw half of those guys before tonight. You know how Achison works. He keeps everything small. Lots of little groups. None of 'em know anything about any of the others. Better security that way."

"Maybe, but I still say I like to know who the hell I'm working with. I don't like to turn my back on somebody I don't know. Don't like to depend on a stranger, either. You never know what a guy'll do."

"Quit griping. In a few hours we'll all be outta here. And with enough money that we won't have to see snow for a year, either. How bad is that?"

They lapsed into silence. Whatever Cohen had told them, it had worked. They were two hundred yards into the trees and still moving. The Executioner was following them step for step. As they walked, they were growing less cautious. Cohen must have sent them on an errand. They sure didn't act like they were looking for an intruder. So much the better.

Glancing over his shoulder, Bolan could no longer see the guardhouse. The trees overhead were moving in a stiff breeze. The clack of their branches would cover his approach. If he were lucky. Brognola had once told him that luck wasn't good enough, and he'd been right. But what Hal never seemed to understand was that, good as he was, he still needed luck on his side. The odds were too great to buck without it.

Suddenly the two men entered a small clearing. Their bulky outlines could be seen against the bright snow. They stopped and looked at the sky. One of them dropped to one knee. The other took out a small torch, shining it on the ground in front of his companion. The kneeling man brushed at the snow with his gloved hands while the other bent over his shoulder.

"What the hell are we looking for, anyhow?"

"Cohen says there's a manhole here someplace. Some cables we have to cut or something. Don't look like it to me, though. Hell, how are we supposed to find anything in this snow, anyhow? That bastard."

Mack Bolan nodded with satisfaction. Cohen had done a superb job. It couldn't have been better. Not only did he get them out into the woods, he had them stationary. And preoccupied.

This had to be done as quietly as possible. And done quickly. It was obvious the men were in no mood for an extended search. Bolan withdrew his combat knife and inched forward. He made sure the Beretta was accessible, but it was his backup.

Concealing himself behind the last line of trees at the edge of the clearing, Bolan coiled for the spring. Like a predatory cat, he leaped, covering the last few yards in midair. Before either man was aware of his presence, he had locked his left forearm around the standing man's neck.

"What the hell—" The words were cut off as Bolan drew the razor-sharp blade across his captive's throat. Surprise turned to a gurgle, as blood and air bubbled out through the severed windpipe. Momentarily frozen, the kneeling man struggled to his feet, but the Executioner was too fast for him. He shoved the dead man forward.

The collision knocked the second man over, the dead-weight of his companion pinning him to the snow. Rolling to one side, he struggled to throw off his burden. He saw Bolan out of the corner of his eye and reached for the automatic on his hip. Bolan dropped his full weight, knees first, on the struggling man's right arm, landing just above the elbow.

The pinioned man screamed as his shoulder was torn from its socket. He scrambled sideways, using his feet and uninjured arm. Like a crab pinned by one claw, he moved in a circle, kicking out from under the deadweight. His efforts tore at the injured shoulder, but he was fighting for his life.

Groping blindly in the snow, the fingers of his good hand closed over the Kalashnikov. He tried to consolidate his grip, but the gun kept slipping free. Bolan plunged his knife deep into the man's chest. The blade scraped across bone as it slid between ribs. Until it found the heart.

With a sigh, the man lay still. The pinioned arm went limp under Bolan's knees. Blood seeped from the slack jaw, almost as an afterthought. Bolan rose, withdrawing the blade as he did so. He wiped the blood on the fur lining of the dead man's parka then slid the blade back into its sheath.

Killing seldom came easy to the Executioner. He felt drained for a moment. In Vietnam he had earned the name of Sergeant Mercy. It was a name he was proud of, and it was rooted in his character. A warrior's strength need not deprive him of compassion. In fact, Bolan believed a warrior without compassion was no warrior at all. He was not even a man.

Looking at the sky overhead, which seemed to have pressed down for a closer look, he wondered. How many men had to die before mankind realized that killing solved nothing?

Bolan walked to the edge of the clearing, turning once to look at the two dead men lying in the snow. They were brave men. Maybe even good men. They were on the wrong side, sure. But people make mistakes. There had to be another way, a better way to solve human arguments.

"WHAT'S GOING ON, ELI?"

"What do you mean?"

"Are we staying here, or moving out? This place gives me the creeps."

"You ought to thank your lucky stars, Louis. You think this place is weird, you ought to walk around that plant a little bit. It's damn spooky. There's enough power in that place to blow New York off the map."

"Hell, man, that's what we're here for, ain't it? I just want to make sure I'm well out of the way when it happens, that's all."

"Don't worry about it. Andrey knows what he's doing. You guys got any coffee in here? It's cold as a witch's tit out there."

"Yeah, there's some on the hot plate. I'll get you a cup. Could use one myself, now that you mention it."

Cohen stood near the doorway, leaning against the wall. The two remaining guards seemed a little on edge. They had been taken aback at his request for the two others to go out into the cold. Having settled into the warmth of the guardhouse, they were angry that something could so easily disturb them. The whole point of guardhouse duty was that it was easy. Now this asshole had changed everything.

Louis rattled silverware in the kitchenette. Rick Edmunds was sitting at the table, playing solitaire. He hadn't said a word to Eli since the Jewish commando had entered.

"Cream and sugar?" Louis called from the cubbyhole.

"No, black's fine, thanks."

Eli didn't like Edmunds, and he knew Edmunds didn't like him. He watched the cards as Edmunds flipped them in threes. The man's jaw was set, the muscles in his cheeks bunched in tight little knots. He was unhappy about something.

He glanced up at Eli in silence for a moment, then said, "Don't watch me like that. It makes me nervous."

"What's the matter, afraid I'll catch you cheating?" Cohen laughed.

"I don't have to cheat, Cohen. I know how to play this fucking game."

"Don't be so touchy, Rick. I was only joking."

Louis returned from the kitchenette, carrying two cups of coffee. He placed the black coffee in front of an empty chair. At the other end of the table, next to Edmunds, he placed his own cup. The coffee was so pale, it looked as if it was two-thirds milk.

He sat next to Edmunds, peering closely at the cards. "Wait a minute, Rick. Put the red six on that black seven."

"Mind your own damn business. You're as pushy as Cohen here."

"Christ, I was just trying to help."

"Don't bother." Edmunds pushed the cards into a small disorderly mound, then turned it on edge, tapping stray cards into place with a few sharp raps on the tabletop. "There, now you don't have anything to mess with."

Cohen watched the two men carefully. His Ingram was still slung over his shoulder, but the close quarters and the table made it difficult to move quickly. While he debated how and why to get to his feet, the phone rang. He took a long pull on the coffee. On the fourth ring, Louis got up to answer it.

"Yeah. Mr. Glinkov, yes, hello. This is Louis. Right. No, no. He just came in. You want to talk to him? Just a minute. It's for you."

Louis extended the receiver to Cohen, who stood up to accept it. He moved against the wall and turned his back to the two men.

"Hello. Yes, Andrey. No, everything's all right. I just stopped in after checking the perimeter. Everything's secure. Tight as a drum. All right, yes. I'll be up in five minutes. Fine."

Cohen hung up the phone and walked back to the table. He picked up his coffee and finished it off without sitting down. Then he unslung the Ingram and waved it casually toward the seated men.

"Don't do anything stupid. Just sit there."

"What the fuck are you doing?" Edmunds demanded.

"Shut up!" Cohen said. He walked carefully around the table, pushing the chairs in to get them out of his way. "Both of you put your hands on the table. Palms down. Don't move. Don't even breathe."

"If this is a joke, it's not funny," Louis said.

"And if it isn't, I'll eat your fucking heart," Edmunds snapped.

"It's no joke, gentlemen, I assure you." He was standing directly across from the seated men. With a sudden sweep, he slammed the side of the SMG into the base of Edmunds's skull. The man fell forward, scattering the stack of playing cards onto the floor. The half-empty cup of coffee spilled among the cards and began to drip onto the floor.

"All right, Louis. Stand up!" Cohen barked.

"What are you going to do?" Louis sounded nervous.

"Don't worry. I'm not going to shoot you. Unless I have to. Now get up!"

Louis got to his feet carefully.

"Find some rope and tie him up."

"Where the hell am I going to find rope, for chrissakes?"

"You got six men tied up in the bathroom. Untie one of them."

"But—"

"Do it, damn it. Now!"

Cohen froze at the knock on the door. Before he could open it, Mack Bolan pushed through, trailing a cloud of whirling snow.

"It's cold out there," he said.

"You ain't seen nothing yet," Cohen said. "Give me a hand here. Mr. Glinkov wants to see me."

"Good." Mack Bolan smiled grimly. "I want to see him, too."

23

The main control room was strangely silent. Andrey Glinkov sat quietly in a chair in front of the control board. The captured engineer sat beside him. Both men were watching the array of dials and gauges. Two guards were the only others present. One of them stood behind the two seated men. The other lounged on the floor just outside the entrance to the room. Every few minutes he'd stand and peer through the thick glass to check on the huddled hostages.

"Shouldn't the temperature be rising more quickly?" Glinkov asked.

The engineer nodded. "There's another way to do it. You can vent the hot water out into the tunnels under the plant. It'll drain off more quickly."

"Why don't we do that then?" Glinkov asked. His voice was controlled, almost polite.

"Because the runoff will flow into the Hudson River. That's where the tunnels lead."

"So? Surely you know by now I am not just playing some elaborate game here."

"Yes. I know."

"Well, then? How do we do that?"

The engineer said nothing. He stared at his hands, watching his fingers twist as if controlled by someone else.

"Mr. Robbins, I don't have all night. I am certain that you are not the only one who knows the answer. Am I right?"

Robbins nodded. "You're right," he mumbled.

"And you haven't forgotten what happened to Mr. Anderson, have you?"

"No, you bastard. I haven't forgotten that."

"Well, then. What happened to Mr. Anderson induced you to cooperate. I imagine that one of your more knowledgeable colleagues can be similarly induced. Don't you agree?"

Robbins was in a bind, and he knew it. The man seated beside him wouldn't hesitate to kill him. He probably planned to kill them all, anyway. On the other hand, if he could stay alive, he just might be able to throw a monkey wrench or two into the works.

The thought of millions of gallons of radioactive water spilling into the Hudson was appalling. The radioactive level of that water, even when diluted by the Hudson, would kill everything it came into contact with. The effects would last for decades. He had no choice. But maybe he could fool his captor. It was worth a try.

"All right," Robbins said. "The control valve for the sluiceways is over here." He indicated a large red button switch on the main control board.

"And what happens when I push it?"

"The hot water drains in the tunnels. It clears out the containment tower."

"Very good. Do you want to push the button? Or shall I?"

"You do it. I told you where it is, but I'll be damned if I'll push it."

"As you wish. Which dial do I watch to determine the progress?"

"Up there, high on the board. That red bulb. When the valve is open, the bulb blinks."

Glinkov depressed the red button with a flourish. He turned a radiant, sardonic smile on Robbins. Gesturing to the guard behind him, he said, "I don't believe we need any more from Mr. Robbins at the moment. I'll call him when it's time to pull the control rods. You can permit him to rejoin his colleagues.''

The guard stepped forward, taking Robbins by the arm. The engineer stood reluctantly. If he appeared too eager, Glinkov might suspect something. The guard tugged his arm, and he moved toward the secondary control room. The sentry rose and opened the door. Robbins was shoved roughly inside by his escort. The door slammed shut behind him.

He stumbled over the feet of another hostage and fell to the floor. The other hostages looked at him questioningly. He shook his head to clear it and crawled to a sitting position. So far, so good.

He hadn't told Glinkov about the evacuation pump or the second valve. Without using the pump, the water would take hours to drain. And unless the second valve was opened, the water would simply fill the tunnels, slowly draining out of the reactor vessel under the influence of gravity. It couldn't reach the Hudson. It seemed like a small thing, but it was all he could hope for. It was their only chance to reverse the madness.

''What's going on out there?'' someone whispered.

''They're draining the reactor vessel,'' Robbins answered. He continued to face front. He tried not to move his lips as he spoke.

''Why? What are they trying to do?''

''I don't know. And I don't want to guess. The more important question is what are they going to do with us?''

''They'll let us go, won't they?'' Another hostage joined the discussion. ''I mean, once they get what they came for, there'll be no reason to keep us here.''

''Don't count on it. As near as I can figure, they want this to look like an accident. They can't very well leave us around to say it wasn't, can they? I figure they plan to kill us all and leave this place so hot nobody will get in to learn the truth for years.''

''Are you crazy?''

''I'm not, no. But I'm not so sure about him.''

''Who the hell is he? Where did he come from?''

''I can only guess. But I'll tell you one thing. The next time that door opens, if I get the chance, I'm going to try to get a gun. If we can do that, we can hold them off in here.''

''For how long?''

''How long do we have without it?'' Robbins asked.

The others said nothing.

GLINKOV WATCHED the temperature gauge for the Unit 1 reactor. It was slowly rising, the needle quivering in place and jumping upward from time to time. In the distance an alarm bell rang continually. It had started as soon as the ventilation valve had opened. The red bulb high up on the control board blinked hypnotically. Glinkov stared at it. Things were proceeding smoothly. More smoothly than he had hoped. In a little more than an hour, he would be on the helicopter Achison was bringing in. The others had served him well but, of course, they would remain behind. Permanently.

There was still one thing needed for an unqualified success, however. Mack Bolan had to be eliminated. Where was he? As long as the Peres woman remained alive, he was certain to make an attempt to free her. He should have been here already. Well, there was still time. For Malcolm Parsons, however, time had run out. He was excess baggage at this point.

Glinkov waved to the guard behind him. ''I have something I would like you to take care of.''

''Sir?''

''Mr. Parsons is no longer essential to our plans here. Dispose of him, won't you?''

"Yes, sir," the guard said without questioning his leader's order. "Where is he?"

"He's on Level 4. In an office at the end of the corridor. One of the men down there can show you to him."

The guard hefted his Kalashnikov and grinned. "I'll be right back."

He crossed the wide floor to the control room exit and walked quickly toward the elevator bank. It was going to be a pleasure. Parsons was an egotistical windbag.

The elevator came slowly, opened with a sigh and closed behind him. When it reached the bowels of the plant, it opened on a dim corridor. The guard moved swiftly, his step almost jaunty. As he neared the end of the long passage, he saw two team members standing guard, one outside of each door.

"Where's Parsons?"

The guard gestured with his head. "In here."

He pushed through the door. Parsons was seated behind a desk, writing busily. He didn't look up when the man entered. The newcomer crossed the office floor and plopped down in a chair alongside the desk.

"You writing another one of your bullshit speeches?"

"That's right, I am," Parsons said.

"Don't bother."

"Oh, but I must. Nuclear energy is one of the greatest social issues of our time. I have a duty to speak out."

"Finish it when we come back then."

"Oh, are we going somewhere?"

"Yup, we are. Let's go."

The guard stood up impatiently. Parsons continued to scribble. "I'll be with you in a moment. I never like to leave a thought in the middle. Sometimes you can't pick it up again."

"I never had that problem," the guard said.

Parsons finished with a flourish and placed his pen down on the paper. He smiled up at the guard. "I shouldn't wonder," he said. "Now, where are we going in such a hurry?"

"Andrey has something he wants you to look at."

The two men left the office and stepped out into the corridor.

"Just a minute," Parsons said. "I forgot to turn off the light." He stepped back into the office. At the desk he reached over and pressed the Off button on the fluorescent desk lamp. The room was coal black.

"Hurry up, Parsons, Andrey's in a hurry."

A moment later, Parsons stepped back into the hallway. He closed the door tightly and nodded to the guard. "Be back in a half hour, Thomas. Please don't let anyone in while I'm gone."

The guard smiled at Thomas behind Parsons's back. "You heard what the man said. Take care of those valuable papers."

If Parsons noticed the sarcasm, he gave no sign. The guard moved on to the end of the corridor and turned right. It was the only direction he could take. The corner was at the outside edge of the largest rectangle on which the plant was built. Ahead of the two men, another corridor, lit even more dimly, stretched as far as they could see.

"What exactly does Andrey wish me to see?" Parsons asked.

"Be patient, old man."

"Old man, is it? I'm not as old as you think."

Maybe not, the guard thought, but you're as old as you're gonna get. He walked behind Parsons and slightly to one side of the older man's left shoulder. All that remained was to find a suitable place to knock off the old windbag, and he could get back upstairs where the action was.

Steel doors, identical to those on the previous corridor, were set into the right-hand wall of the passage. They were spaced farther apart. That meant the rooms were larger.

Probably for storage, the guard thought. A good place to take care of business.

"Is it much farther?" Parsons asked.

"The next door," the guard answered. Why in hell not, he thought. He had a master key. He could open any goddamn door in the place.

Parsons stopped in front of the door. He turned the knob. The door was open. He stepped on through into the darkness.

"Get the light, would you, Malcolm?" the guard asked as he followed the antinuke leader into the room.

Parsons did nothing. Cursing under his breath, the guard reached for the wall switch. He flipped it on, and the fluorescent lights overhead flickered once and then bathed the room with sickly white light. The room was filled, ceiling to floor, with cartons and old office furniture. But where the hell was Parsons?

"Malcolm? Come on, quit playing games. We have work to do." The old man was nowhere to be seen. "Malcolm, I'm getting pissed off. Come on, where are you?"

The guard stepped forward, working his way into the passage between two tall stacks of cartons. This was a pain in the ass.

"Malcolm?"

Shoes scraped on the concrete floor behind him. The guard turned to see Malcolm Parsons standing at the mouth of the cardboard canyon.

"What the hell are you doing?"

The guard stepped toward Parsons. The antinuke leader raised the Walther automatic Glinkov had given him at the farmhouse and shot him in the face. Twice. One bullet smashed into the guard's left eye, then bored its way on through the back of the skull, scattering sticky gray tissue the length of the short passage. The second bullet pierced the forehead, struck the occipital bone and rattled uncertainly around the interior of the cranium, scattering bone fragments before coming to rest not far from its point of entry.

Malcolm Parsons had been pushed too far.

The guard, of course, was dead.

24

Bolan trained his Ingram on Louis and Edmunds while Cohen unlocked the bathroom and freed the hostages. Eli noticed the body of the dead guard in the corner, but said nothing. One by one, the five captives emerged, rubbing their wrists to restore circulation. As each man came out, Bolan waved him to one side. The men were too stunned to ask what was happening. When the fifth man had been freed, Cohen returned to the front office.

Finally, angry and puzzled, Matt Stevens, the chief of the guardhouse detachment, spoke. "Who are you guys? Are you with them? Or with us?"

"There is a third possibility," Bolan said.

"Like hell there is," Stevens snapped. "Look, I'm pretty damned tired of being herded around by assholes with guns. They killed a good man, a good friend, for no reason. I have a right to ask who you are. Who are those guys? Why are you all here?"

Bolan gestured to Glinkov's men. "This scum ought to be tied up first, don't you think?"

"I'd like that fine," Stevens said.

Bolan liked the guy immediately. He obviously had guts. His temper might be getting the better of him at the moment, but he sure didn't hide what was on his mind. And he and Cohen were going to need him. Matt Stevens just might be it.

Stevens went back to the bathroom, returning with several lengths of rope. Quickly he bound Edmunds and Louis. The process was swift, and none too gentle. "Take these bastards into the back and watch 'em," he said to his men. "And while you're at it, dig up some spare uniforms. It's too damn cold to stand around in skivvies."

Cohen interrupted. "Mack, I wasn't kidding. Glinkov wants to see me. I'd better get a move on. You'll handle things on this end?" Cohen smiled. "Sorry, I guess that was a stupid question, wasn't it?" He looked at Bolan and then added, "Yeah, it was."

"Eli, I'm going with you."

"So am I," Stevens said. "These pricks have a lot to answer for. No way I'm going to miss it."

"I guess I should have expected that," Cohen said. "Let's figure out what we're going to do then."

The guards were busy slipping into ill-fitting uniforms and grease-stained jeans. Anything that came to hand was better than trying to fight in their underwear. When they finished, Stevens sat down at the table and gestured for Bolan to join him.

"Look, I don't know who you are, but it's seems clear you're on our side. What can we do to help?"

"Are there weapons here?" Bolan asked.

"Some. Not many. A couple of pistols and an M-16. That's about it. We got ammo, but nothing much to use it in."

"The first thing we have to do is get you some guns. You heard what Eli said. We don't have much time. And we don't know exactly what they plan to do with the reactor. But we can't wait. There are fifteen to twenty more terrorists inside the plant. Most of them are in the main building. They've got hostages, but we don't know how many."

"About thirty, I would guess," Stevens said. "That's the usual night crew. Not much goes on here at night. I better call out for help."

He walked to the phone console and punched an outside line. Angrily he punched another, then a third. In disgust, he slammed the phone back into its receiver. "There are no lines to the outside. The only thing working is the intercom."

"We don't have time to wait for help. We'll have to do this ourselves," Bolan said. "We can get you some weapons. Eli, take one of these guys in the Jeep and get the Kalashnikovs we stashed. Grab everything that shoots."

When Cohen left, Bolan turned back to Stevens.

"You know the inside of that place. I don't. Educate me."

Stevens walked to a wall cabinet, returning with a ring binder and a map of the installation. Quickly he and Bolan thumbed through the binder. Bolan needed some idea of the layout of the plant before entering. Surprise was their ally, but it wouldn't last long. And when it was gone, there would be no substitute for knowledge of the plant.

Glinkov and his people had prepared well. They had known exactly what they were doing. That meant they had access to information, and plenty of time to digest it. The rough sketch Bolan was getting was no match for that kind of planning. But it was all he had.

"Any ideas, Matt?"

"Well, not many. But my best guess is that the hostages would be kept in this building here." He placed a fingertip on the main building of Unit 1. "That's where most of the staff would be anyhow, and there's no point in herding people all over the place."

"Where in this building?"

"Well, if you're going to fuck around with the reactor, you got to be in the main control room. That's the easiest place to direct things from. Unless you just want to blow the damn thing sky-high. But that would take a lot of explosives."

"No. They want to fake an accident," Bolan said. "You're right, the control room is the best place for that."

"Hell, man, you can't mean they just waltz in here, fake an accident and waltz out. No way. Too many people know what happened. Unless..."

"That's about it, Matt. No survivors. They're going to kill everybody. They have to."

"Holy shit!"

The door banged open. Eli and the guard had returned. Each carried two Kalashnikovs. "There's two more out in the Jeep," Eli said.

Stevens looked at the weapons. "I heard about these bastards, but I never used one. Anybody know anything about it?"

One of the other guards nodded. "I do. Let me get the others, and I'll give you a lesson." He banged through the door, returning a moment later with two more rifles and several ammo clips.

"Matt," Bolan asked, "can you scan the inside of the plant from here with the television monitors?"

"Not completely. But we can check out the lower levels and some of the corridors. What are you looking for?"

"Not what. Who. And we don't have a clue where they're keeping her."

"Let's check it out then," Stevens said.

He punched in the manual control code for the security cameras. The images on one of the four screens stopped jumping about.

"Check the lower levels first," Bolan directed. "Wherever they've got her, it's bound to be out of the way."

Stevens selected the cameras on Level 4. One at a time, he worked his way from camera to camera. The effect on the screen was that of taking a quick walk along the halls.

In the dim light, it was difficult to see more than a few yards on either side of each camera. Stevens was working his way along the outermost corridors. On the third side of the large rectangle marking the boundary of the plant, he stopped.

"Look at this. I think we got something."

Bolan noticed two men leaning against the wall. They were positioned between two doors, both of which were closed.

"Where is that, Matt?"

"The lowest level. It's on the west corridor. Unless they're hiding out for a smoke, I'd say they're guarding something. Or somebody."

"Is there anything important on that level of the plant?" Bolan asked.

"No. It's storage and offices. Big rooms mostly and a couple of engineering labs. But they're not being used much yet."

"That's got to be where they're keeping her." Mack Bolan got to his feet. "We're going to make plans. Then we have to get moving. As near as I can figure it, we have less than two hours. These animals have to be out of here by dawn."

Cohen paced anxiously while Bolan sketched out his plan of attack. As soon as Bolan finished, Cohen picked up his Ingram and opened the door. As he stepped through, Bolan grabbed him by the shoulder. "We get Rachel, first thing. No matter what."

Cohen smiled grimly. "You'd better believe it." His voice was metallic, deadly flat.

"Okay, this is it," Bolan announced as he followed Cohen outside. As Stevens and the others stepped out into the open, an earsplitting hiss issued from the plant. Bolan stared up at a serpentine cloud of steam. The cloud snaked skyward, gradually torn to shreds by the cold wind.

"Holy shit," Stevens yelled.

"What's wrong, Matt?"

"The reactor's venting. There's only one reason it'll do that. The reactor core is melting down. That steam is radioactive."

Stevens didn't have to tell them what it meant. They sprinted across the frozen snow.

Eli Cohen reached the main entrance to the Unit 1 reactor first. Bolan, Stevens and Tony Giancana, one of Stevens's men, were well behind him and to the left. While Eli approached the entrance, the others angled in toward the side of the building, keeping to the shadows.

One man had been sent over the fence to find a telephone. The remaining two were to sweep the rest of the plant for strays, then join the others.

Cohen nodded to the guard on the door and pushed on it. As soon as the door closed behind him, he turned. Poking his head back out, he called to the sentry. "Got a cigarette?"

The man reached into his pocket, pulling out a pack of Camels. He tapped one free and extended it to Eli.

"Thanks," Eli said, stepping back outside. He fumbled in his coat for a lighter. The guard snapped his own lighter, and Eli bent into the flame. "I hear they got a girl locked up someplace inside."

"Yeah. Good-looking broad, too. Wish to hell I pulled guard duty on her instead of standing around in the cold."

"Who is she?"

"I don't know. They got her on Level 4 someplace. Way to hell and gone downstairs. David Lawrence is watching her. If I know David, though, he's doing more than watching her, you know?"

The guard never heard Bolan move in behind him. The big guy locked an arm around the man's neck. With a swift jerk, he snapped it. The dead man dangled just briefly in Bolan's grip, then Giancana dragged him into the shadows.

"Okay, Tony." Stevens said, "You wait here for Daniels and Grissom. As soon as they get here, move in. We'll be on Level 4. Once we get Rachel out, we'll need all the help we can get taking the control room."

Bolan and Stevens joined Cohen inside the building. The concrete floor echoed hollowly under their feet. Bolan was silent. Glinkov would be in the main control room, he knew. The dim lighting in the broad corridors was almost ghostly. Everything in the plant was built on such a colossal scale that he felt insignificant.

"Come on, she's on Level 4. Let's go."

The three men rushed to the elevator bank. Bolan and Cohen each pressed the down button at the same time, their thumbs colliding. The elevator took a long time to arrive. Its slow climb marked on the bank of lights gave Cohen time to think. The cameras had shown at least two guards. The attack force had been spread rather thin, so he doubted there would be more. On the other hand, where the hell was everybody?

"Something's wrong...."

"What?"

"I don't know. But I don't like the way it smells."

Of the remaining men, he had seen only three, one at the outside door and one at the control room door. That left more than a dozen men unaccounted for.

Before he had a satisfactory explanation, the elevator arrived. They stepped inside. Cohen pressed the button for Level 4 and walked to the rear of the large car. Then it hit him. It was a setup. Some of the others were below. Glinkov didn't trust him.

"That's it. Mack, it's a trap. I knew it was too easy. I couldn't figure out where everybody was. Now I know. They're waiting for us down there."

"No, Eli. They're waiting for *you*. They don't know Matt and I are here. That gives *us* the edge. Let's take advantage of it."

When the elevator reached the lowest level of the plant, the door opened with a soft sigh. Eli stepped cautiously into the corridor. To the left, there was nothing. To the right, he could see the dim outlines of several doors along the near wall. The opposite wall was blank. He waved Bolan and Stevens out.

"Eli," Bolan whispered, "wait here. Give Matt and me two minutes. We'll work around to the other side. When you get to the guards, make sure they're both watching you. We'll hit them from behind."

Eli nodded. Bolan and Stevens turned to the left and sprinted down the next passage. Eli counted the seconds. The hands of his watch barely seemed to move. Finally the two minutes were up. Slowly, keeping close to the wall, he headed down the corridor. In the dim light he couldn't see very far ahead.

The first door on the right was closed. Cohen opened it with a turn of the knob. The room was pitch-black. He felt for a light switch. When it clicked on, the room was bathed by flickering fluorescent illumination. It was an office of some kind, empty except for its furniture.

Cohen walked on to the next doorway. Another empty office. And another. Six in all. There was a long blank space. At its far end, barely discernible in the dim light, was the figure of a man.

He walked more quickly now, approaching the guard with a confidence he didn't really have.

"Rachel Peres around here anywhere?"

The guard tilted his head to the door beyond.

Beyond the guard, he couldn't see the second sentry. It puzzled him, but there was no time to worry about it.

And beyond the guard, Cohen saw Matt Stevens. And the Executioner.

Mack Bolan reached into his coat for the Beretta. It was risky, but there was no choice. Eli Cohen knelt to tie his bootlace.

With a clear shot, Bolan squeezed. The Beretta coughed. The slug bored through the guard's temple. Blood sprayed over Cohen's neck and hands. Catching the slumping body before it fell, he placed the dead man against the base of the wall.

The door was closed. He turned the knob and pushed the door open. It was dark inside. As with the other offices, he reached for a light switch. Nothing happened.

Cautiously Cohen stepped into the dark room.

"Rachel? Are you here? Rachel?"

Silence. He could hear his own breathing, coming faster and faster. His mouth was dry. Something was very wrong. As he moved slowly forward, he reached out blindly with his hands, waving them back and forth until he finally found something. It felt like a desk.

Carefully he groped along the edge of the desktop. His fingers encountered a wire, which he followed to the base of a desk lamp. He depressed the push-button switch. There was a brief glimmer, more darkness, then a flash of light. Four men stood behind the desk. Their weapons were pointed directly at him.

This was going to be tougher than he thought.

25

Mack Bolan and Matt Stevens held their breath. When Cohen flicked on the light, its blaze cast a stark white rectangle on the corridor floor. The sudden blaze was followed by silence. Something was wrong.

"Fancy meeting you here." The voice belonged to Eli Cohen. He wasn't talking to Rachel. Bolan eased closer to the doorway. He couldn't risk charging the room unless he had an idea where Cohen was. On the opposite side of the door, Stevens fingered his rifle nervously.

"You know, Cohen, I never did like you." The voice was low and rasping, full of Hollywood menace—a wiseguy putting on a show for his buddies.

"The four of you never did much for me, either," Cohen said. He was raising his voice just slightly. Bolan smiled. Eli was telling him what he needed to know.

"I guess those AK-47s make you big deals, huh?" Cohen continued.

"Hey, Bobby," another voice joined in. "What are we wasting time for? Why don't we get it over with? I don't like it down here."

When Bolan got through, he'd like it a lot less.

"What, exactly, is it that you have to finish?" Cohen's tone was mocking. He wanted to get them on edge, but knew he couldn't push them too far too soon. "You know, you guys won't make it out of here, no matter what happens to me."

"Says who?" Bobby demanded. "You?"

"Not me, no. But think about it for a minute. Who are you working for? Not Peter Achison. He's a gofer just like you. The Russian is pulling your strings. And when he's got what he wants, he's gonna cut them. Dead."

"No way, man. When we finish here, it's gonna be hot sun and sandy beaches for me."

"I wouldn't count on it. You never know where you're gonna wash up once you're cut loose."

"Let's just grease the bastard and get on with it," a third voice said.

"Shut up, everybody. Cohen, put your gun on the floor. Slowly. Then turn around." Bobby must have sensed the play slipping away from him. He was trying to force things back into his control.

Bolan heard the clink of the Ingram on the concrete floor. He moved.

Wheeling back away from the door, he sprayed hellfire into the room. Eli was bent over, and the bullets skimmed just over his stooped form. At the first sound, he dived for a corner of the room, rolled once and slammed into the wall.

The four men inside were taken by surprise. Bolan's first burst of fire caught Bobby in the throat. Blood spouted from three holes just below his shoulder line. Stunned by the impact of .45 caliber slugs he slammed back into the wall, but refused to fall.

As Bolan sprayed a figure eight to the left of the dying man, he caught a second punk in the shoulder. The bone-cracking slaughter chewed him to pieces before he dropped.

Bolan stood framed in the doorway, an easy target, but there was no other way. Matt Stevens slipped in behind him. Down on one knee, he sprayed his own death stream into the room like an angry fireman hosing down a three-alarmer.

The two remaining men had taken refuge behind a standard-issue steel desk. Bolan slammed a new magazine into the Ingram. He drilled the desk with cold fury, working his fire in a wavy line. Hole after deadly hole opened in the flimsy sheet metal. The desk shuddered, slowly sliding back toward the wall.

Bolan entered the office as Eli retrieved his weapon. Eli walked to the desk and pushed it aside. His shoulders arched, and with a rush he spewed the contents of his stomach. He shook his head as if to clear it, spitting to rid his mouth of the bilious aftertaste. "I don't think I'll ever get used to this," he said.

But Bolan was transformed. His large frame seemed made of harder steel. The set of his jaw was something Cohen hadn't seen before. The Executioner was all business. He crammed a new magazine into the Ingram and tossed the empty one over the ruined desk. It clanged once and was still. Cohen recognized the sound. It was a death knell.

"So where the hell are they keeping her?" Bolan asked the question as if the walls should answer him.

"There are a few more rooms down here," Stevens said. "If she's on this level, we should be able to find her."

"We'd better."

Cohen said nothing.

"Let's hit it then." Bolan started down the hall, moving away from the elevator bank. He tried the first door, banging it back against the inner wall with a dull echo. He clicked on the light, but the room was empty. Stevens moved on to the next. It, too, was deserted. Cohen came up empty on the third.

On the fourth try, the door was locked. "Check those bastards, Eli. One of them might have a master key."

Cohen sprinted back down the hall to the scene of the firefight. In a minute he was back, dangling a key on a heavy metal ring.

The intricately etched key ground in the lock. The door opened with a cavernous boom. Bolan flicked the light. The room seemed as empty as the others. Then something caught Bolan's eye. It was a shoe, lying just to the side of the office desk that occupied one corner.

The Executioner ran to the desk and pushed it aside. Rachel was lying on her back, her eyes closed. "I've got her! Give me a hand!"

He knelt beside the still form.

"Rachel, Rachel. Can you hear me?"

Cohen and Stevens pressed in behind him, but Bolan was oblivious to them. He chafed the woman's wrists, then patted her cheeks gently. Cohen marveled at the gentleness of the huge hands. Too frightened that she might not respond, Cohen turned away. He closed his eyes. His fists were white.

Then, there was a moan. Music to their ears. "Rachel, it's me, Mack." Bolan bent closer, placing an ear to her lips. He noticed they were raw. A large bruise on her cheek had faded, but it didn't escape his eye.

"Eli? Is Eli there?"

"Yes, Rachel, he's here."

Bolan's memory returned to another frail form, in another place. That woman hadn't been so lucky.

He helped Rachel to sit, and Cohen slipped in beside him. Mack Bolan stood while Eli Cohen continued to revive his sister.

As he watched the two of them, he remembered the pain of his own sister's loss. So many victims. The war went on and on. And always it was the innocent who suffered. It didn't matter that Rachel had more guts than most, had chosen to fight back. Compared to the animals, compared even to himself, Rachel Peres was an innocent. It was she, and those like her, who made the war necessary. And who made it possible to continue.

And he *would* continue.

For sure.

Her voice roused him. It was weak, sure, but it sounded no less determined than the last time he had seen her.

"We have to get a move on," Matt Stevens said. "Judging by that plume of steam we saw on the way over, the reactor is getting hot. Fast. If we're going to take these bastards down, we have to do it now."

"I know," Bolan said. "Don't worry. We'll take them down. Hard."

Rachel struggled to her feet, and Cohen assisted her to a seat behind the desk. "Rachel," he said. His voice was so soft that Bolan barely heard it. "We need help. Do you have any idea what's supposed to happen here?"

"They're going to trigger a meltdown. They're draining the reactor coolant. When they're ready, they'll pull the control rods for the final step."

"The hostages. What about the hostages? What are they going to do with them? Do you have any idea?"

"I heard Glinkov talking. I think he said they're going to be put in the building with the reactor. Something about the radiation helping them out."

"The containment building," Stevens said. "The radiation level is already up in there. That's where that steam came from. If he uncovers the core of that reactor, the radiation will kill anybody inside. And when the fuel burns, that place will be so hot, nobody will be able to get in there for years."

"That's just what the bastard wants," Bolan said. "Enough time to cover his ass. And a shutdown of all the nuke plants in the country."

"How many men, Eli? How many left?"

"Twelve, I think."

"And where the hell is Parsons? And Achison?"

"I saw Parsons a couple of hours ago," Rachel said. "I don't know where he is now. Or even if he's still alive. Achison is supposed to bring a chopper in for Glinkov's getaway."

ANDREY GLINKOV WATCHED the dials. The needle on the containment building radiation level was still rising. At ten thousand rems it would be time to move the hostages. The television monitors flickered as they jumped from one image to another. In the bottom of the cooling tower, he could see the water slowly rising. It was highly radioactive waste water leaking from the reactor pressure container. As the core heated, seals and joints on the coolant conduit system began to give, spilling waste water indiscriminately.

Radioactive hydrogen was beginning to accumulate at the top of the cooling tower. The gas was generated by the breakup of the remaining coolant water. An errant spark would detonate the explosive gas. Unless the volume was large, the four-foot-thick concrete walls of the containment building should be equal to the task.

Pressure valves released the gas, together with radioactive steam, whenever the pressure grew too great. Already the runaway reactor had begun to leak deadly gas into the atmosphere around the plant. In the cold air, the radioactive steam condensed in small, deadly clouds for a few moments. Then, borne on a stiff winter wind, it vanished into thin air to become a slowly drifting invisible killing zone.

The temperature gauge was most interesting. It was slowly climbing as the coolant drained away, rushing into the complex of concrete tunnels that honeycombed the earth under the plant. It was already nearly six hundred degrees in the containment building, and the core was hotter still. Glinkov was still unaware of Robbins's ploy. With the evacuation pump out of action, the water was running off at a slower rate than was possible. And the tunnel exits were still sealed.

From time to time, the Russian glanced at the security monitors, but his hands were full. He had no time to watch what was going on in the bowels of the plant. Had he been more alert, he might have seen three men and a woman move past one of the cameras on Level 4.

Had he been more attentive still, he might have seen another shadowy figure as well. This one moved with less urgency, seeming almost lost in its tentative wandering through the maze of underground corridors.

He hadn't heard from the hit team waiting for Eli Cohen. It was taking a long time. On the other hand, perhaps Cohen had simply taken as long to get below as he had to check the plant perimeter. Death is patient, Glinkov knew. Cohen's time would come soon enough. And that would leave one final victim.

Mack Bolan.

Surely he wouldn't fail to show. Everything in his KGB files said that he would. A man who dared to chew at the Soviet beast from its very heart as Bolan had done in Moscow itself, wouldn't balk at the opportunity so carefully and generously extended to him here.

By his own estimate, Glinkov had less than an hour. Achison would be arriving in fifty minutes. By then he would have completed his sabotage of the reactor. The hostages would long since have been sealed in the containment building, to be found God knows when, but certainly long after their discovery would be a threat to him. That left only the assault team itself to deal with.

They, too, were expendable. Their work finished, some of their number would turn on the others. They would be eliminated quickly and painlessly. He and Achison would finish the job from the chopper.

Years later, with little left but radioactive bones, no one would care how they had died. They would be written off as victims of the tragic accident of Thunder Mountain—if anyone still cared.

It was time to check on the hostages.

Glinkov gestured to the sentry posted outside the backup control room.

"How are our guests, Warren? Resting comfortably, I trust?"

Warren smiled before answering. "Hell, yes. They don't have a care in the world."

"It will be time to move them very shortly. You had better get the rest of the team. We'll need them for the last part of our operation."

"Where to?"

"On Level 4. There's a double-airlock entrance to the reactor containment building down there."

"What about Cohen?"

"Don't worry about him."

"Bobby taking care of him?"

Glinkov nodded.

"Too bad. I wanted to waste him myself," Warren said. "That bastard was getting way too big for his boots."

"I shouldn't wonder," Glinkov said. "Mossad agents are not known for their modesty."

"Mossad! Are you kidding?"

"Most assuredly not."

"Why'd you wait so long to ice him?"

"He was useful. A man should never lose an opportunity to let an opponent do his work for him. It is most efficient. Even Moscow Center is budget conscious these days. Tools are everywhere, Warren. But it takes a craftsman to recognize them. And an artist to make the most of them."

"Yeah," Warren said, laughing. "I guess you could teach a course on that subject."

"Perhaps I will, Warren. Perhaps I will. Even you might learn something."

"I'll bet," Warren said.

Glinkov just smiled.

26

Fortunately Rachel was resilient. She had already regained her energy and now toted an AK-47 taken from one of her erstwhile captors.

"We're going to have a real problem upstairs," she said. Her voice betrayed no emotion. Bolan knew it was partly self-control and partly realism.

"What's the situation up there?" he asked.

"If they haven't moved anyone, all the hostages are in the secondary control room. I don't know how Glinkov has his team deployed. But I do know there's only one way into that room."

"Are there guards in with them?"

"There was one on the door. That's all I saw."

Bolan turned to Matt Stevens. "Is there any way we can get to the main control room without being spotted, Matt?"

"Depends on where they are. We can get close, but unless the door is opened from inside, there's only one way in."

"How?" Bolan's voice cracked sharply. The concrete walls echoed as if it was a pistol shot.

Stevens reached into his pocket and withdrew a flat plastic security pass. About the size of a credit card, it was magnetically coded. There was a lock on each of the doors. The card would permit him to open them one at a time. "The problem is, this can be overridden. If Glinkov spots me, we're out of luck."

"Would he be able to tell you were there? Is there an alarm or something that indicates that the card is being used?"

"No, no alarm. But there is a set of lights on the console. If he sees them, and if he knows what they mean, it's all over."

"Then we have to keep him busy," Eli said.

"How?" Rachel demanded.

"I'm supposed to be dead, right?"

"So?"

"So what if he finds out I'm alive and well? Matt, is there any way I can call attention to myself someplace in the plant?"

"How much attention?" Stevens asked.

"Lots of attention."

"Hell, the easiest thing is just call him on the intercom."

"No good. Too obvious."

"The TV security monitors," Stevens suggested. "You could take a few of them out. He'd have to notice the blank screens."

"Listen," Mack Bolan said. "We have to know what we're up against before we try anything. We make one mistake, and we lose it all. Everything."

"You got any ideas, then, Mack?"

"Look, we know there's a guard on the control room. We also know there's another guard in the backup control room. That means there are at least ten men someplace in this plant. They have guns, and Glinkov needs them."

"But how do we find them?"

"We don't. They find us."

"But the hostages. As long as Glinkov has them, we can't take any chances. We can't jeopardize their lives."

"Their lives are already in jeopardy. And Glinkov wants us to worry about them. He also wants to get out of here alive. He can't afford to get caught here. If he kills the hostages before he gets us, he has no leverage at all. None. I think we should hit him head on. Go right to the control room.''

''Then what?''

''If he knows we're coming, we smoke out the other gunners. We take them down, and our problem gets a whole lot easier to solve.''

''Mack's right,'' Eli Cohen said. He stood and picked up his Ingram.

''I don't like it. Those people are friends of mine,'' Matt Stevens said.

''You have any other ideas, Matt?''

''No. . . I don't.''

''Let's do it.''

Matt Stevens found the group anticontamination suits, which they put on before sprinting for the elevators. Rachel had recovered most of her strength, but she still lagged behind the others.

It was beginning. Mack Bolan felt the juices flowing. For the first time since getting into the plant, he felt like a soldier instead of a bag man. Head on, that was the way to deal with slime like Glinkov.

Glinkov was going to meet a warrior. Bolan knew men like the Russian always counted on caution. They used it against you, and then they laughed all the way to their sanctuaries. But this time it would be different. Mack Bolan was nobody's victim.

It was time to play hardball.

And Mack Bolan knew the rules.

Back on the main floor, the four soldiers had a quick conference.

''Look, keep this in mind,'' Bolan whispered. ''Either way, we win. If we get inside the control room before he notices, we've got him. If we don't we smoke out the other goons. Matt, you said there's a second set of doors into the control room, right?''

''Yeah, but I only have one card.''

"It doesn't matter. Eli, you and Rachel get to that other entrance. Make a little noise. Let him know you're there, but watch your back. If he tries to run, he'll come our way. Otherwise we get to him."

As they made ready to leave, two of Stevens's men slipped in through the main entrance.

"Find anything?" Stevens whispered.

"Nothing. The place is deserted. It's spooky."

"We'll have our hands full here," Bolan interrupted. "One of the guys go with Eli, the other come with Matt and me."

"What's going on?"

"You'll see soon enough."

"Matt, how long will it take to get to the other door?" Bolan asked.

"Two or three minutes. Adam knows the way. And now we've got another security card. Adam can get in the other door."

One of the new men nodded.

"Okay. Eli, we'll wait five minutes. Then we'll make our move. Make sure he knows you're there. If there's a guard, you'll have to take him down. But don't take any foolish chances." Bolan looked at Rachel. She avoided his gaze. The steel in those hard blue eyes frightened her.

"Right."

The three moved out, working their way along the darkened corridor to the opposite approach to the control room. While they waited, Bolan and the others were silent. The Executioner was zeroing in on the job ahead.

Glinkov was a pro. And he was good. He wouldn't have gotten this far if he wasn't. He was also unpredictable. Despite his calm exterior, Bolan knew he was risking lives, lives that weren't his to risk. But he had no choice.

To hesitate was to lose. And Mack Bolan hadn't come this far to lose it all at the wire. Too much had to be accounted for. Hanley's kids were fatherless. That counted. An innocent guard at the plant was dead. That counted. Bolan wasn't going to rest until he could cancel the debt. Completely. Paid in full was the only settlement he would accept.

THERE WAS A GUARD on the door. He was pacing back and forth in front of it, smoking a cigarette. A pile of butts lay against the wall. The man was either bored or nervous. Cohen smiled grimly. In a minute he'd be neither. In a minute he'd be dead.

The distance was too great to cover without being seen. On the other hand, they were supposed to create a diversion. Well, here it comes, Cohen thought.

The guard continued his pacing. He was heading toward them. At about fifteen feet past the door, he would pivot and move back the way he had come. Pivot, strut. Pivot, strut.

Cohen timed it perfectly. He had one minute. The guard paced, and Cohen watched. And waited. Pivot, strut. Cohen didn't want to shoot him in the back. He wasn't a grandstander, but he wasn't a backshooter, either. If he didn't have to be.

The guard turned again, his AK-47 slung carelessly over his shoulder. The man stopped to light a new cigarette from the stub of his last one. He dropped the butt to the floor and ground it under his heel, then kicked it into the pile. Cohen made his move.

"That's littering, pal." He stepped into view, his Ingram held waist high. "You should be more careful."

The moron didn't know any better. He reached for his Kalashnikov, and Cohen squeezed the trigger. The Ingram belched one short burst. It caught the guy just above the belt line, nearly cutting him in two and slamming him backward.

Blood gushed over his belt, cascading down over his pants. He had been so surprised, he hadn't said a word.

Quickly Adam and Eli dragged the lifeless body against the wall, dropping it over the heap of cigarettes. The SMG's suppressor was a good one. Eli doubted Glinkov even heard them.

Cohen looked through the small glass panel in the door, but he couldn't see anyone in the control room. Rachel walked back to the intersection to keep watch. Adam slipped his card into the first security lock and began punching in the code number to release the lock. None of them heard the approaching footsteps.

THE FIVE MINUTES WERE UP. Mack Bolan stepped around the corner and made for the guard. Facing away from him, the man didn't notice Bolan's approach. Bolan's Ingram was ready to spit fire.

Bolan narrowed the gap. He could hear Stevens and the other plant guard right behind him. Their footsteps sounded like thunder in Bolan's ears, and still the guard didn't turn. With twenty yards still to go, at last the guard looked at them. His face, behind a bright red beard, froze. Bolan fired.

The deadly rain of .45 caliber slugs chewed into the guy from the neck up. The man's skull shattered, and he struck the floor. As they reached the still spastic figure on the concrete, Bolan tugged the dead man's Kalashnikov free and slung it over his shoulder. The ruptured skull oozed blood and brain tissue. The man's face was gone, as if it had never been there at all. One eye lolled over a shattered cheekbone, like a cherry on its stem.

The three warriors covered the remaining distance to the first door without opposition. While Stevens worked on the lock, Bolan peered through the large window into the control room. Glinkov was absorbed at the control console. He was intently watching the array of gauges and dials. The inner guard was seated casually before the secondary control room. Its door was closed. Neither man seemed to have heard anything.

If luck were with them, Cohen and his team would be working on their doors by now. The eerie silence was broken by a sudden burst of gunfire from the opposite side of the control room.

"That's at the other door!" Stevens shouted.

Bolan knew Eli was in trouble. And Rachel was with him.

"Matt, keep at it. I'll be back as soon as I can. If you get it open, go in. And watch yourself." He sprinted across the floor, heading for the corridor leading to the other doorway.

The gunfire continued. It sounded like a small war. Cohen must still be alive, or the shooting would have stopped. At the mouth of the passage, Bolan paused. A security mirror high on the wall showed him the full length of the corridor. Adam lay in a pool of blood, sprawled in front of the unopened security door.

Three of Glinkov's men were at the other end of the passage. Cohen peered from the scant cover of an open office door farther down the hall. As Bolan watched, Eli sprayed hellfire along the corridor without aiming. He was holding the Ingram in his left hand, extending it just enough to hold off the attackers with blind fire.

Rachel was nowhere in sight.

Checking his own SMG, Bolan put in a fresh clip and waited. There was a time to plant, and a time to reap. The Executioner was going to plant some lead. The Grim Reaper would bring in the crop.

The passage intersected another at right angles. Bolan could fire down the hall and cross to the opposite side while the gunners dived for cover. With a little luck, he might nail one of them. Watching the mirror closely, he waited. Eli pulled his weapon back to reload. The three men charged. Bolan made his move.

With the Ingram held at waist level, he began firing as he stepped into the intersection. The lead man was chewed up; the deadly spray from Bolan's SMG had punched through his chest wall. Wild return fire ricocheted off the concrete walls as the remaining two men dived for the floor. Eli rejoined the firefight with a short burst, and Bolan was across the hall.

If he remembered his quick lesson in the layout, he could work his way around behind. He fired another quick burst and sprinted for the next intersection. The gun battle continued behind him, its echoes resounding along the maze of concrete passages.

He skidded to a halt at the next passageway, checked it for opposition and rushed on. The noise died abruptly. Bolan increased his pace. The next passage was just ahead. As he ran, he changed clips in the Ingram, slipping the half-empty one back into his coat.

At the corner he stopped. There was another mirror, and he scanned it quickly. He knew they could see him as well as he could see them in it. But the hallway was empty except for Adam's body and that of the man he had nailed in crossing the hall.

All right.

He changed back to the half-empty clip, wasted the mirror, then reloaded. He'd rather fight blind than give them the advantage of the glass. He tossed the empty magazine into the corridor. It bounced once, twice, then disappeared in a hail of bullets and concrete chips.

So they were still there.

But where was Eli? And Rachel?

The architecture of the damn building was an obstacle. All right angles, there was no way to get from A to B without exposing oneself. It hadn't been planned as a hell zone.

And while he waited, the clock ticked. If Stevens managed to get the door open, he'd need all the help he could get. Things had to be wrapped up on this end. Now.

What the hell, he told himself. Sometimes you have to take the bull by the horns. Steeling himself, Bolan charged into the open corridor. He watched both walls, looking for the first sign of movement. He sprayed a burst the length of the hall. No one returned fire. Charging ahead, he reached the body of the dead man. His weapon was gone. Ahead on the left, a door yawned open.

Inside, he answered one of his questions. The other two lay dead. Somebody had nailed them already. From behind. Bolan pushed on to the next office. Three empty clips lay just inside the door. But the room was vacant. No Eli. And no Rachel.

Adam's security card, what was left of it, dangled from the mangled lock. It was useless. And Bolan doubted the outside mechanism would function. He rushed back to the main control access. Stevens was nowhere to be seen. Another of Stevens's men, Donny Grissom, lay dead on the floor. Approaching cautiously, he peered through the master window, just in time to see Glinkov vanish through the opposite door. A klaxon somewhere deep in the plant began a mournful uproar.

Stevens was just inside the first door. He had been wounded. Blood soaked his right sleeve. He was still struggling with the second lock.

"What happened, Matt?" Bolan demanded.

"I don't know. Somebody blindsided us. They killed Donny, but he was between them and me. I got the door open just in time."

"Did you see Eli?"

"No. Why?"

"He's missing. So is Rachel."

"Adam? Is he okay?"

Bolan said nothing. Stevens collapsed to the floor. "Those bastards."

"We'll get them, Matt."

Stevens grabbed the bloody sleeve of the anticontamination suit and ripped it loose at the shoulder. "Help me wrap this."

Bolan bound the ugly wound in Stevens's upper arm. The security chief turned back to the lock. He punched in the combination code, pressed the release and the door hummed open. Inside, the sound of the klaxon was insistent.

There was no one in the control room. Bolan ran to the backup control room door. The lock was destroyed. He stepped back and planted a sharp kick just above the damaged lock. The door swung back with a crash. The room was empty except for two dead men lying against one wall.

Bolan looked at the security man. "Do you know anything about this reactor? Can you work the controls?"

"Nothing. No, nothing."

Two more flashing lights joined the carnival array high on the board. They felt the rumble before they heard it. It grew slowly and sounded as if it would never stop.

27

The deserted control room echoed with the sound of alarms. Blinking lights were everywhere. Bolan stared at the flickering monitors. The images were randomly selected. As he watched, a group of shadows zipped past on one screen. As he moved in closer, the image changed.

"Matt, is there any way to select the cameras for these things?"

"Sure. What do you want to see?"

"I don't know. I thought I saw Rachel and Eli. But there were three figures. They were gone before I could get a fix on it."

"Okay, I'll run through the cameras one at a time. Keep an eye on the top left-hand screen. If you see something, holler."

Stevens sat at the security console. One by one, he scrolled through the cameras. Bolan watched intently. He was beginning to doubt that he had seen anything at all. Image after image of the gloomy depths of the plant flew by—corridors, storage rooms, work areas dominated by huge conduits and rumbling machinery.

"Hold a minute. Go back." Bolan shouted in his excitement. "No, one more. There."

The three figures he had seen were back. It was too dimly lit to be sure who they were, but despite their suits, he knew one of them was a woman. Their backs were to the camera, and they were stooped over, moving cautiously.

"Can you move in closer, Matt?"

"Hang on."

Stevens looked for the right button. When he found it, the image on the screen grew larger. The figures were still dark, but there was no question. He had found Eli and Rachel. But who was the third person? He had to know.

"What's that location?"

"It's on Level 4. The southwest quadrant."

"Matt, you stay here. Don't let anyone you don't know in here."

"Where the hell are you going?"

But Bolan was already gone.

The elevator was interminably slow. When it finally arrived, Bolan rushed in. He hit the button and waited for the doors to close. The ride down took forever. It seemed as if he had done nothing but ride up and down the damned elevator.

On the lowest level of the plant once again, he rushed through the elevator doors before they had fully opened. The corridor was even darker than it had been. He paused to get his bearings, then ran to the corner of the hall. The long concrete passage stretched dimly ahead. He heard and saw nothing.

Wherever Eli and Rachel had been going, they were in a hurry. That could mean only one thing. They knew where the hostages had been moved.

Bolan was running at top speed. The concrete echoed with his heavy steps. The corridor seemed endless. Suddenly he was in the open. The right-hand wall ended, and he found himself in a wilderness of throbbing machinery. Huge conduits ran in seemingly endless banks overhead.

It was a steel jungle. The hum of the machines was off-key somehow. He knew the reactor was overheating. Something was getting ready to blow. Unwilling to run into opposition at full tilt, he had to slow his pace. Listening for anything that didn't belong, he worked his way among the towering structures.

A huge generator loomed just ahead. He was at the heart of the plant. Beyond was another jungle, a mirror image of the one he had just passed through. He paused again. The area looked familiar. He was certain it was the area through which he had seen Rachel and Eli pass.

Bolan dropped to the floor, peering into the murk, trying to see under the tangled pipes and bunched cables. Visibility was limited. He saw nothing.

Getting to his feet, he moved around the generator. He had to be getting close. But where the hell was everybody? Bolan fingered the trigger on his SMG. The wilderness stretched ahead of him, vanishing in the dark.

The generator was behind him now, groaning like a wounded beast. If he didn't find them soon, he might have to continue in total darkness. There must be an emergency system. He wished he had thought to tell Matt Stevens to kick it in. Too late now.

Bolan thought he was approaching the bottom of the containment building. There was a double-locked access. If Glinkov planned to herd the hostages into it, it would have to be done from nearby.

The first burst of fire caught him by surprise. He hit the deck, straining to place the point of origin. A second burst was louder. The thunder seemed to echo through the bowels of the plant as if it, too, wanted to get out. This time he got a fix on it.

Regaining his feet, he bent low and moved toward the sound. He couldn't tell whether the fire had been returned. It might have been somebody on edge. Nerves were bound to give way in the eerie half-light.

Behind him Bolan heard the sound of the generator. It was rising and falling. Then it died altogether. It was pitch-dark. Bolan froze in his tracks. For a long moment he heard nothing, then shouts were followed by more automatic weapon fire. It was close. He couldn't afford to use a flashlight. Any moving light would be an easy target.

Another burst of gunfire cast ghostly shadows that vanished immediately. He moved closer. Like dawn breaking, a dim light began to appear. Stevens must have kicked in the emergency generator. The light wasn't bright, but it was better than nothing.

Just ahead, he saw a figure crouched behind a huge, dead machine. The outline was too vague for him to tell who it was. He circled around behind the machine, keeping his eye on the hiding figure.

As he got closer, the figure left its cover and moved forward. There were two others off to its left. They too were crouched and moving forward. The last figure moved again, passing just beneath one of the emergency lamps. It was Rachel.

Bolan sprinted to her side.

She turned to him. "It's about time you showed up."

"What's going on?"

"They moved the hostages. They're locked in a storeroom up ahead."

"How many of the goons are there?"

"Eli thinks ten, maybe twelve."

"You know what they're planning to do, don't you?"

She nodded. "I know."

Cohen was crouched behind a stack of metal drums, ahead and to the left. Bolan whistled, and Cohen turned. He broke into a grin.

"Who's your buddy?" Bolan asked, indicating the third figure, kneeling in the shadows beyond Cohen.

"Parsons," Rachel said.

"What?"

"He says he didn't know what Glinkov was planning until tonight. Glinkov was going to have him shot, but he greased the guy who was going to do it. With a gun that Glinkov had given him. How's that for poetic justice?"

"It's not bad for a fairy tale. I don't buy it."

"I didn't either, at first."

"You do now?"

She nodded. "I do. He saved our lives. We were jumped while we were working on the door to the control room. They killed Adam."

"I know."

"Parsons hit them from behind. If he hadn't, we'd have been blown away."

"Do you trust him, Rachel?"

"Do we have a choice?"

"I guess not. I'll be back. I want to talk to Eli."

Bolan crossed the dim expanse between Rachel and Cohen. "Where are they holed up?"

"Most of them are straight ahead, up near the wall. I hope they're all there. If they get around our flank, we're in big trouble."

"Maybe we shouldn't give them the chance," Bolan said.

"Lead on, Macduff."

Bolan hefted his Ingram and moved to the right. "When I give you the sign, we'll move," he whispered. "Let's stay spread out, so they can't gang up on us."

"You got it. Tell Parsons."

Bolan looked at Cohen without saying anything.

"I mean it, Mack. Tell him. Listen, we need all the help we can get."

Bolan slipped through the shadows, taking a position just behind the older man.

"Did you hear that?" Bolan asked the antinuke leader.

Parsons nodded. "Mr. Glinkov has been anxiously awaiting your arrival. If we're going to have a chance here, you'll have to live up to your reputation, Mr. Bolan."

"Don't worry about it," Bolan snapped. "We don't have much time, so here's what we're going to do. In two minutes, the three of us will hit them head-on. Rachel will cover our rear."

Bolan turned to leave. Parsons grabbed his arm. "Listen, Mr. Bolan. I don't blame you for feeling the way you do. But I swear to you, I had no idea this was going to happen. All I wanted was to close the plant down. I never meant for anyone to get hurt."

"It's a little late for that, isn't it?"

Parsons said nothing. After a moment of awkward silence, Bolan slipped away to rejoin Rachel.

"You're going to have to watch our backs," he whispered.

"Mack, be careful. And look out for Eli. He can be a little reckless."

"He'll be fine. Caution is a luxury we can't afford."

Bolan cocked his Ingram and gestured to Cohen and Parsons. At the sign, the three men pressed forward, sliding in and out of the shadows. It was fifty yards to the blank wall. It was the longest fifty yards Mack Bolan had ever walked. He checked his watch. There was less than an hour left now.

Parsons was on the right wing. The old guy moved well for an inexperienced man. Eli Cohen was on the left wing.

Mack Bolan took the point.

Parsons slipped through a notch between two columns of piping. Gunfire chased him back into the shadows. The dim light and the banshee wail of the ricocheting slugs chilled Bolan to the core.

In the shadows ahead, several men shifted positions nervously. They had the edge in numbers, and they had the advantage of defending from cover. Bolan's group had no choice but to expose itself from time to time as it moved in.

Parsons was using a Kalashnikov. He sprayed fire randomly, and Bolan jumped ahead. Bolan fired and Cohen leaped. Cohen hosed the shadows and Parsons moved. Foot by foot, they moved forward.

The progress was agonizingly slow. Time was slipping away, and they had yet to get a clear shot. It was time to quit fooling around, Bolan thought. Time to make a difference.

Slipping off to the left, Bolan sprinted into the darkness. The overhead lamps were few and far between. It might have been an illusion, but it seemed to the Executioner that they were fading.

If he could get an angle on the bastards, he could neutralize their cover. Watching front and side wouldn't leave them any place to hide. The first moments were going to be crucial. He hadn't told Eli he was slipping away. He didn't want any mistakes, and he couldn't take the chance the gunners would realize his intentions.

Flat on his belly, Bolan slid under some yard-high conduits. He wormed forward, the suit scratching on the rough concrete floor. The hiss of the cloth was serpentine and menacing. It seemed louder than it was in the lowering darkness.

While he worked forward, he could hear an occasional short burst from Eli's Ingram and Parsons's AK-47. He only hoped neither of his men would mistake him for the enemy. It was a chance, but he had to take it. Another ten yards, and he would have a clear angle of fire.

He slid forward under another bank of conduits. Just ahead, there was a stack of wooden pallets standing on end. Bolan cleared the pipes and got to his feet. Sprinting the few remaining feet, he ducked in behind the pallets.

The flimsy wood wouldn't offer much cover. But he was close now. He could hear the surprised breathing of one of the terrorists as yet another burst of fire came in from Eli's position. One of the stray slugs whined overhead, and Bolan ducked down instinctively. Deadly fire wasn't particular when it came to choosing a victim.

Now.

Three men were exposed to Bolan's Ingram. Cautiously he raised the weapon. He wanted to take them all out.

Whittling the odds was all well and good when time wasn't a factor. But not this time. The targets were fidgety. One of the guys was shifting back and forth on his feet. His profile slipped in and out of the shadows. The other two were stationary. Choosing the moment, Bolan squeezed. The sound of the SMG bounced off the tangled pipes and concrete floor. It exploded in his ears.

Spraying his fire in a wide arc, Bolan saw one of the guys go down. The hellfire seemed to lick out of the Ingram's mouth like a dragon's tongue. The second guy heard the fire from his side and turned. Three slugs smashed into his face and blew it away. In the dim light, his backward sprawl seemed staged, like Hollywood's idea of bloody murder.

The third man was quick. But not quick enough. As the chattering Ingram swept its tongue toward him, he moved back into the shadows, but there was no room. His dodge bounced him violently back into the path of the incoming fire. With a groan, he was down. But not out.

He began to haul himself behind cover, using one arm. The other dangled uselessly at his side. A dark stain covered his left shoulder. Bolan couldn't see its color in the twilight. He didn't have to. He knew it was bright red.

The guy struggled to get out of the way. Bolan rammed a new clip into the Ingram and let loose. The gun bucked in his hands as he walked his fire across the concrete floor toward the crawling man. Two ricochets caught him in a spray of concrete chips, then three more punched through rib cage and shoulder blade.

The man lay still.

28

Three down.

After the first burst, Cohen and Parsons caught on. They were alternating fire, just enough to pin the others down. Bolan angled closer to the wall. He could see the huge steel door of the storeroom where, he knew, the hostages waited.

A large shadow detached itself from the darkness. Supple movements and swiftness combined to create the impression of a large predatory cat walking on its hind paws. Bolan caught a glimpse of the movement. But he was too late. The stalker found new cover.

Bolan was now vulnerable. If he moved to the right, he'd be exposed to fire from his own side. If he moved to the left, he'd be an easy target for the enemy. Quickly he searched the immediate area looking for something, anything, to tip the odds back in his favor. Overhead, the conduits seemed to extend to heaven. Steel beanstalks, he thought. He could climb them to the giant's castle, if he dared.

But he didn't have to climb that high. A little more than fifteen feet up, a yard-diameter conduit met the column he was hiding behind. The right-angle intersection led to a point directly over, and eventually behind, the remaining terrorists. If he could mount the pipe without being seen, he'd have a chance to end the fight immediately.

And in transit he'd be a sitting duck. He'd have to attain his position without being seen. If they spotted him, it was all over. He couldn't carry the Ingram with him, so Bolan laid the SMG carefully on the floor.

Standing on tiptoe, he could just reach the first flanged joint in the vertical length of the conduit. It was wide enough to afford him a grip. He pulled himself up far enough to reach the next joint.

Painfully he hauled himself aloft. At the intersection, he paused to catch his breath. Beneath him, the firing continued sporadically, but it seemed distant and ancient. It was as if it were another fight, one he had left behind long ago.

As he gathered himself for the perilous crawl out over the gunners' positions, he saw Eli Cohen place a new clip in his SMG. At the same time, Malcolm Parsons slammed a new magazine into his Kalashnikov. Suddenly there was a piercing whistle. Both men began firing.

There was a spurt of shadow off to one side. For a moment, he couldn't place it. Then it hit him. It was Rachel. She was trying the same thing he was, but she kept to the floor to do it. She darted in and out among the shadows, swinging off to one side, trying to slide in behind the attackers. She was holding her fire, hoping for an edge.

Quickly Bolan made his decision. If he could get into position on the opposite side, they could squeeze Glinkov like a walnut. Cross fire wouldn't be a problem, because they were on two different levels. It was a three-dimensional assault.

Bolan slid forward on his belly, clinging to the broad, round surface of the pipe. He had to lift himself over each joint without losing his grip. His progress was slower than Rachel's but she had farther to go. If it worked, they'd reach their goals at the same moment.

So far the stalking figure below had remained motionless. Either he hadn't noticed Bolan's ascent or he was biding his time. Rachel nipped in beside a broad stone column that supported the building above. Bolan was directly opposite her position, but five yards higher.

He unzipped the anticontamination suit and unholstered Big Thunder. The .44 AutoMag felt cold in his hands. Its familiar weight was comforting after the feel of the MAC-10. One by one, he sought the positions of his opponents. Straining to peer into the darkness, he checked their locations relative to himself, to Rachel, to Eli and Parsons, and to one another. When he pulled the trigger the first time, he wanted to know where he was going with his second shot. And his third.

Rachel had settled on a risky firing position. Unless she nailed two men immediately, either of them would be in a position to fire back. Bolan made his target priority dependent on Rachel. She didn't seem to realize the second of the two men was there. She sighted in on the first guy, who was hunkered down out of the stray fire coming from Eli and Parsons.

Bolan drew a bead on the second man. With a little luck, no one below would even realize he was there and firing. And it was getting late. He was due for some luck.

More than a little.

Rachel opened up, and Big Thunder bucked in Bolan's hands almost simultaneously. His shot plowed into the crouching target, striking him in the forehead just below the hairline. The impact of the heavy slug drove him down and backward. The AutoMag's roar was lost in the cavernous, echoing firefight raging below him.

The stalker had moved again, this time placing a pillar between himself and Bolan. The man seemed intent on something other than the firefight. And Bolan was the only one who had seen him. He moved once, then again. It seemed as if he were more interested in escaping than in engaging in combat.

He moved farther still. And finally Parsons saw him. The old man gave a start. He thought at first they had been encircled, but a nervous scan showed that no one else had moved. He called to Eli, but Cohen didn't hear him. Eli was moving forward now, pressing Rachel's advantage.

Bolan moved another five yards along the conduit. He reached the point where it penetrated the stone wall, then swung down to the concrete, landing on the balls of his feet at the base of the wall. Ahead of him, the remains of Glinkov's attack force was firing frantically.

Bolan sighted in on his first target. A squeeze, and the AutoMag moved on. Another squeeze, and two were down. One of the terrorists realized Bolan was there. Turning, the man sprayed Kalashnikov fire in a jagged line that swept the wall just behind the Executioner's diving form.

Bolan squeezed off another round, but the gunner ducked away from Eli's fire. The Stony Man warrior's slug slammed into the column a scant three inches above the gunner's head.

Four terrorists formed a line and pressed forward. Their heavy fire drove Eli backward. Parsons seemed to have disappeared. As the charge advanced, Bolan realized it had to be halted at once. If they drove Eli back far enough, two of them could turn back toward Rachel, cutting her off and pinning her against the wall with minimal cover. Eli would have his hands full. He wouldn't be able to help her.

But they didn't realize the Executioner was also behind them. The diving gunner was a problem that had to be solved first. Bolan moved in, deliberately exposing himself to the hidden man's position. The guy took the bait. He raised himself carefully, sighting in with deliberation. A look of celebration slipped over his heavy features. It was premature.

Very.

Bolan drilled him just above the left eye. The explosive force of the AutoMag's 240-grain projectile ruptured the gunner's cranium as if it were a ripe pumpkin. The splattered gore on the stone behind him was as dark as death. And just as silent.

Now for the four horsemen, Bolan thought.

Eli was holding his ground. Occasionally he searched the area to his right, looking for Parsons. But there was no sign of the old man. There was no time to look for him now. The men were making a push, although none of the four seemed aware of the deadly presence behind them. They were alternating their fire, two shooting and two advancing, then switching. Suddenly the four of them surged forward in unison. Their deadly fire poured in, and Cohen had no choice but to run.

Pinned down, the advance pressing him too hotly for escape, Eli sprayed fire without looking. His SMG chattered and then went silent. It was too soon for a new clip, Bolan thought. He heard Eli tug on the empty magazine, but it wouldn't budge. A stray slug had struck the weapon. It was jammed.

Bolan was pressing in now. He fired twice, taking one of the four just above the left shoulder blade. The gunner fell like a sack of wet cement. His three buddies pushed on. They were in the open and had no choice.

Bolan moved forward, pressing his advantage. When the goons realized Eli wasn't firing back, two of them turned to the threat from their rear. The third continued in Eli's direction.

Rachel rushed forward, calling out to her brother. She reached an opening just as the onrushing gunner flanked Eli's position. She closed her eyes and sprayed .45 caliber poison in a broad figure-eight pattern.

The hellish spray nailed her target from head to hip. Blood spurted from his neck, and he fell forward heavily. Drenched by the bloody spray, Eli caught the falling corpse in his arms.

The remaining two belonged to Mack Bolan. He reholstered Big Thunder and relieved his last victim of a Kalashnikov and two magazines. He slipped a new one into place and dived to the right, hitting on his shoulder and rolling on to regain his feet behind a thick stone column.

He was acutely aware that thirty odd lives hung in the balance, trapped in a room just behind him. Rage at such intentional barbarity gave a manic edge to his movement. What Glinkov was trying to do was beyond loathsome. For Mack Bolan it was beyond all comprehension. Now Bolan was close to pulling the plug on it. He wanted desperately to do it. Do it now. He wanted to shut Glinkov down, but there was a succession of gunners and slugs to go through first. Each one made him a little more angry.

He raised the Kalashnikov and squeezed. The two men in front of him dropped in their tracks. The relentless fire seemed like the voice of outrage as it chattered and roared. And then was still.

The gun was empty.

The last two gunners lay in their own blood.

Bolan wanted Glinkov.

He wanted him bad.

And he would have him.

ELI AND RACHEL HURRIED the hostages back to the surface. The elevator was running on emergency power, and there were too many people for a single load. On the way, Rachel explained what she knew of the situation. It was decided that the first group to go up should be technical people. Without them there was no chance to reverse the process Glinkov had set in motion. With them, there was precious little, but even a slim chance was worth taking when it was all you had.

Stevens was still in the control room. There had been no attempt to break into it. Everyone else in the plant had gone to Level 4—the hostages at gunpoint, Glinkov's men prodding them like wayward cattle, and the others in pursuit. And Stevens had waited. He was determined to get even with the bastards who had killed his friends.

When Eli Cohen arrived, he knew there was still a chance. But first they had to prevent a meltdown. Eli was no engineer. All he could do was sit and watch the dials. And wait. And pray.

And his prayers, if not answered, were at least being acknowledged. With the hostages free, there was still a chance to stop the nightmare.

Anxiously the security chief paced behind the console as Stan Robbins tried desperately to reverse the damage and prevent a meltdown. It was too late to reinsert the control rods. The interior of the reactor was too far out of control. All he could do was try to cool it down.

Robbins told Eli that the fuel was already disintegrating. The reactor's internal alignment was so out of whack that there was no hope of a mechanical solution.

Both men paced and watched the dials. It seemed absurd that an array of colorful lamps could signify so much destruction. There had to be something useful they could do. It didn't seem right to sit and do nothing.

Finally Eli spoke. "Matt, we have to get outside."

"What's up?"

"There's a chopper coming. To pick up the Russian."

"No way. No way in hell that son of a bitch gets out of here."

"Let's go, then."

"Stan, you'll be all right here?" Stevens asked.

The engineer nodded without taking his eyes off the console. "But you should start getting everybody else the hell out of here. There's not much more I can do. And if this doesn't work, I'll be in Boston before I stop running."

Stevens clapped him on the shoulder. "I'll tell somebody on the way out. I have some business to take care of."

Rachel joined them, handing Stevens an AK-47. "You'll need this," she said.

"Not if I get close enough to use my bare hands."

29

Andrey Glinkov was running for his life.

The footsteps following him grew louder. Ahead, like the mouth of hell, yawned a fifteen-foot circle in the floor. A steel ladder led down to the floor below. Parsons descended.

The Russian had underestimated the man called Bolan. It would cost him dearly. Just how dearly, he wouldn't know for some time. If he managed to escape with his life, there was still the question of his superiors. There was no way to obscure the KGB presence in this fiasco. No way but one.

Peter Achison was supposed to meet him in a stolen attack helicopter. The original intention was to use the chopper only for his escape. But it was heavily armed. And there was still a chance. If he could hold the world at bay long enough, the reactor would do the rest of his job for him.

He'd already set in motion the forces of the chain reaction that would ultimately destroy the reactor complex. He might not be able to lock the hostages into the containment building as he had planned, but they were still in the plant. If he could keep them until he put his plan into action, the radiation would preserve the secret of his participation. But only if no one got out alive.

Especially Mack Bolan.

Right now, the odds did not favor that outcome. But it was still possible. Whoever was following him in the tunnel would have to be eliminated first, of course. Then he might still be able to hook up with Achison. It would be a simple matter to use the chopper's firepower to prevent escape from Thunder Mountain. As long as the reactor was unchecked, it would eventually achieve his purpose.

Sweat began to bead his brow as he ran through the tunnel. He could hear the footsteps of the man behind him. He didn't know who it was, but he couldn't afford to use his flashlight. It would give him away more quickly than it would pick out his pursuer. And if the pursuer were Mack Bolan, he wouldn't make it to the chopper.

The echo of his footsteps began to pound in his ears. He had to catch his breath. He looked into the dark toward the man chasing him. Far behind, he could see a dim light descending to the floor of the tunnel. Another man had joined the chase. Was one Mack Bolan?

He pushed on. A sharp pain stabbed through his chest. Each breath brought with it the edge of a razor blade. The slicing of the air into his lungs hurt like hell. His legs were beginning to feel leaden. His feet felt as if they were encased in concrete.

It began to get warmer. The air around him seemed to dampen and heat up. The first slosh of water underfoot went unnoticed. And the second. By the third, he realized he was running in shallow water. It wasn't until the fourth step that he began to wonder where it came from.

The tunnels, he knew, were part of a vast complex that radiated in all directions from the heart of Thunder Mountain. They were all tied together to serve as emergency coolant conduits. If it became necessary to flood the reactor with large quantities of cool water, the tunnels would handle the runoff. If it ever became necessary to drain off the reactor coolant, the tunnels would handle that, too.

He had begun draining the reactor. The water under his feet might be some of the coolant. It might be radioactive. He had to find out whether he was heading in the right direction. He needed someplace to use a light for a minute, a place to get his bearings. A place to look at his map. He had to know whether he was heading toward the reactor or away from it. The water under his feet would mean certain death if it were radioactive.

Shielding a small flashlight with his palm as he ran, he sprayed a small beam against the wall for a second or so at a time. He was looking for someplace to duck in out of the main tunnel.

Every so often, he knew, there would be a ladder. They led from one level of tunnels to another. If he could find one, he could climb out of this tunnel into another, higher one. Once there, he could use his light to find out where the hell he was. And to ambush the men on his trail.

The beam wavered. Snapping it off and on, he was taking the chance that he might miss one of the ladders. The third time the light went on, he saw a dim shadow against the wall. Long and thin, it had to be a ladder.

He doused the light and began to clamber up the rungs, taking care not to let his feet on the metal give him away. At the top of the ladder, there was the mouth of a second tunnel. He climbed into the higher tunnel and ran thirty yards into it. Flicking on the light, he tried to place himself by referring to the map. With no idea exactly where he stood, he'd have to find a marker.

He played the light along the wall, moving farther into the new tunnel. Somewhere, he knew, there had to be a sign. Something with a number on it. There had to be some key to enable someone inside the tunnels to locate himself. After another thirty yards, he found it. There was a small metal sign bolted into the wall.

It identified the tunnel he was in, and the section. With some careful scrutiny, he placed it on his map. He'd been heading toward the Hudson River. That was good and bad. Good, because it would get him closer to the place where Achison was supposed to land the chopper, but it also meant he was heading in the same direction as the reactor. He had no idea what the consequences would be if he was exposed to the draining coolant.

He had no idea how deep the water might get, or how much of it he would encounter. At the moment, he could avoid it by keeping to one side of the tunnel. The rivulet of water in the middle of the tunnel bottom might just be draining snowmelt. If he was lucky. But he hadn't had much luck so far.

The footsteps of the approaching man started to boom through the high mouth of the tunnel. Whoever it was was getting closer. Glinkov doused his light and moved swiftly back toward the main tunnel. He had to move cautiously. He couldn't afford to run off the floor of this tunnel into the main tunnel. The drop was high enough to break a leg.

And someone was chasing him.

Someone who wanted him dead.

Someone who was willing to see to it.

In his gut, Andrey Glinkov knew that Mack Bolan was right behind him.

Glinkov had to get out of the tunnel. And Mack Bolan was determined that he would never make it. Glinkov was too uncertain of his path to outrun the pursuit. He had to stop and find out where he was from time to time.

Glinkov knew that timing was his only hope. He couldn't outrun the people behind him. If he got where he was going and the chopper wasn't there yet, he was finished. If he got there and the chopper had come and gone, it was all over. But if he made it out while the chopper was still there, he had a chance.

As if from another world, distant echoes drifted through the network of tunnels. Barely perceptible, Glinkov had the brief impression that they might have been older than he was, the last dying sounds of a long-dead war. Or the last stand of his crew, hastily assembled as it had been. Idiots, most of them. How could he have expected to succeed with such incompetent help?

And in his heart, he knew it was a sham. He knew he couldn't truly blame his failure on the men who followed him. But it didn't much matter. They were finished. If he survived, his version would be history. If he didn't, he wouldn't much care, either.

The footsteps stopped. Somewhere in the dark, not fifty yards away, a man waited. That man, if given the chance, would kill him. He didn't know the man's name. And it made no difference. He would have to kill him first, and there was nothing more anonymous, in the final analysis, than a dead man.

Glinkov held his breath. In the darkness, he could hear the whisper of running water. And the sound of rubber on metal. The ladder was being climbed. Slowly, carefully, climbed.

Glinkov slid forward. His weapon clinked on the hard stone. There was a whisper behind him, his cuffs dragging on the concrete. He stilled his movement. He waited.

The ladder thumped softly. The climber placed each foot carefully, quietly. But the care wasn't sufficient. The quiet, not enough. Slowly Glinkov rolled sideways. He could recall approximately where the ladder entered the tunnel mouth. It was on the left-hand side, extending just two or three inches above the lip of the opening.

The Russian strained his ears. He heard nothing from farther off. Whoever else was following had either turned back or stopped, waiting to see what happened. The closer man hadn't been Bolan. Of that Glinkov was certain. It reassured him. But suppose Bolan had caught up? Suppose Bolan had switched places? Suppose it was Bolan climbing the ladder?

Could it be? Could he afford to believe it wasn't? What the hell should he do? The Russian asked himself a hundred questions. Time was running, just as surely as water ran in the tunnel below him. The seconds clicked off in measured rhythm as steadily as the water dripped on the rock behind him.

And another step on the ladder. Whoever was coming had a foot less to go. Glinkov placed his flashlight parallel to the barrel of his weapon. If he used the light, he had to be ready instantly to shoot at what he saw. Nervously he rubbed the slide switch on the flashlight. He moved his fingers side to side, unwilling to risk accidental illumination.

And the stalker rose another rung on the ladder. That made at least four. One more, and his head should be above the floor of the higher tunnel. One more step, and he would risk the light. Glinkov was silent. No one could possibly expect him to be there. Even Bolan would believe he was long gone. Running was the only sensible thing for him to have done. So, of course, he hadn't.

But the Russian knew that Mack Bolan was too experienced to make book on such things. It happened so quickly, Glinkov wasn't even sure who it was. He flicked on the light. The piercing eyes burning back at him scared him into an involuntary contraction of the trigger finger.

In an instant the man was gone. The face dissolved in bloody spray and there was nothing but the pale, ghostly beam of his torch, dying just as it reached the opposite wall. The man's hair had been gray. The man had been Malcolm Parsons.

And Glinkov gave him credit. He would never have suspected the old man of having such nerve. He must have been mortified to have been so easily seduced. His vanity had gotten the better of him. A less vain man would have left pursuit to the likes of Bolan. Too bad. But then a less vain man would not have been tricked so easily, would not have been in Parsons's predicament to begin with.

But was it really Parsons? Maybe the light had tricked him. Maybe the beam had been so close it had bleached Bolan's darker hair. Maybe the man he killed had been the Executioner. Maybe there was no Executioner to fear now.

It was tempting to hope so, to think so. And Glinkov held his breath, waiting for a sign. And he wasn't waiting in vain. And the sign came, and when it came, it chilled him to the bone.

"I'm coming for you, Glinkov."

The voice was cold, brittle. Deep and resonant in the stony catacombs. He knew it was only a dream. Parsons was dead, after all.

And Mack Bolan was on his trail.

The echo seemed to spread out in all directions. Glinkov couldn't tell where Bolan was. He might be just below, waiting at the foot of the ladder. Or he could be behind him, in the feeder tunnel, creeping up on him even now. Or maybe he'd gone on past the feeder tunnel, waiting for him to blunder right into his hands.

In any case, it didn't matter. It would soon be over.

STAN ROBBINS KNEW water was the only answer, lots of it. But first he had to do something about the temperature in the containment buildings. If it went any higher, the whole thing might blow.

He knew the tunnels to the Hudson were closed. Even at gunpoint, he'd made sure those gates stayed shut. He'd snookered the Russian. Now he hoped he could snooker fate. With a prayer, he opened a second set of valves. The first step was draining the radioactive coolant from the bottom of the containment building. Then he turned on the pumps. He had to flood the reactor with new, fresh water from the river to get rid of the radioactive waste.

As it was, this place would be off-limits for some time while they tried to clean it up. But if he couldn't cool the core in the next few minutes, there might be nothing left to clean. Out of the corner of his eye, he watched the warning lights blink on and off. Finally he saw what he was looking for. The blue light was on, indicating that the complete circuit from the Hudson through the containment building and on into the emergency tunnels was opening.

Two million gallons of water would slosh around the ruins of the Unit 1 reactor until they were ready to be purged. One more glance, and he bit his lip as he pressed the button. The surge of vented waters was something he could only imagine.

MACK BOLAN HEARD IT. The water was rushing into the tunnel at an alarming rate. He stepped on something resilient. With a start, he realized it was Parsons. Snapping on his light, he nearly gagged. It was too late for Parsons. Way too late. The faceless corpse lay on its back in the middle of the tunnel.

He ran to the next ladder on the tunnel wall and began to climb. Behind him, he could hear the rushing flood. Stifling heat surged ahead of the incoming water. He wouldn't know until it was too late, of course, but drowning was definitely not the way he wanted to end his life.

No way.

One tunnel ahead of him, Andrey Glinkov heard the deluge begin. The inrush of the water galvanized him. He shuddered at the sound. Screaming as if confronted by a ravening beast, he climbed desperately to the next level in the honeycomb. And the roar of the water seemed to follow him.

Climbing hand over hand, he reached the next tunnel and ran for his life. The sound of the water grew louder. He reached the next ladder and began to climb. Rung after rung. He stopped to look behind him but could see nothing in the dark.

He climbed still higher, his rifle rattling against the steel rungs as he turned to look down again. He turned on his torch and pointed it down into the abyss. Just beyond the beam he could see, or thought he saw, the whitecapped waves of a raising tide. The water, too, was climbing the ladder.

Glinkov knew that he was in a race for his life. Either he would soon get out of the water's reach, or the water would rush past him to claim his rightful place at the head of the line. And there could be only one winner in this race.

Then, suddenly, it was over. On his cheeks he felt fresh air—cold winter air. The lock on the grate above him was a simple latch affair. He loosened it and pushed the heavy plate aside to haul himself out into the winter darkness.

Fifty yards away, Mack Bolan did the same. He looked anxiously about for the Russian. And both men heard the roar at the same time. The chopper was right on time. Achison had made it. Would it make a difference?

30

The incoming helicopter roared overhead. Its running lights were incredibly bright against the dark sky. Bolan recognized the profile immediately. It was a Cobra gunship. Bolan had seen more than enough of the deadly choppers in Vietnam. The night was split apart by the roar of the 1,100-horsepower engine.

Behind him, the plant loomed ominously. It was wounded and, like a wild animal, it was more dangerous that way. Glinkov had to be nearby. Bolan had seen him slip into a vertical shaft and head out of the tunnels. With the flood raging in behind, there had been no time to follow the Russian. But he must be on the surface by now.

The chopper hovered just over a stand of trees, then drifted slowly left toward a clearing in the woods. Glinkov had been the consummate professional up to this point. That meant there was a prearranged LZ for the chopper. The Russian wouldn't have left his most crucial rendezvous to chance.

Rather than waste time trying to find the KGB man in the darkness, Bolan headed toward the LZ. The chopper touched down, but was still visible behind a thin stand of evergreens. The engine chugged away, whirling the forty-four-foot rotor. Cobras could carry an array of armament, Bolan knew. Anything from machine guns to pods of 2.75-inch missiles. And there was no way this one was unarmed.

The pilot had to be Peter Achison. Rachel had said he was coming to meet Glinkov in a chopper. That meant he would have a shot at the man who had killed Robert Hanley. Bolan had been trying to piece things together since he'd first seen Achison at the Parsons place. There had been something familiar about the tall, balding man. Now he knew why. Achison was the same man he'd seen through the window at Hanley's farm—the guy who had slipped out at the last minute, after shooting the defenseless engineer in the head.

It was all coming together now. All the scores Mack Bolan had to settle, all the debts he had to pay. Everything could be taken care of right here. The slate could be wiped clean.

No, not could be.

Would be.

In the distance, Bolan heard the wail of approaching sirens. Somewhere out in the darkness, police cars were rushing to the plant. Matt Stevens's man must have gotten through. But there was no time to wait for the cops. If Glinkov made it to the chopper, he'd be gone. If he got out of Thunder Mountain, there'd be no way to catch him.

Crunching across the frozen snow, Bolan knew he was only going to get one shot at the Russian. And if he didn't nail him, the Cobra was capable of finishing what the Russian had started. In its crippled condition, the reactor was a time bomb, just waiting to go off. Rockets from the Cobra could destroy the containment tower. If it blew, the whole complex could blow. And if that happened, the lower third of the Hudson Valley was going to be a dead zone for decades.

As he neared the trees, Bolan saw a shadowy figure a hundred yards ahead of him. The guy was running straight for the chopper. It could only be Glinkov. Bolan fired a burst from his Kalashnikov. He sprayed deadly 7.62 caliber fire in a narrow arc. The man was well within the AK-47's effective range, but he was dodging among scattered shrubs.

The figure disappeared, and Bolan thought for a moment that he had nailed the Russian. Return fire told him he hadn't. Glinkov had cut loose with his own weapon. The slugs tore up the snow just ahead, and Bolan hit the deck.

He had to nail the bastard before he got to the chopper. If Glinkov got airborne, Bolan would be a sitting duck. As it was, the chopper wasn't a threat. The trees were too thick for it to fire on him.

Bolan waited until the shadow resumed its flight. When Glinkov made his move, Bolan was right with him. In better shape than the Russian, he was closing the gap, but there wasn't enough time. Glinkov was too close to his goal.

Behind him, Bolan heard a shout. He turned to see Eli and Rachel racing toward him. Eli knelt to fire toward the tree line. If they could rotate their fire and keep Glinkov pinned down, Bolan could catch the Russian.

Eli emptied his magazine, and then Rachel began firing. Bolan waved and resumed the chase. Angling to one side to keep out of the line of fire, Bolan didn't bother about his own weapon. When he reached the undergrowth, he had closed the gap to fifty yards. Glinkov had seen him but held his fire.

As the undergrowth thickened, the big guy's progress was hampered. And he lost sight of the Russian. The firing continued from behind him, so Glinkov was still visible to Cohen and Rachel. Working his way through the bushes, he could hear the chopper off to his right. He stopped to peer through the trees. The chopper was outlined against the snow. Only one man was visible in the cockpit.

Another ten yards, and Bolan would be between the chopper and the fleeing Russian agent. The odds were getting better. And time was getting shorter. The sirens were drawing closer as the police raced toward the main gate to Thunder Mountain.

There was a deep rumble, and the ground shook for an instant. The sound died away slowly as the lights on the plant winked once, went out altogether for a moment and then came back on.

Glinkov was still pinned down among the trees, but he'd have to make his move without much delay. Bolan pushed on. He could just make out the clump of trees in which Glinkov had taken cover. There was another rumble, this one deeper, and sounding as if it were close by. Then a geyser of steam and hot water shot up among the trees.

There was an earsplitting hiss, and the water continued to spew into the air, drenching the tops of the taller trees. The snow on their branches melted, and a large circle of earth appeared as the snow melted around the mouth of a tunnel access grating.

Another hiss and another geyser. Then a third. All through the trees, the coolant was gushing into the air. With the Hudson drainage valves close, and water from the river pumping through the containment building and into the tunnels, the pressure buildup was forcing the water to the surface.

Then Glinkov bolted. Heading straight into the open, he dodged through the few small bushes that rimmed the clearing. The chopper sat in the center of the clearing like an insect. Its rotor whumped away in the darkness. The air was full of mist, wind-borne from the fountains spraying the forest on all sides.

In the clearing, the running man was an easier target than he had been earlier. Bolan fired a short burst, then the Kalashnikov was empty. He had no more magazines for it. Hurling the weapon aside, Bolan hauled Big Thunder from its sling and charged after the Russian.

Eli and Rachel had reached the far side of the woods and were plunging into the trees. Bolan aimed carefully and squeezed. Just as the AutoMag barked, Glinkov tripped and fell headlong. The skull-busting .44 caliber slug sailed harmlessly over his head.

The Russian was up in an instant.

Bolan heard the rumble before he noticed the hole opening in the earth in front of him. He dived to one side just as a deep chasm opened in the snow.

The rushing torrent underground had been too much for the tunnel walls. Weakened by the huge volume of superheated steam and water, they had given way under the intense pressure. Gnawing its way to the surface, the water had begun to spread out under the whole area, drenching the earth with its poisons.

While Bolan watched helplessly, Glinkov climbed into the chopper. The Executioner cursed. The man was getting away. He fired twice. The first slug bounced harmlessly off the chopper's fuselage, the second flattened against the bulletproof glass of the cockpit.

Eli and Rachel had caught up to him. Eli hit the ground, hauling Rachel down with him. The chopper's engine roared as its gun pods rotated, seeking them out. There was a burst of fire, and the earth exploded around the three warriors.

"Holy shit," Eli whispered when the firing stopped. "What the hell is that?"

"That's a 30 mm cannon," Bolan informed him. "Three barrels and remote controlled."

"Damn. We're in for it now."

"We can't let him get away," Rachel cried.

"Anybody got an idea?"

Another surge of cannon fire tore into the earth. The three fighters hugged the ground, trying to burrow into the snow. Just to their left, the sound of the rushing flood grew louder. The hole was beginning to widen.

"We can't stay here," Bolan shouted above the roaring water.

"Why the hell isn't he taking off?" Eli asked.

The shadows in the cockpit were stationary for a moment, then changed places. The chopper lifted off sluggishly. Glinkov was inexperienced, at least with the Cobra. At a height of fifty feet, the chopper spun on its axis. Bolan stood helplessly. But the helicopter wasn't going anywhere.

With a roar, it loosened a salvo of rockets. The three warriors on the ground watched as the missiles crashed into the containment building near its curved peak. The roar was deafening.

The top of the building disappeared in a shower of flame and smoke. The ground trembled. But the concrete held. Four feet thick and reinforced with steel, it was built to withstand incredible stress.

The machine wobbled under Glinkov's uncertain hand. Again the chopper belched fire, and a second cluster of rockets flew toward the building. But this time the pilot's shaky control was costly. The cluster of rockets sailed past the containment building. They vanished into the trees and exploded harmlessly against the mountainside.

The Cobra descended abruptly. As it touched down, the cockpit door slid open. There was the distant sound of an argument, barely audible over the roar of the chopper's engine. A second later, there was a muffled gunshot, and Peter Achison tumbled out into the snow.

The chopper's engine surged again, the rotor spinning faster and faster. The machine wobbled slightly, lifted off and bounced down hard. In an instant, Eli was on his feet. He tossed a pair of grenades to Bolan.

"I'm going to draw his fire. How's your arm, Mack?"

"Eli, don't be an idiot," Rachel said. She jumped to her feet and grabbed Cohen by the arm.

He shook her off and ran toward the chopper. At first Glinkov didn't see him. Eli was counting on the Russian having his hands full controlling the chopper's flight. He dodged back and forth like a halfback in broken field.

Charging straight ahead, Eli tried to draw attention to himself. Bolan saw the cannon turret swivel and leaped to his feet. Behind him, Rachel was screaming over the roar of the rushing water. The turret swiveled again, drawing a bead on the running man. Bolan plunged on behind him.

For a moment the chopper wavered, then lifted off the ground. It hovered in the air, wobbling like a dead puppet on its last string. The turret swiveled again, this time seeking Bolan. Glinkov seemed uncertain of himself. Cohen was closer, but he knew Bolan was the bigger threat.

The first burst of cannon fire passed harmlessly over Eli's head. It plowed the earth between the two running men. Cohen rushed on. His Ingram was spitting at the chopper, but the slugs bounced off harmlessly. The air was full of the chopper's roar.

Then, getting control of the machine, Glinkov rose higher. Fifteen feet in the air now, and rising. Eli ran right under it, and out of range of the deadly cannons. Glinkov would have to move to find him again.

The chopper slipped sideways, and Eli was back in the open. He stood motionless, fighting to get another clip in his Ingram. When the gun was reloaded, he backed away, trying to get an angle of fire that would let him chew at the chopper engine's air intakes.

The cannon turret swiveled again, and Eli began to fire. The cannon barked, and hellfire rained all around Cohen's figure. This time Glinkov didn't miss. For a second everything stopped. Then Bolan heard Rachel's scream over the noise of the engine.

Pulling the pin on his first grenade, Bolan chucked the M-56 in an arc. It bounced off the fuselage just in front of the air intake and fell into the snow. Bolan hit the deck as the grenade went off, sending razor-sharp steel fragments whizzing overhead.

Glinkov banked the chopper slightly to the left, and Bolan was on his feet. The turret swiveled as the Russian tried to draw a bead on the man below. Bolan pulled the second pin and sprinted straight at the chopper.

The angle was too tight for effective control of the cannon turret, and Glinkov tried to raise the chopper. Bolan let go of the second M-56 as the helicopter pitched forward and roared over him. The grenade sailed just over the lip of the intake, and the Cobra surged ahead.

Bolan dropped down and dug into the snowy crust. The grenade went off, and the chopper pitched wildly to one side. The fuselage burst into flame. The Cobra yawed and staggered. The entire area was bathed in light from the burning fuel. Its engine mangled, the rotor shaft seized and one blade snapped off.

The chopper fell like a stone. Its fuel tank exploded as its nose tipped forward. The ruined machine was consumed in flame for an instant and then fell into the churning maelstrom of radioactive waste. The hiss of the extinguished flame was applause to Bolan's ear.

Bolan sprinted to Achison and rolled him over. There was a jagged exit hole where his forehead had been. Splinters of bone stuck out at odd angles. The gore oozing from the ruined skull had already stained the snow in a small circle around the dead man. Robert Hanley would never know it, but his account had just been closed.

Turning back toward the plant, Bolan stood motionless for a long moment. He didn't want to face Rachel. Eli was dead, he knew. There was no way in hell he could have survived the burst of cannon fire that took him down.

Rachel was bent over her brother's body. His head was cradled in her arms, and she was rocking back and forth. She crooned softly, as if to a child.

Bolan knelt beside her.

He put his hand on her shoulder. She turned her face toward him for a moment but said nothing. Her face was streaked with blood and tears. Her lips moved spasmodically for an instant, as if she wanted to speak. But when the words didn't come, she turned back to her brother, bending low over the motionless body, and kissed him softly on the forehead.

"Please, go away," she whispered.

Bolan knew he had no choice.

Epilogue

Thunder Mountain was down, but not out. The extensive damage would take years to repair. The cleanup years more. But the Hudson had been spared, thanks to guts and quick thinking on the part of Stan Robbins. Matt Stevens was appointed to a special Congressional panel on nuclear power security. He had lived through hell and was better able than anyone else to advise on how a recurrence might be prevented.

For Mack Bolan, though, it was another battle in the endless war. But a special battle. Thunder Mountain would haunt him. There were times when he would wake in the night, the sound of a surging flood filling his ears. It had been close. Closer than he cared to think about.

But the image that would stay with him the longest was the one he could bear the least. Rachel Peres, and the empty look in her cold eyes as she glanced away from Eli's lifeless form lying there in the cold snow. For them, the battle would never be over. Never mind the war.

And Rachel Peres? She had gone back to Israel. She thought Mossad was something she wanted to get away from. It was a part of her past. The contract assignment for the CIA was to be her last job. Until that night. There in the darkness, she came to understand that a real warrior doesn't walk away from a war. War doesn't let go that easily, and the warrior doesn't quit while there's something worth fighting for.

And if Mack Bolan knew anything at all, he knew that there would always be something worth fighting for. And he knew that somebody had to stand up and lead the battle. Somebody had to draw the line. Somebody had to say "enough." And most of all, Mack Bolan knew, even if no one else did, that he would be that person. As often as he had to. Until the war was over.

Or until he stopped breathing.

AVAILABLE SOON!

SuperBolan #7

Sudden DEATH

EUROTERROR:
the latest buzzword in the pantheon of fear

Someone is killing the leaders of Europe. And the eyes of the world are focused on the most rabid terrorists. But they all have iron-clad alibis.

No statesman is safe from a master assassin who stalks the corridors of European power, not even the President of the United States, who is on a goodwill tour of France.

America turns to Mack Bolan—the one man who can stop these deadly hits. This special hunter unravels a bizarre plot that has its roots in World War II. In a stunning climax he comes face-to-face with the man who would change the world.

Available soon wherever paperbacks are sold or through Gold Eagle Reader Service. In U.S.A.: P.O. Box 1394, 901 Fuhrmann Blvd., Buffalo, New York 14240-1394. In Canada: P.O. Box 609, Fort Erie, Ont. L2A 9Z9.

SB7

TAKE 'EM NOW

FOLDING SUNGLASSES
FROM GOLD EAGLE

Mean up your act with these tough, street-smart shades. Practical, too, because they fold 3 times into a handy, zip-up polyurethane pouch that fits neatly into your pocket. Rugged metal frame. Scratch-resistant acrylic lenses. Best of all, they can be yours for only $6.99. **MAIL ORDER TODAY.**

Send your name, address, and zip code, along with a check or money order for just $6.99 + .75¢ for postage and handling (for a total of $7.74) payable to Gold Eagle Reader Service, a division of Worldwide Library. New York and Arizona residents please add applicable sales tax.

Remove from pouch...

unfold once...

unfold twice...

and they're ready to wear.

GOLD EAGLE

Gold Eagle Reader Service
901 Fuhrmann Blvd.
P.O. Box 1325
Buffalo, N.Y. 14240-1325

Offer not available in Canada.

GES1–RRR

You don't know what
NONSTOP HIGH-VOLTAGE ACTION
is until you've read your
4 FREE GOLD EAGLE NOVELS

LIMITED-TIME OFFER

Mail to Gold Eagle Reader Service

In the U.S.
P.O. Box 1396
Buffalo, N.Y. 14240-1396

In Canada
P.O. Box 603,
Fort Erie, Ont.
L2A 5X3

YEAH! Rush me 4 free Gold Eagle novels and my free mystery bonus. Then send me 6 brand-new novels every other month as they come off the presses. Bill me at the low price of just $14.95 -- a 13% saving off the retail price. There are no shipping, handling or other hidden costs. There is no minimum number of books I must buy. I can always return a shipment and cancel at any time. Even if I never buy another book from Gold Eagle, the 4 free novels and the mystery bonus are mine to keep forever.

_____
Name   (PLEASE PRINT)

_____
Address   Apt. No.

_____
City   State/Prov.   Zip/Postal Code

_____
Signature (If under 18, parent or guardian must sign)

This offer is limited to one order per household and not valid to present subscribers. Price is subject to change.
166-BPM-BP6F

MYSTERY BONUS GIFT

HV-SUB-IRRRF